SO OTHERS MAY LIVE

B. William Hoolihan

Publisher Name: Sabal Palm Press
Print ISBN: 978-1-969718-00-7
LCCN: 2025911828

This is a fictional story based on real-life experiences. However, all characters are fictionalized, and any resemblance to a person living or dead is purely coincidental. Names, characters, businesses, places, events, and incidents are either the products of the author's imagination or used in a fictitious manner.

Credits:
Cover Design Copyright 2025 © Michael Dorer

*This book is dedicated to the brave men and women
of the United States Coast Guard.
And to a few inspirational characters I've met along
the way.*

TERMS

Bravo Zulu – a flag signal meaning "well done." Widely used across the maritime community to express appreciation for good work.

Chief Petty Officer – highest of the noncommissioned officers in the United States Coast Guard (USCG). There are three classifications within this group. Chief, Senior Chief and Master Chief being the most senior. All may be addressed as Chief.

Coastie – informal nickname that depicts the identity and camaraderie among those who serve or have served in the Coast Guard.

SAR – Search and Rescue.

Semper Paratus – The Official Motto of the Coast Guard, which means…Always Prepared.

So Others May Live – The Unofficial Motto of the Coast Guard.

Gulf of America
Fort Jefferson
Key West
Marquesas
Stock Island
N
W
E
S

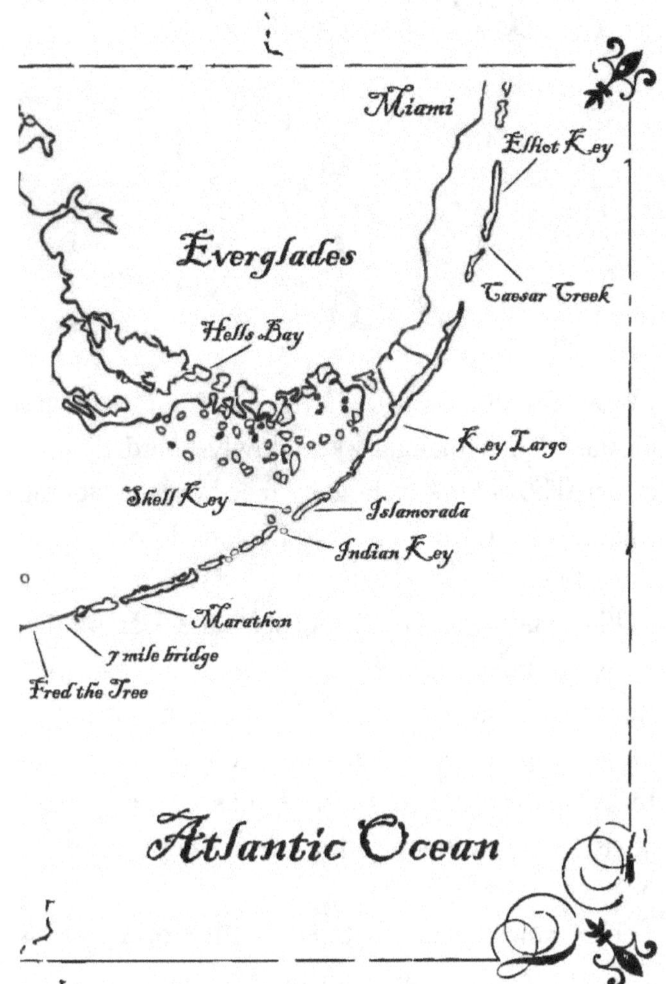
Miami
Elliot Key
Everglades
Caesar Creek
Hells Bay
Key Largo
Shell Key
Islamorada
Indian Key
Marathon
7 mile bridge
Fred the Tree
Atlantic Ocean

PROLOGUE

Key West Harbor
1783

Wind-driven torches lit the faces of two stern Tequestas as their haggard kin slowly boarded an old schooner. The elder's mahogany face bore the etchings of a harsh life, further engraved by the burden of his people's fate.

This small band of Tequestas, the last of their kind, were boarding *La Exquisita*. She had been chartered by Jesuit priests who were transporting the destitute people to Havana, Cuba, ninety miles to the south. The priests had offered these proud people sanctuary in exchange for their conversion to Catholicism.

The Tequesta had inhabited South Florida for two thousand years. They were an ancient, peaceful people who lived off the land and sea. Their name for their homeland was Ikanay, which meant "Our Land Blessed by the Sun, the Moon, and their Children the

Stars."

With the arrival of Europeans and the Seminole and Pahokee tribes, their kind was pushed further and further south. Eventually, they were driven to the very end of the geographic line—Cayo Hueso, also known as Key West.

The elder Tequesta was Quetzal, the son of Kalos, a storied elder who, years earlier, had befriended the legendary pirate Black Caesar. Black Caesar sailed the waters off Elliott Key, to the north, in search of bounty and counted Blackbeard among his friends.

Before Quetzal boarded the old schooner, he addressed his son Tulec by the windblown torches. "Tulec," he began, "I have a quest for you that's crucial to our people's survival."

"Yes, Father, anything," Tulec replied quickly and confidently.

Tulec was a strong, young warrior raised in the swamps and waters of the Everglades. Skilled with the large bow unique to the Tequesta people, he could live off the land and waters indefinitely. His strength, stamina, and wisdom would serve him well in the task ahead.

Quetzal continued, "There are events which I have not told you concerning Kalos, Black Caesar, and the legacy they left our people.

"Black Caesar and your grandfather were blood brothers who relied on each other to survive. They were each deeply indebted to the other. For this reason, Caesar entrusted Kalos with the location of his treasure.

"The treasure was hidden in two locations. Caesar carved secret instructions on separate pieces of wood that only a clever and deserving person could decipher. To a casual observer, it would resemble scrimshaw—the carvings sailors made all over the world.

"When Kalos learned that Caesar and Blackbeard were captured by the English, in the Carolinas and hanged, he put Caesar's plan into action. He hid the first scrimshaw inside a stone turtle on the north end of Elliott Key."

"And the second?" Tulec asked impatiently.

"The second scrimshaw, named the Kahatee, was never hidden. Kalos fell ill and was unable to conceal it, so it was passed on to me. Now, I give it to you, my son." With that, Quetzal produced a dark piece of wood from his threadbare cloak. The scrimshaw was made of lignum vitae, the hardest wood in the world, and grew only in the northern part of the Keys.

"It's not likely that we will ever return here to Ikanay, so I'm entrusting you to find a secret location for the Kahatee. Can you manage this task, his son?"

"Of course, Father."

Quetzal then handed the mysterious scrimshaw staff to his son, who swelled with anticipation of this great responsibility.

The Jesuits were now shouting in Spanish for Quetzal and Tulec to board quickly. No Tequestas were to be left behind. The *Exquisita*'s sailors were urgently tossing lines and raising sails as the boat began its departure to Cuba. Quetzal grabbed the stern backstay and swung himself stiffly on board. He turned and stared deeply into the eyes of his son. Tulec acknowledged his father's gaze, then slipped silently into the dark harbor water and vanished.

An osprey screeched above as Quetzal wiped the tears running down his weathered face. He would never see his son again. His sorrow eased, knowing he had taught his son well, and that Tulec would be the salvation of the Tequesta people.

ONE

"This is the United States Coast Guard! Step towards the bow … the pointy thing! I'm going to shoot your engines! *¡Esta es la Guardia Costera de los Estados Unidos! ¡Pasa hacia la proa! ¡Voy a disparar tus motores!*"

Master Chief Rik Meade put the hailer mike down and thought, *Man, I just love saying that!* Usually a quiet and somewhat introverted man, Rik came alive on these missions. Snipers and marksmen are solitary people, but this was his calling. This was when he felt alive.

He was wedged in the doorway of a Dolphin helicopter, a two-hundred-mile-an-hour narco-intercepting machine. He and his crew were chasing a go-fast boat through the Cay Sal Banks, a remote Bahamian island chain and favored drug-running route.

He repeated the phrase in English and Spanish and the two strung-out narcos looked at each other quizzically. In their drug addled minds they had two choices.

First, they could lay their bodies over the engines hoping Chief Meade was bluffing. Hard to imagine, right? Fear is an unbelievable motivator and they knew there is nothing so fearsome and cruel as an angry cartel leader. The narco crew knew all too well, what happened to associates, who failed to protect their illegal and insanely valuable product. Key word, *knew*.

Option two was they could walk to the pointy end of the boat, as instructed.

The narco crew chose the latter, so Rik smiled, exhaled. He then whispered the sniper's mantra. *Slow is smooth. Smooth is fast.* Then squeezed off three .50-caliber rounds from his trusty Barrett M107. Three holes appeared in the engine cowlings, which instantly oozed hot, black oil. He felt like a hunter who had just dropped a bounding mechanical beast.

Like a dying animal, the boat came off plane, sinking lower in the water with white smoke billowing out of the engines. The two compadres sat dejected as they contemplated their fate. The Tabasco cartel loathed having tons of their finest Peruvian marching powder adorning the Coast Guard docks in Miami Beach.

Tony, the helicopter's pilot and Rik's longtime friend, said over the intercom, "Nice shooting, Rik. What that's now? Number nineteen?"

"Twenty," was the quick reply, "but who's counting?" Well, that was some grade A bullshit. Rik loved counting his "kills." In fact, every cowling the team took out was hanging like the *Mona Lisa* at their Opa Locka, Florida air base. All with neatly placed holes in them.

Master Chief Rik Meade was an Aviation Precision Marksman assigned to HITRON, the United States Coast Guard's Helicopter Interdiction Tactical Squadron. He had the best job in the world and worked with the best crew imaginable. This was his destiny. He was born to be a guardian. Fitting that he joined the Coast *Guard*.

But now, perched in the Dolphin's doorway, Chief Meade had no idea that his perfect world was about to be turned upside down—and inside out.

TWO

After their mission debrief, Rik sat in the mess with the pilots, gunners, and crew chiefs, shooting the bull. This was a common occurrence after a successful mission. Unlike other service branches, different Coastie ranks got along well with each other.

They were less concerned about spit-shined shoes and snappy salutes than the real job of saving lives and defending America. They prided themselves on always being ready to serve. In fact, the USCG motto, Semper Paratus, meant just that. Always Prepared.

Somewhere between analyzing the Miami Dolphins' recent lackluster game and wondering about the marital status of the new curvaceous flight instructor, someone yelled, "Who's up for Ball and Chain?" This statement was accompanied by a chorus of hoots and hollers. Rik, normally a loner, was feeling good, and with a couple of good-natured jibes, his Coastie buddies convinced him to join the fun.

For the uninitiated, Ball and Chain was a legendary Miami bar nestled smack-dab in the middle of Calle Ocho in Litte Havana. Its namesake had been a famous bar in Cuba in the '50s before Castro and his henchmen ruined the party. So, the current incarnation had done its best to bring back the Havana party vibe and over time it had become the official and sometimes raucous party bar of USCG Air Base Miami.

The owners had just won a contentious legal battle with a local politician nicknamed Crazy Juan and celebrated their victory by offering half-priced drinks for a month. Using the rationale of work hard, play hard, the boisterous Coast Guard crews headed down to the land of mojitos, salsa music and sultry long-legged girls who could shake it like a Polaroid picture.

Rik parked Roxanne, his old ragtop Jeep, on a shady tree-lined street around the corner and soon found himself at the bar with a large minty mojito. This well-crafted concoction was provided by Enrique, the B&C's longtime bartender. "On the house," he said. "We heard about number twenty." Rik thanked him and tried sipping the delicious cocktail slowly, but he was thirsty and soon he was staring at a tall, empty glass filled with crushed mint leaves.

Enrique was back in a minute and handed him a different drink. It had an orange hue reminiscent of the official USCG color scheme. "Here ya go, Rik. I had a moment of divine inspiration and just invented it. I call it the Coastie Shooter in honor of your latest accomplishment! A couple of these and you'll wake up wondering where all the glitter came from?"

Rik thanked him and tasted his latest concoction.

Enrique had his ups and downs when it comes to new "creations." Who could ever forget his Smokin' Monkey Butt cocktail? Its secret ingredient was two muddled ghost peppers. Did anyone enjoy that delightful concoction? Certainly not the four customers who'd downed it and immediately visited the nearby urgent care facility.

Rik took a wary sip of the Coastie and thought, *Damn, this is pretty good.* "Hey, Enrique. This is great. What's it in it?" he asked.

"Ah…I could tell you but then…oh, never mind. I'll text you the recipe."

Rik's Coastie buddies soon flooded in, and the party was on. Salsa, timbales, short skirts, Tito Puente, dark rum, contraband Cohibas. Platters of much-needed late-night Cuban comfort food started coming out of the kitchen. *Vaca frita, pollo a la plancha, plátanos maduro, frijoles negros, flan, cafecitos.* The entire night was a much-needed break from the stress of aerial operations and narco dickheads.

At one end of the bar, Rik observed a tall dark-haired woman in a short silvery dress. Her shiny black hair was pulled tight in a long ponytail. Her heels could have been on loan from RuPaul. How did he know this? Well, it was literally a rite of passage for everyone in South Florida to attend Fantasy Fest in Key West at least once. Down there anything and everything goes.

But more on that later.

Fueled by liquid courage in the form of one mojito and two Coastie Shooters, he approached his target and turned on the Ol' Riky Rik charm. "Hi ya," Rik said, "I'm Rik, can I buy me a Coastie? I mean a Coast Guard. I mean an orange drink. Not named Julius."

She smiled and seemingly understood his anxiety. She then said in an understated but distinct Latin accent, "You have *meent* on your teeth. Are you grr-owing plants, *mi amigo*?" Her *r*'s vibrated like a Florida panther's purr.

Rik's mind went into high gear, motivated by her titillating accent and rolling *r*'s. *Shit. The mint from the mojito. Think fast…you have exactly two milliseconds with this hottie.* Then his training kicked in. Semper Paratus. He held a cloth napkin over his face, swallowed the cud-like blob, dropped the cloth, and displayed his now-unencumbered pearly whites. "Ta-da!" he announced, "I'm a magician. Enjoying the show so far?"

Whether she was genuinely interested or taking pity on a service member, she replied in a Sofia Vergara–esque accent, "Sure, Riky, I'll try a Coastie thing."

She leisurely sipped Enrique's new beverage and over the next few hours, just as slowly, she revealed her life to Rik. Her name was Carmen and she was from Cali, Colombia. Despite its crazy reputation,

Colombia was a beautiful country and Cali was known for its beautiful women.

Periodically Rik's buddies would stop by to check on him but also to get a closer look at Carmen's neckline. Perhaps to ensure she wasn't a drag queen. This was Miami, after all, and anything went. They were doing their best to be good wingmen. Trying to build him up, so to say. Larry tried singing "You've Lost That Loving Feeling" à la Top Gun and Tony was always addressing him as "Admiral Meade, sir!"

The six-piece band started playing "Oye Coma Va," Tito's version, not Santana's, and he asked her to dance. Rik held Carmen tight and tried to make his gringo hips move like Jagger, but they were failing. And so were his neck and shoulders. The more he tried to move to the beat of the congas and timbales…the more his Anglo body let him down.

But not hers. She moved for the both of them. Lithe and sensual. Graceful and rhythmic. In perfect time to the Latin beat. Time stood still for Rik. She was the only thing in this world. As she held him tight, he inhaled her delicate perfume and melted. What a night!

As the song was ending, she whispered in his ear, "I'm late, Rik. But I want to see you again. Check the bar." With that she twirled and ran outside. There was a shiny, black Suburban waiting for her. She jumped in the back seat and disappeared into the humid Miami night.

What the hell just happened? he thought. He moved quickly to their place at the bar, and there, on a thick B&C coaster, was a phone number. Hers, he hoped, and not the beefy guy who winked at him occasionally. As I said, this was Miami.

Seeing Carmen drop him like a first-period French class, his crew wandered over and started the collective urge to bust his balls … in a typical guy, muy macho, testosteroney kind of way. But seeing his eyes, the eyes he had before he pulled the trigger, they stopped.

The impromptu party wound down and the group eventually ambled to their motley collection of jeeps, pickups and one ridiculously loud Harley and headed back to base.

The party at the Ball and Chain had been everything Rik hoped for—a night of laughter, camaraderie, and the kind of wild freedom that everyone needed. But as he lay in his bunk at the base, with the coaster and Carmen's number in his hand, the night's events replayed in his mind like a looping soundtrack. The combination of her perfume, charm and the enigmatic nature of her departure had left him craving more than just another drink or dance.

Carmen's exit left a void. He couldn't shake the feeling that there was something more to her than just a fleeting bar encounter. The mystery of her leaving and the brief connection they'd shared kept him wide awake, staring at the ceiling, wondering if their paths would cross again.

Finally, as the first light of dawn began to seep through the window of the barracks, he decided to act. Carmen's number was more than ink and cardboard; it was a link to something unexpected and real. He needed to find out more, to see if the connection could be more than just a fleeting moment.

He picked up the phone and dialed the number scrawled on the coaster. She didn't answer, so he left a simple message. "Hi, this is Rik from the Ball and Chain. I'd love to see you again if you're interested."

All the while a song played in his head. *Oye coma va, me ritmo...*

THREE

"Hey, man, quit moping around! I got a sweet gig for us!" Tony's words were followed by several swift kicks to Rik's bunk.

"Dammit, leave me alone, Tony, I've got work to do," was Rik's sad sack reply.

"No, you don't. You're just pouting about that Carmen chick. Forget her, dude. I just got you assigned to a special task force."

Rik's head peeked out from under the blanket. "The only 'task force' I'm interested in is three days in bed with Carmen."

"Relax, horndog. She'll show up. In the meantime, meet me in the mess. I'll tell you all about it."

Reluctantly, Rik dragged himself out of bed and into the mess hall, where three cups of the strongest coffee he could find barely took the edge off. Only then did he sit down across from Tony, whose energy was bordering on terrier puppy hyperactivity.

"Okay, spill it. What's the deal?" Rik asked, rubbing his temple.

Tony leaned back, hands behind his head. "You,

my friend, are now a proud member of the Joint US Coast Guard and Royal Bahamian Defense Force Helicopter Task Force."

Rik squinted at him. "What the hell does that mean?"

"Well, someone in Washington thought it would be a good idea for us to train with the Bahamian Commando Squadron and, and I quote, 'improve the interoperability and effectiveness between the countries' defense forces.'"

"That's Pinder's group!"

James Pinder was a commanding officer in the Royal Bahamian Defense Force, more specifically of their Commando Squadron. They're trained for a wide variety of water borne missions but lately their focus was on counter-narcotics operations. Pinder and his guys were as tough as they came. And loyal.

Tony continued, "Are you seeing the light? We head over to Nassau, pick up James and head to South Andros, train, then do a little diving and fishing, then come home."

Rik replied in the affirmative. "It would be good to see Pinder. He's good people. And makes a world-class conch salad."

Six hours later, Rik and Tony were walking to the helipad with all their gear. But Tony headed for a different bird than Rik was used to. The tail number had an X on it, which indicated it was experimental.

Rik looked at Tony with a puzzled face. The pilot replied, "She's new. The engine and rotors have stealth features, making her extra quiet. On the way back we're gonna fly by Autec and see what their sensors say."

Again, Rik looked puzzled.

"You never heard of Autec?"

"Nope."

"The Atlantic Undersea Testing and Evaluation Center. That's where the US and Britain evaluate their subs. There's a trench just offshore, east of Andros. It's six thousand feet deep—one of the deepest in the Atlantic Ocean. In the sixties they built test facilities there to see how quiet our subs are. They've recently added aerial sensors too. It's a fascinating area. I hear there's good yellowfin tuna fishing there."

All Rik really heard was *'good yellowfin fishin.'*

Takeoff was uneventful, and they were soon flying two hundred miles per hour over the indigo-colored waters of the Gulf Stream towards Nassau. Rik thought it might be quiet outside, but they sure as heck needed headsets inside.

They landed on a little-used portion of Lynden Pindling International Airport and were met by Lieutenant Commander Pinder sporting his black beret with a red dagger insignia. He had been instrumental in getting this designation for his team of warriors. In the special ops world, everyone knew these guys were the real deal. Especially around the water. Few nations had a special forces outfit where the members had grown up literally in the ocean; a Hawaiian sling in one hand and dinner in the other.

The three exchanged salutes followed by manly hugs. It had been a while since Rik had seen his brother from another mother.

They hopped into Pinder's Jeep and ended up at a local beach shack that made great island fare. After Pinder made sure his guests had a heaping pile of fresh conch salad, crackers, Tabasco, cracked conch and ice-cold Kaliks, he said, "So tell me about this Carmen woomahn?"

Rik cast a questioning glance at Tony, who clearly had spilled the beans. "Well, first, it's none of your Bahamian business, and second, I want you both to be in my wedding party."

Tony and James stared at each other; slack jawed. Both knew Rik better than most on this earth and they couldn't believe their ears. If ever there was going to be a lifelong bachelor, it was Rik Meade.

James continued, "What did she do? Cast a spell on you? Use voodoo?"

Rik's mind retreated for a moment. Carmen. She'd completely scrambled his head. His luck with women was lousy, but something about her was different. He had called her number, but he wasn't sure he'd ever hear from her again. This assignment was exactly what he needed—a break from overthinking everything.

Ignoring James's question, he announced, "Tell you what, guys. We don't fly out till the morning. Let's have another round of Kaliks."

The next morning found the trio flying the short hop to an unnamed and uninhabited island at the southern end of Andros. Andros was geographically the largest chain in the Bahamas and the least populated. Filled with hundreds of tiny islands and unnavigable sandbars, it was the perfect place for this type of military training. Their destination came into view, surrounded by turquoise waters.

The next few days were consumed with a wide range of helicopter-related skills for Pinder's men. They practiced hot loading and unloading, fast roping, combat offloading and a few other skills that cannot be mentioned for security reasons. Suffice it to say that by the time Friday rolled around, all were exhausted.

Pinder's men shipped out back to Nassau on the HMBS *Lawrence Major*, but James stayed behind to show Tony and Rik the local sites. Saturday morning, they explored several blue holes, and in the afternoon, they went spear fishing with slings and pole spears and also did some conch collecting. Rik brought along his underwater GoPro to record their exploits.

Tony was in charge of the conch operation as he wasn't as skilled at free diving. That night, under a million stars, they built a small fire on the beach and grilled lobster and mutton snapper along with some corn, peas, and lots of butter.

As they were eating, Rik said, "Hey, Pinder, how'd you get the mutton? I saw a couple but couldn't get near them."

He replied, "Well, first of all you have to speak mutton. Growing up in Spanish Wells we were taught the language of all fish."

Tony and Rik pondered this for a second before Rik shouted, "Bullshit!" No one laughed harder than Pinder, and after a few swigs of Kalik he responded seriously.

Pinder looked all around him, as if someone were listening, then said, "Well, first of all you need good lungs. You need to hold your breath for at least two to three minutes. The muttons like to be near reefs but spend a lot of time in the surrounding grass. Once you find a good area, you swim down stealthily and land in the sandy area between the reef and the grass. Then you grab small handfuls of sand and let it pour slowly out … like a broken hourglass. The muttons spook easily but they're also curious. If you're lucky, one will come within range. And when that happens—bam, headshot and you have dinner. But then you have to watch out for the tax man."

Tony looked confused and said, "Tax man?" Rik knew what James meant but stayed silent.

"You know, the man in the gray suit. Sharks."

Tony quickly said, "I didn't see any sharks."

At this point Rik and James laughed. "Well, they were there."

Tony, being less experienced in the water, practically shouted, "Well, why the hell didn't you tell me?"

Without missing a beat, Rik replied, "Because then we wouldn't have five beautiful conch over there."

Tony, hopefully believing that these two maniacs wouldn't let anything happen to him, finally said, "Well, I gotta tell you…this is the best seafood I've ever had."

Rik joined in. "Tomorrow, thanks to you, we're gonna have James's famous conch salad. And I do believe they teach that in the schools here!"

Tony next asked, "So I get how James learned to dive, but what about you Rik?"

Rik never liked talking about his childhood but these guys were special. "Well, it all goes back to my uncle Jax. He raised me after my parents disappeared. We lived in a small house in West Miami but on weekends we spent time on his ramshackle houseboat docked next to Alabama Jacks.

From there he took me on numerous nautical adventures. He taught me to skin dive, scuba, use a Hawaiian sling and spear gun. He showed me where to find lobster, stone crabs. Fish for yellowtail, grouper, mahi, wahoo. You name it. We caught it, cleaned it, and ate it. It was a good life and he was a good teacher."

"As I got older I started working as a mate at Ocean Reef. I thought that would be a good life … being a charter captain. Like the old Crunch and Des stories. Anyhow I grew tired of tending to rich, entitled northerners and Uncle Jax felt I had a bigger calling."

"You don't talk about him much. What did he have in mind for you?"

"It was a weird time. He didn't plan on being a father. He was more of a teacher or mentor. He meant well but there wasn't a lot of love or emotion around. But he did impart his life code on me. Defend those who can't. I believe he felt guilty because he didn't guard someone or something he should have."

"What did he do?"

"He worked for Uncle Sam in a military capacity but we rarely talked about it. I know he spent time in Vietnam in special ops but again it wasn't discussed. From tidbits he dropped I feel like he was CIA or in the Green Berets. He was deep in the jungle working with Montagnards. And the US certainly didn't treat them right."

"Sorry I'm not familiar?"

"Nobody talks about them much. They were one of the countless victims of the Vietnam war. Anyhow one night Uncle Jax had too much to drink and muttered the following. I'll never forget these words."

'The Montagnards didn't take orders—they sized you up, to see if they would fight with you. 'They came out of the jungle with a crossbow and a machete and they'd move through triple canopy like ghosts.'

'When the war turned ugly—the Montagnards paid the price. Families killed. Promises broken. We left too many behind.'

'I carry that. Some of us tried to make it right. Some still are.'

"Then he fell asleep. He seemed to carry that burden all the time. And I felt like he was training me to carry on when he no longer could."

"Where's he now?"

"I'm not sure. After I joined the Coast Guard he would disappear for months at a time. I haven't heard from him in a year. But he'll turn up. He always does. Probably with some wild ass story!"

Rik chuckled at the thought, then suggested they turn in. With that they put out the fire and headed back to their rustic but habitable accommodations. Rik's last thoughts before falling into a deep sleep were of Carmen, of course.

The next day James gave the two Coasties a lesson in making conch salad. The first thing he did was to poke a hole in the cone of the shell and pry the conch out. He beat the hell out of it and trimmed the meat into small pieces. Then he found an old board and left the conch to sit out in the sun for a bit. Oh, and he squeezed a generous amount of fresh lime juice on it.

While the conch was marinating, James sliced up onions, red and green peppers and one of his secret ingredients: cucumbers. He eventually mixed everything together with even more lime and his second secret ingredient: orange juice. He put the entire concoction in the small fridge and said, "When we get back…this will be perfect."

The rest of the day they fished offshore. Pinder had borrowed a small boat, and they caught several mahimahi as well as deep jigged. Using this technique, with braided line, of course, they brought up two very nice black grouper.

Once again, they found themselves at the end of the day on the beach, under the amazing stars, dining on some of the finest seafood in the world.

Pinder showed Tony how he liked to put a spoonful of conch salad on a cracker topped off with hot pepper sauce. He offered one to Tony, who ate it in one bite. His eyes bulged out and tears ran down his cheeks, but he took it like a man as Rik and Pinder laughed their asses off. Recovering from his encounter with a Scotch bonnet pepper, he asked Rik how he'd met James.

Still chuckling at Tony's teary-eyed face, Rik replied, "We met under unusual circumstances.

Basically, I found him floating in the Gulf Stream in a large Igloo cooler. We were both fishing for mahimahi that day, but James's boat had some issues. Hull integrity issues. I knew I liked him 'cause he still had a line out and had a schoolie on."

James quickly interjected, "Schoolie? It was a big bull, forty-pounder at least!"

"Yeah, right. Anyhow, James stayed with me and Uncle Jax in Miami until the authorities could straighten his paperwork out. In the meantime, we bonded like brothers while we fished and dove Biscayne Bay and ate like gluttons in Little Havana. The guy could eat his weight in black beans and rice. Who knew our lives would be intertwined now?"

As the dinner wound down, Rik proposed a toast: "To the two best friends a guy could ever have!" And with that they headed back to the old lodge, where they all had a restful sleep.

The next morning, Pinder said his goodbyes as he decided to stay an extra day and do some bone fishing with a guide friend a few islands to the north. Rik and Tony spent the day drafting reports documenting their training exercises. It was dusk by the time they lifted off.

Rik glanced out over the Andros shoreline, reluctantly leaving. "Man, I'm gonna miss this place," he muttered. He took a few photos with the GoPro hanging from his neck, thinking he would send copies to Pinder and Tony when they returned to base.

As Rik settled into his copilot seat, Tony said, "It's going to be sporty." A front was moving in that would stir up the air and the waters below. They were both used to bumpy flying, but together they each knew it was no day to be on a boat in the Gulf Stream. They lifted off and the string of islands looked even more stunning from the air, with its endless mangroves and shimmering water.

Their flight path took them north initially, and Tony pointed forward and said over the headset, "There's the Autec site. I'll get 'em on the horn."

Tony raised them on an encrypted channel. The Autec ops director instructed him to make four different passes at five hundred feet over the base. The audio would be recorded, analyzed by their massive Cray supercomputers, and sent back to some obscure site in the middle of nowhere for analysis. Probably Area 51.

After the last pass, they headed northwest for what appeared to be a typical if bumpy flight home. About ten miles into the flight there was a flash and an explosion. The helicopter shook intensely. Tony's expression turned grim as he fought the controls. "Oh, no! No, no, no!"

"What's happening?" Rik asked immediately.

"Tail rotor's gone!"

FOUR

Tony's terse words were said through gritted teeth while he wrestled with the helo's cyclic stick. Simultaneously a myriad of alarm sounds erupted from the helo's instrument panel. None of them particularly good.

Before Rik could fully process Tony's words, the helicopter began to rotate violently. Tony shouted into the radio, "Mayday, mayday!" But he never finished his sentence as their world became a spinning blur before they hit the water.

The impact was brutal. Rik's head slammed against the panel and water flooded into the cabin immediately. The helicopter tilted, then flipped onto its side. Fighting fear and disorientation, Rik and Tony clawed their way out before the helo sank.

They surfaced gasping for air, only to be met by towering, angry waves. The weather had turned worse while they were in the air, and now they were floating in ten-foot seas with no immediate sign of rescue.

"You okay?" Rik yelled at Tony.

"Yeah. I'll make it. Where's the life raft?" he

yelled back.

"It didn't deploy!"

Without wasting a second, Rik dove for the sinking helicopter. He saw it thirty feet down in the limited light, sinking fast. This was a depth he could normally free dive to, but his life preserver's buoyancy stopped him. He quickly punctured it with his survival knife and kept swimming and kicking for the sinking craft as if his life depended on it. It did. And Tony's too.

His lungs were bursting when he reached the side cabin door. He braced his feet on the helicopter's fuselage and pulled and yanked on the handle, but the door was bent from the crash. It wouldn't open. The copter was sinking faster now, and Rik realized if he hung on any longer, he would never be able to reach the surface. As he pushed off the craft skyward, he glanced at the tail rotor. It had been blown apart.

After a frightening ascent, he surfaced, gasping for breath. Luckily, Tony was near, and he grabbed onto him.

"I couldn't get to it. The cabin door was fucked up. I'm sorry," Rik lamented.

Tony immediately noticed Rik's punctured life preserver. "Man, you didn't have to do that."

Rik replied stoically, "I had to. Don't worry, I'm tougher than I look. Does ATC know our position?" he yelled over the roar of the waves.

Tony sputtered and yelled back, "I don't know. It happened so fast. They should see our ping disappear off the radar. I put out a mayday, but I don't know if anyone heard. When they realize we're no longer pinging, SAR ops will start, but we have to survive till then."

Their training began to kick in and they went through their survival vests. They simultaneously reached for their Personal Locator Beacons and turned them on. Nothing happened.

"Aren't they supposed to flash red when working?"

Neither were. "The batteries are dead. How can that be?"

"Well, at least we have the survival radios." Again, they reached into their survival vests and turned on their radios. Dead. "This can't be happening. This is impossible. At least they know the last spot from helicopter's pinger. They'll start a grid search from there. Hopefully, we don't get pushed too far away from it."

Rik knew the chances of them being found were slim to none in ten-foot seas. He had been on enough SARs to know the higher the seas, the harder people were to find. Plus, every minute they were in the water took them farther from the ping sight. The SAR team would use computer models to project their location, but they weren't always reliable.

He was starting to get annoyed by the little camera around his neck. He was about to discard it when he realized he and Tony's last moments on earth were hidden inside. He kept it, thinking one day someone would find it and bring their memories to life.

They did find two chem lights. They lit one, saving the other for later. Its green glow gave them comfort as they could see each other's faces while the sun set.

They floated in silence for a few moments in the maelstrom, but it was apparent Rik wouldn't be able to tread water forever. If the seas were calm, he could float on his back, but this wasn't an option.

Rik knew what he had to do, but Tony said it first.

"Take off your flight suit," he said firmly. "We need to inflate it."

As Rik stripped off the suit, Tony proceeded to tie the ends of the arms and legs with tight knots. Next, they held the neck open and plunged into the foamy water, so the bubbles filled the suit with air. Then they rolled it up, creating temporary but lifesaving buoyancy for Rik. They would repeat this tiring process every twenty minutes. It was better than the alternative.

Their dire situation was sinking in. As pros, they knew their team would find them. They just had to stay alive through the night.

"You know that's a terrible look," Tony sputtered.

Rik didn't understand. "Naked. You're naked in the Gulf Stream. You look horrible." They both laughed weakly. Anything to put their predicament temporarily out of their minds.

Tony took out his survival knife (at least something worked) and began cutting the bottom half of his flight suit off. He then cut it into long strips, which he then used to tether the two of them together. They had a greater chance of being spotted and surviving as a duo than if they drifted apart.

"We gotta conserve energy," Rik said, panting. "Float on your back when you can. Let the vest do the work."

Tony nodded but still had enough cheek to quip, "And here I thought this would be all sun and rum punch."

The night dragged on. Rik would occasionally catch a flash of lightning on the horizon, illuminating the massive, dark waves. The two men traded short conversations, if only to keep each other awake and sane. Rik was remined of a saying he heard at Cape May, '*The sea is a mean teacher. She gives the test first, then the lesson after.*' He now saw the truth in that adage.

Around two in the morning, they were bumped into by something large. And hard. Rik immediately thought it was a shark. Oceanic whitetip, to be exact. Ten feet long. Four hundred pounds of instant death.

He'd seen them inhale one-hundred-pound yellowfins off Great Isaac Light. He started saying his prayers.

But it wasn't a fish. It was telephone pole. Thanks to the many hurricanes in the Caribbean, you wouldn't believe what you could find floating in the Gulf Stream. They often harbored a wide variety of fish, including tripletail and mahi. But tonight, the pole held two exhausted Coasties.

They clung to the pole until dawn, when a particularly large wave bounced them off.

The sun rose like a molten coin, scorching and relentless. With no shade or fresh water, dehydration began to set in. Their tongues felt thick, their lips cracking.

The skies darkened, and the seas turned choppy. A storm rolled in, bringing driving rain and fierce winds. "The rain!" Tony shouted. "We can drink it!"

They removed their flight helmets, tipping them back to catch the rainwater. It wasn't much, but every drop felt like a lifeline.

The storm raged, tossing them around like driftwood. Rik's muscles burned from clinging to the tether they'd rigged. His mind wandered back to Carmen. He couldn't die out here. Not without seeing her again.

The morning dawned clearer as the storm had spent its fury. Rik blinked against the sunlight, his body aching from the constant battle against the waves.

Tony squinted toward the horizon. "Hey… do you see that?"

Rik followed his gaze. A faint speck moved against the shimmering line where the sea met the sky. Was it a ship? A plane? It was an orange helo. The Coast Guard baby.

Tony lit the other green chemical light they had saved and waved it high as they both gestured their arms maniacally at the crest of each wave.

They grew tired, and horrible thoughts began to ebb in their subconscious state.

It was Rik who rallied first. *No, goddammit. Not here. I've got to live. I've got to see Carmen. And Tony has to return to his daughter. I don't mind dying*, he thought. *But not today.* His mind started firing internally like a camera. It was true. Your life flashed before your eyes like a camera.

A camera!

He grabbed the camera from around his neck and started taking photos of the distant copter. Tony stopped waving and questioned Rik's sanity. "Are you crazy?"

"No, brother…it's the flash. They'll see the camera's flash."

Rik kept his finger on the shutter button and just when the camera's battery was about to expire…the helo turned eastward. "They see us!" Tony shouted, his voice cracking.

Soon they were engulfed in its welcomed rotor wash. The rescue swimmer started to jump and they waved him off. They didn't need rescuing in their mind. They simply needed a lift back to shore and signaled for the winch and harness to be dropped.

Rik pushed Tony in first, insisting he had a daughter and he was priority.

Tony was too exhausted to argue and he rapidly soared into that beautiful orange creature hovering overhead. Rik was hoisted next and finally slid into the cabin. The flight crew turned in his direction and everyone erupted in nervous laughter, including Tony.

Rik looked down. He understood. There he was naked, holding onto his blown-up flight suit like a pool floatie. He started laughing too as the pilot spun the helo around and headed for Opa Locka.

On the flight home, as Tony downed several bottles of water and continuously muttered, "Worst vacation ever," Rik was feeling pretty darn grateful but couldn't shake the suspicion that someone was behind their troubles.

FIVE

Tony and Rik required an overnight stay at Jackson Hospital for observation, but they emerged from their ordeal relatively unscathed. From Rik's perspective, he practically forgot about the misadventure when Carmen called.

They arranged a lunch date by the pool at the Biltmore Hotel. On the appointed day, Rik took the cover off Roxanne and headed down the fast and furious and occasionally death-defying I-95 to pick up Carmen. She lived in a gaudy, even by Miami standards, condominium on Brickell Avenue. He pulled into the "Chez I'm Really Rich and You're Not" and circled around to the valet stand. Alarm bells went off and valets hastily approached Rik and his "rustic" Jeep.

The first valet put his hand on Rik's shoulder and said, "Food deliveries use the service entrance… sir!" The sir was certainly not meant with respect and was a bit condescending. Nope, it was really condescending. Perhaps Rik should have dressed up more, but he was in no mood for jerks that day. So, he grabbed the valet's fingers and began bending them backwards, curious to see which one popped first. His money was on Mr. Pinky Finger, but who knew?

"Marco, Marco, he's with me!" Carmen walked up and was even more stunning in the daylight. Perfectly underdressed in a baseball cap, tight buttoned cotton shirt and Daisy Dukes. Or Carmen Mirandas. Whatever the term was for Latin short shorts.

Rik released Marco and his nervous fingers and Carmen slid effortlessly beside him. As fancy as her surroundings were, she was right at home in his lowbrow Jeep.

She kissed him on the cheek, and he melted when he smelled her perfume. He was instantly transported to their magical night at the Ball and Chain. *"Hola, mi amor,"* she said, and with that they headed towards Coral Gables and the iconic Biltmore Hotel.

The Biltmore was one of Miami's oldest hotels and one of the most stylish. Its architecture was a combination of classic Italian, Moorish, and Spanish influences. Rik knew this because he was pulling out all the stops with Carmen, including reading architectural magazines.

As they drove down the oak-lined streets of Coral Gables, she asked about the Jeep. "Why do you call her Roxanne? Was she a girlfriend? A lover? A mistress, perhaps?" The last phrase was said slowly and mischievously as if all those scenarios would be okay with her. Even encouraged.

"Nope," he replied, "She's named after the Police song about a woman of the night. My girl likes her top off too, so the name stuck." Carmen started to say something about her top, but she was cut short as they turned into the Biltmore's parking lot.

Rik's high school friend Bob was in charge of the hotel's food and beverage operations for years, and he'd come through in a big way. He reserved the best poolside table for the excited couple. The hotel was fantastic, and the pool was equally outstanding. It was gigantic, a beautiful shade of blue and surrounded by gorgeous tanning men and women. There were even several secluded cabanas that could be used for, shall we say, discreet moments.

They sat down and Rik felt like a million bucks. Carmen looked great and all was right with the world. After ordering, they started a bit of small talk. Rik opened with, "Carmen, I feel like I've known you forever, but I know so little about you. Tell me more about your life in Colombia."

"Well, as I told you, I grew up in a small town outside of Cali. I had an uneventful childhood. I enjoyed school, but my parents did not want me to go to college. I had a simple life. Despite what Americans say about my country, it was a wonderful place to grow up. I was happy and never saw the horrible things in the newspapers."

Her body language told Rik she was uncomfortable talking about herself. As if on cue, she said, "But tell me about you. Your life is so exciting. Tell me, *mi amor*."

"I was born and raised right here in Miami. One of the few natives. I grew up on the water, fishing, diving. I love it here. As a kid I sold mangos every summer from a stand my uncle built for me."

"How did you end up in the Coast Guard?"

Part of Rik's job was classified, but there was certainly no harm in telling her why he'd joined. So, he continued.

"Well, growing up in Miami I often saw the Coast Guard helicopters and boats speeding off over the horizon on lifesaving missions. They were always on the evening news too. They were military, but their job was to save people and that was something I could relate to. I always felt a calling to help people. So, after high school I applied and was accepted."

"And what do you do exactly?"

He fibbed and said, "I'm involved in aviation maintenance."

"Interesting…tell him more. Do you work on helicopters or fixed-wing aircraft?"

Her question caught him off guard. He was hesitant to expand on the topic, so thank goodness the food arrived and the conversation drifted elsewhere. She was very interested in the details of his job, but he let it go.

The poolside lunch under the pink-and-purple bougainvillea trellis continued and they each had a great time. He was comfortable with Carmen. Their backgrounds were so different. Perhaps opposites really did attract? After lunch, they walked the grounds to stretch their legs and eventually toured the ornate lobby. They stared upward and gawked at the colorful frescoes painted on the ceiling.

All good things must come to an end, so rather than stretching their date out, Rik took Carmen back home but planned for date number two.

The next few days passed quickly for him as suspected drug trafficking picked up significantly. Rik and his team flew several missions, but no shooting was involved. This was all good as he literally couldn't wait to see Carmen.

Several days later he pulled into Carmen's opulent circular driveway and saw Marco retreat strategically into his valet hut. *Good move, Marco*, Rik thought. *Roxanne wouldn't like your paws on her anyhow.* Carmen was standing in the lobby and she hopped in eagerly.

They were soon headed down Old Cutler Road to the world-famous Fairchild Botanical Gardens, the site of their second date. Fairchild is a botanical wonderland and sometime respite for Rik from the concrete jungle that Miami had become. His mother would take him here when he was a little kid and he especially enjoyed the annual White Elephant sale. But like many good things, those days were long gone.

Once they entered the grounds, the two began walking silently through the garden, hand in hand. Words weren't needed at the moment. They strode past lily pad–covered ponds, under flame-red poinciana trees and through orchid-clad rainforests. They smelled jasmine and wandered through the Lower Keys habitat. Having spent much of his youth in the Florida Keys, Rik felt particularly drawn to this area of the garden.

After a bit, he broke the silence and said, "Come with me. I want to show you a secret spot." They walked back through the rainforest, past the ancient cycads and down a limestone path that descended slightly and ended up in front of a small waterfall. The couple was surrounded by roughhewn limestone walls covered in orchids and green moss. The air was cool, and the little grotto was very secluded. The only sound was the music made by the water as it tumbled over the rocks and splashed into a small pond.

Carmen stared at him and said, "It's so beautiful. I love you for taking me here."

And with that, they embraced and kissed deeply. Their souls reached out and entwined. *This is crazy*, he thought, but he wasn't so crazy as to stop kissing her. They finally came up for air and slowly sat down on a small bench.

Carmen's facial expression was changing. She wanted to say something. Much of his training involved observation and he was good at it. Now he was observing her face and body language. She was nervous and was holding back. "What is it, Carmen?"

"I'm ashamed. I haven't been honest with you."

Rik was confused—a normal state of affairs when he was with women, but in this case, he was really confused. He was falling hard for this mysterious Carmen. *She's probably going to tell me she married or some BS like that.*

"Rik, I'm married."

Rik was startled by hearing these words. On the other hand, he was impressed by his own intuitive powers. At that moment he wanted to run out of there screaming like a banshee.

But then Carmen uncrossed her sculpted, tan legs and that little spot in a man's brain that made them stupid kicked in. "Go on," he said, "you can tell me anything."

"I'm married, Rik. I'm married to a horrible man. A violent man. I came to Miami to get away from him. He lives in Colombia, but he's a bad man and I'm scared. I'm scared he followed me here."

Rik's face was stern as she continued.

"I didn't plan to meet you that night. I just had to get out, I was going stir-crazy. I'm so sorry for misleading you. But you melted my heart, *mi amor*." She leaned in and kissed him. This kiss was different. Like two old souls who had been separated and were now together again. Time truly stood still. Some tourists strolled down to the grotto, but Rik's glare sent them retreating quickly to the Rare Plant House, where making out was very much frowned upon.

They eventually stopped and after a pensive moment Rik made some decisions. Decisions clearly influenced by that kiss and other carnal interests.

"Carmen," he started, "I haven't told you much about my job with the Coast Guard. Some of what I do is classified. But I have access to resources. And friends. Both of whom can help you and keep you safe. Help the two of us, actually. I want to be with you, and I don't want you to be afraid anymore. What's your husband's name? My friends can check him out, even in a foreign country."

"Roberto Allende," she replied hesitantly.

Huh? She couldn't mean the notorious drug kingpin. "You don't mean Roberto Allende of the Tabasco cartel?" She nodded shamefully.

"Not El Pintor! Not the Painter?"

"*Sí*, that's him," she said, staring a hole though the rock floor beneath her feet.

His mind was racing. Roberto Allende was the son of Chi-Chi Allende, the head of the Tabasco cartel and one brutal SOB. He was called the Painter because, like Van Gogh, he was missing a significant part of his left ear. To maintain his machismo air, he attributed it to a brutal knife fight, but word on the street was he'd lost it in an unfortunate shaving accident.

The Painter ran the transportation end of his father's druggie kingdom and allegedly was personally responsible for the submarines and other crazy vehicles used to move their contraband. Lately their strategy had evolved to take advantage of the popularity of large go-fast boats with four outboards or more, up to five hundred horsepower each. The tactic involved simply blending in. Like hiding under the cover of daylight. This tactic had suffered lately, however, due to increased intel and the efficiency of airborne units like Rik's. These guys had the Coast Guard's attention. And vice versa.

Rik thought, *This knowledge changes things. Changes our relationship. I'm sure there's a rule in the Coast Guard that requires a guy to fill out a form when you're in contact with the wife of a drug kingpin. I wonder if there's a check box for making out?*

His mind was cluttered, and he needed a break. Rik suggested returning to Brickell, where he dropped Carmen off. Marco was nowhere to be found.

SIX

"We need to talk."

Most men feared those words. But in this case, Rik initiated them. With good reason. Carmen's husband and father-in-law were the worst of the worst narco-terrorists. They were involved with the manufacture, transport, and distribution of cocaine, heroin, fentanyl, and methamphetamine.

If that wasn't enough, they were also engaged in human trafficking, smuggling migrants, extortion, and kidnapping. The tools of their trade were all forms of violence, including assassinations, armed confrontations, and acts of terror. In summary, they were huge pieces of shit.

Rik couldn't believe Carmen could be involved with these dirtbags. So, he really needed to talk. Rik preferred to discuss their situation in person, away from cell phone towers and prying eyes. Carmen suggested meeting on her boat, which was docked in the small private marina behind Chez Taj Mahal. This seemed like a good plan or a very bad plan depending on the moon phase. Either way Rik was there the next day.

His new best friend, Marco, greeted him promptly too. "Hello, Mr. Meade, sir. How are you today? I understand you are visiting Mrs. Allende. Would you like to leave your vehicle on the ramp?"

"You mean park my beat-up ol' Jeep between the Ferrari 296 and the Lambo Aventador? Well, I guess so." Rik really drew out the "guess so" part for some emphasis. Either Marco's fingers were doing the talking now or Mrs. Allende's reputation had gotten around. Rik suspected it was a bit of both.

Carmen met him in the lobby, but they quickly departed and walked around to the concrete docks and then straight to her boat. And by boat, I mean a sixty-five-foot fisherman's wet dream. It was a cold-molded, custom Carolina-built Spence called *La Exquisita*. Everything about her was top-of-the-line. She had a sweeping Carolina flare and a deck you could play Olympic volleyball on. Teak cockpit, air-conditioned bridge and a tuna tower that kissed the sky (yes, a Jimi Hendrix reference). She even had a flats boat for a tender. When Rik was done drooling, Carmen smiled, then ushered him into the salon.

Rik focused and began strategizing a plan for their dilemma. In a nutshell, Rik was in love with a cartel member's wife. But she was separated, so in his mind everything was going to be okay. Not to worry. She'd divorce him. They'd marry. Move to the suburbs, white picket fence with three-phase electrodes and live happily ever after. And security. Lots of security. And dogs. Lots of nasty dogs. Big cane corso types with spike collars.

They sat silent for a moment and then Rik said, "Why don't you start at the beginning and tell me what happened?"

She sighed and started her tale. "I met Roberto when he was working in Cali after high school. He was handsome and charming. I knew his family had money, but he said they owned large farms and cattle and other enterprises. We eventually got married. I was naive. But we were in love, or I thought we were.

"But over time our love deteriorated. He became angry and violent. He was never home. When he was home, there were always thugs around. He claimed we needed them because we were rich. But these were just henchmen on drugs.

"After several years I couldn't take it. He told me to take a break. Go to Miami. Have fun. Go to the spas. But he had an agenda. He wanted me to pick up *La Exquisita*. I was the only one he could trust with a ten-million-dollar boat. Well, I've been here almost a year, and I don't want to go back. But he wants me. And his boat. I'm beginning to suspect he was going to use it to transport drugs. A new approach for him.

"So here I am. Scared. Alone. I have enough money for several lifetimes. But if I don't return with the boat, he'll kill me."

Rik thought, *Me too, if he finds me on board with his wife.*

She was exhausted and teary-eyed after revealing her tale. Carmen moved into his arms, and he held her closely while they rocked gently with the small marina waves. They kissed and then she looked deeply at him and took his hand. He followed her into the stateroom. There was not a lot of sleeping that night.

The next morning, Rik awoke to the scent of the best coffee he'd ever smelled. He followed the aroma of caffeine into the galley, where Carmen had brewed a delicious pot of Colombian coffee. As she poured a cup, she winked and said, "See? There are other benefits to dating a girl from Colombia." His mind drifted momentarily to last night and he thought of several other benefits.

Over a Colombian breakfast of *huevos pericos* and a few Cuban *pastalitos con guayaba*, his mind started to clear and work for their benefit.

"Carmen," he said, "There is a way I can help you. I haven't told you everything about what I do. Much of it's classified. I'm taking a big risk telling you. A career-ending risk. A future of showering with rough guys kind of risk."

"You can trust me. I love you!"

That declaration caught him off guard, but he continued.

"Carmen, I'm part of a task force that intercepts illegal contraband coming into the United States. There are people in this unit who will protect you. And you could share any knowledge you have of Roberto's operations."

The color left her face. "I know very little. Even if I did, Roberto would kill me and my family for collaborating. This is no option for me … *mi amor*."

"If you truly want to get away, leave him forever and have a life with me, we need the power of the US government and the people I trust. The US Coast Guard. There's no other way!"

Carmen's eyes met his, a mix of fear and resolve. "Rik, I'm terrified. But I trust you. How do we even begin?"

In the quiet aftermath of their emotional disclosure, Rik's mind raced with strategic calculations. He knew that engaging his Coast Guard contacts was risky, but it was a calculated risk that would secure their safety. *It's about leveraging federal resources*, he thought, *but more than that, it's about outsmarting one of the most cunning and ruthless cartels in the world.*

Meanwhile, Carmen was grappling with her own turmoil. "He's dangerous, Rik. And he's vindictive. If he even suspects…"

"We'll need to plan carefully," Rik replied. "First,

we secure a meeting with my task force—off the record. They need to understand the threat level and what's at stake. Then, we'll need a safe house, something off-grid where you can stay until we sort this out."

The logistical nightmare of safeguarding Carmen, while his own career was in jeopardy, wasn't lost on Rik. Yet the thought of losing her to the cartel's grasp was unimaginable. He pictured their potential life together, far from the shadow of her past, somewhere quiet, where the drama of their current life couldn't reach.

"We'll make sure he doesn't know," he said, his voice a blend of assurance and steely resolve. "We'll use burner phones, coded messages, whatever it takes. I know people who specialize in this—people who've kept witnesses safe against odds you wouldn't believe."

She thought for a moment and came to her senses. "Okay, I'll talk to them."

Their strategy session stretched into the afternoon; each detail meticulously plotted like coordinates on a nautical chart. As the sun dipped below the horizon, casting a golden glow over the marina, Rik and Carmen emerged from the boat's salon. The marina was quiet, opulent yachts bobbing in the calm evening tide, oblivious to the storm of human drama unfolding aboard *La Exquisita*.

Dinner was a quiet affair, eaten mostly in silence. Their shared secret bound them in a mutual resolve, each bite punctuated by unspoken vows of protection and defiance.

"It won't be easy," Rik said as he held Carmen close, watching the distant Fowey Rocks lighthouse blink against the darkening sky. "But I swear on everything I am, we'll get through this. We'll start fresh somewhere, and all this will be a distant memory."

Carmen nodded, her head resting against his chest, her voice barely audible against the wind. "With you, I believe it's possible. With you, I have hope."

As they stood together, the challenges ahead loomed large, yet the resolve in their hearts burned brighter. Tomorrow would bring hurdles, but tonight, they had each other, and for now, that was enough.

SEVEN

The next few days were a whirlwind of meetings, not just with Rik's guys at the Coast Guard but with nearly every other agency out there. Carmen's defection was huge. The kind of intelligence coup that had every lettered agency drooling. She was the first real insider from the Tabasco cartel to flip.

They were both exhausted. Rik stayed by her side through it all. Some of his superiors threw suspicious glances his way—Carmen wasn't just any informant. But their skepticism was tempered by their ambitious visions of taking down one of the most infamous cartels in the world.

In Miami, Carmen had been moving frequently, taking every precaution to keep Roberto and the cartel off her trail. But now, with so many agencies and personnel involved, the pressure was starting to get to her. Soon, though, they would be relocated to a base far from Miami and its many prying eyes.

They needed a break. So, Rik decided to take *La Exquisita* down to the Keys. It had been a while since he'd run a boat like that. They traveled light—just a few small duffels packed with clothes, swimsuits, and some dive gear. Of course, he packed a pair of Glock 19's and some extra clips. Carmen's safety was his top priority.

They left the marina and headed south, down the Intercostal Waterway, passing under the towering Rickenbacker Bridge before making their way toward Biscayne Channel. They had a few options to reach the Keys, but Rik figured Carmen would like to see Stiltsville—a group of quirky wooden houses perched on stilts seemingly in the middle of the ocean. There weren't many left, but they were fun to see. Carmen loved seeing them and wrapped him in a hug as they passed by.

Once in deeper water, they turned south and made a beeline for Key Largo. Rik had a discreet friend with a house and dock where they could lie low for a few days. Along the way, he made a detour near a small island called Boca Chica, where he knew a great spot for spiny lobsters.

He anchored in thirty feet of water and slipped over the side with his snorkel gear, a tickle stick, and a net. Sure enough, there they were—hiding under a small rock, but their antennas gave them away. Three dives later, he had three lobsters ready for the grill that night. After raising and then rinsing off the anchor, he continued south, eventually turning west in sight of the Carysfort Lighthouse.

His buddy's house was like something out of a tropical dream—Key West style, with a metal roof, a wraparound veranda, rocking chairs, a pool, and an adjoining tiki hut. Perfect for their getaway. Oh, and not to mention, a fully stocked bar and kitchen.

Carmen was thrilled as they idled up to the dock. Without missing a beat, she called out, "I'll get the bow line and then the spring!" Her Charo-esque accent made Rik grin. You know you're lucky when your girlfriend can help dock a boat like *La Exquisita*.

After a quick tour of the house, Carmen looked at Rik with those big, doe-like eyes and whispered, "I'd do anything for a delicious seafood dinner."

His mind wandered in a mischievous direction, but he simply handed her a pen and paper and said, "Good. Write them all down."

Rik was starving too, so he got to work. The first thing he did was tail the lobsters and clean them, using their own antennas to clean out their canals—it was a little gross, but fast and efficient, one of nature's quirky tricks.

He butterflied the lobster tails and placed them on the grill. When they were almost done, he brushed on a light smattering of BBQ sauce and flipped them facedown for a finishing touch. Inside the kitchen, he had some drawn butter ready, a side salad prepped, and just enough time to whip up some fried green tomatoes.

To top it off, his buddy had left him a Key lime

pie. Rik grew up with a Key lime tree in his backyard and literally ate three pies a week as a teenager, so he considered himself an aficionado. His friend's was very good, but one day he'd make Carmen his own special version.

They sat down to this delicious meal, and as they ate, they started to talk about the future.

"Rik, this is amazing," Carmen began, her voice soft. "I want to spend the rest of my life with you."

He was caught off guard, but he had been thinking the same thing too.

"Carmen," he said, pausing to collect his thoughts. "Let's be realistic—how could we ever truly escape and be free?"

She looked at him steadily. "If it's money you're worried about, I have more than enough. Enough for several lifetimes. We'll never have to worry about anything ever again."

At that point, Rik felt like he had an angel on one shoulder and a devil on the other. It would be nice to relax, not to have to worry about putting food on the table. And traveling the world with Carmen—it all sounded so tempting.

"Where would we go?" he asked.

"Anywhere. Fiji, Australia, Croatia, the Mediterranean—anything we want. We could get another boat, many boats. We could live the life we've always dreamed of."

Every word Carmen spoke sounded amazing, casting Rik into a deep moral quandary. They owed their security to the United States Coast Guard and Uncle Sam. The thought of fleeing, vanishing into the unknown, tugged at his conscience. It felt like a betrayal, yet the lure of untamed adventure was irresistibly thrilling.

After finishing their meal, Carmen and Rik stepped out into the balmy evening air, finding comfort near the softly lit tiki bar. They sipped on another round of cocktails, the tropical flavors mingling with the salty breeze. As the night deepened, they nestled into a hammock, swayed gently by the southeast breeze. Wrapped in each other's arms under the vast, star-studded sky, the world beyond their quiet sanctuary faded away. There, suspended between duty and freedom, they drifted into dreams, the ocean's rhythm lulling them into a serene slumber.

EIGHT

The next few days were relatively calm. The coastal waters were free from drug traffickers, and Rik and Carmen were free from their influence, at least for now. Given his new state of affairs, he had been temporarily reassigned from HITRON to an administrative role at Coast Guard Miami. It was boring, but he was much closer to the Chez-A-Lago and Carmen. He spent most of his free time there, and they would stay up late laughing and planning their future together.

One typical rainy afternoon, as Rik was wrapping up some Coast Guard paperwork, his cell phone rang. It was Carmen. She sounded hysterical.

"Rik, Rik, he found me! He found us! They hurt me, Rik. Please, come quick—I'm on the boat." And with that, the phone went silent. Rik was in a rage, but he had to keep his wits about him. He yelled for Charlie and Jim, two members of the base security team, and told them to grab sidearms and come with him.

They all jumped into Roxanne and sped across

MacArthur Causeway to Carmen's marina. They left the Jeep running with Marco and sprinted to the docks and onto *La Exquisita*. Carmen was crying on the salon settee. Her blouse was torn, her right eye was turning green-blue, and her lip was dripping blood. Someone had roughed her up good.

Rik quickly assessed her injuries—no other obvious ones aside from what he could see. He looked at her, his heart breaking. She glanced up at him, tears streaming down her cheeks. "I'm sorry, *mi amor*. He found us. His men found us and did this. They told me: Come home to Colombia, or die in the US."

If Roberto had been standing in front of him right then, Rik would have killed him with his bare hands.

Charlie and Jim searched the boat and then took up fore and aft defensive positions without saying a word. They were good. He didn't know them well, but Coasties took care of their own.

"Who were they? Where did they come from? Not through the lobby?" Rik demanded.

"No, *mi amor*," she said slowly. "They came by boat. From the ocean. I knew them. My husband's goons, enforcers. Sicarios. Trained from childhood. I hope they die."

Just then, Carmen's phone rang. Rik knew who it was. He answered, his grip tightening around the phone. It was Roberto. Rik yelled, "I'm going to kill you, you piece of shit!"

"Ah, Master Chief Petty Officer Rik Meade. I see you've met *mi esposa, mi Carmencita.* She can melt a man's heart. Like what my men did to her? I told them to stay away from her face and just break a leg or an arm, but boys will be boys. *Bueno?"*

Rik shouted into the phone, "Listen to me, *pendejo.* I'm going to find you. And I'm going to put a bullet in your temple and another in your heart. *Comprende, cabrón?"*

"No, you listen to me, *puta madre*! I'm coming to Miami, Chief Rik! Me and my army of loco SOBs. We are going to kill you and all you gringo Coastie fucks! Then, after *mi Carmencita* sees your bullet-riddled, fly-ridden corpse, I'm going to take her back to Colombia to renew our vows. *Comprende?"*

The phone went silent, and Rik's blood was boiling. His uncle Jax trained him to be a guardian and the Coast Guard trained him to be cool and calm. But not now. Now, he wanted to gut that piece of dogshit like a bull gator for his hide. But he needed to calm down. He needed to protect Carmen and get her to a hospital. And he needed to plan.

NINE

The seeds of an escape plan were slowly growing in the back of Rik's stressed mind. But there were so many moving parts to his current situation that he couldn't come up with a solid strategy.

He had to move his things out of the Opa Locka Station, so he headed up to the base. As he was walking gloomily to Roxanne, boxes in hand, he heard the flight mission alarm sound. This meant there was a potential interdiction. His adrenaline kicked in, but he said aloud to himself, "Down, boy, you're no longer part of that world." Carmen and the Coast Guard brass had seen to that.

He had no regrets, but nevertheless, he could use some action. And flying over the Straits of Florida would be great. Not to mention the feeling of having his Barrett tucked in tight by his side.

Tony saw him and yelled through the security fence, "Rik, where ya going? Are you deaf?"

"No, man, I'm sidelined. On the bench. Season's over. You know that."

"Didn't you hear? Terry, your replacement, has Ebola or some shit. He's been puking all morning. C'mon, gear up. We need ya, brother. Wheels up in ten. I hear this is a hot one."

Tony didn't have to ask him twice. Rik ran back inside, jumped into his flight suit, grabbed an armament bag, and climbed aboard. He'd straighten his gear out in the air. As they went airborne, he glanced at the base's orange windsock. For all the incredible technology at their fingertips, nothing beats some of the old aeronautical ways. And that ol' windsock's direction and horizontal attitude told him it was going to be a sporty mission.

They headed west briefly, then turned south over the Everglades to avoid civilian traffic. Their destination: his old friend, the Cay Sal Banks.

Fat Albert, the radar-equipped blimp flying over Cudjoe Key, had picked up five fast-moving targets headed through the Cay Sal area. The most they had ever seen were two boats, so this was all very suspicious. And odd.

Soon, they were on the scene, and there they were: five identical, low-visibility gray boats. Each with two occupants and a thousand horsepower, doing sixty to seventy miles per hour on a northerly heading into high seas created when the Gulf Stream collided with a strong northerly wind. They made a low pass over this narco navy to get their attention. They succeeded.

Upon seeing the chopper, as if on command, the boats immediately headed in different directions.

"Shit," Tony shouted into the intercom. "Now what'll we do?"

Rik's intuition kicked in, and he yelled, "Stay with the middle boat. It's headed to Miami."

Tony nodded, dropping the helo lower and flying parallel to the middle boat's course. Rik looked through his scope. Holy fuck, it was the Painter. Yep, messed-up ear and all. He was in a bit of shock, but his training kicked in, and he grabbed the hailer mike.

"This is the United States Coast Guard. Step away from the cockpit! I'm going to ventilate your engines!" Rik put the hailer mike down and wondered what the hell this Roberto prick was doing. All he could come up with was that he was trying a new transportation strategy where one or two boats would certainly make it through. He wondered if these guys used their own product. Apparently so. After all, Roberto *had* said he was going to pay him a visit.

The Painter looked up at the Dolphin and grinned maniacally. He even gestured, flipping them off, indicating they were number one. He knew Rik was up there.

Rik thought he could kill this guy right now and no one would care. But he had a duty. The Coast Guard saved lives, not took them. He rested the Barrett on the nylon sling he used to steady his shots and prepared himself.

He aimed for the center of the cowlings, exhaled, and whispered his mantra. *Slow is smooth. Smooth is fast.* He then squeezed off three .50-caliber rounds from his M107. Simultaneously Roberto smirked, his boat hit a large wave, and the helo lurched.

Three holes did not instantly appear in the engine cowlings. Instead, El Pintor's cabeza turned into a bright red ball of mist. One minute it was there, and the next… poof. His headless body stood erect for a moment before it realized it no longer had a command center and fell forward onto the driver.

Shit. What just happened? Had he involuntarily taken out that now-headless pile of shit? The son of the most violent narco-terrorist in the Western Hemisphere? No, he was doing what he was trained to do. The boat lurched; the helo swerved. Or at least he *thought* that was what happened.

The next few hours were a blur. He had never killed before. There was an intense debrief at the base and a visit from their staff psychiatrist. She said that he would experience powerful feelings of remorse. But he felt nothing like that. He'd felt more guilt smashing a palmetto bug on his kitchen floor. They, at least, had a right to live. But not Roberto. He and his father brought immeasurable pain and suffering to the world. Nobody would miss him. And when he met Saint Peter, Rik hoped he would stand proud before him.

Reality soon set in. Rik still couldn't shake the feeling that there could be a mole in the Coast Guard. Their crash off Andros and the problems with their survival equipment were just too improbable. Sadly, any evidence lay at the bottom of the Straits of Florida.

With that in mind, and the knowledge that cartel families were known for exacting horrible vengeance, Carmen and Rik needed to disappear. Fast.

The brass didn't know what to do with him. Or Carmen. There was nothing in the USCG playbook that covered what to do with a Coastie who fell for a narco-terrorist's wife, got her to assist Uncle Sam in its fight against drug trafficking, and—oh, right! Said Coastie blew Mr. Narco-Terrorist's head off with a .50-cal. At least he didn't *think* there was. Shit, who knew anymore? It was a complicated world, after all.

Rik had Carmen safely hidden for now and was reviewing his options. None of which added up to much. Even if the Coast Guard could see their way around him bumping off suspects—yeah, yeah, yeah, the whole innocent until proven guilty thing, blah, blah, blah. Fuck Roberto—there was still the matter of Chi-Chi, Roberto's father. The same father that would not be attending an open-casket funeral. On a positive note, he could save some coin and purchase a smaller one.

They needed to disappear. At least for now. A plan started to come together in Rik's admittedly foggy brain. But he had to move fast—for his sake and Carmen's.

Once again, he had to rely on a friend. A very discreet friend. He reached for his cell phone and made a call.

TEN

Charlie and Jim made quick work untying the dock lines. They asked no questions and the guys added another level of security for their departure. Yep, it was time to get outta Dodge. Once on board *La Exquisita*, with its four thousand horses and two thousand gallons of diesel, and a nearby country with no extradition treaty, Rik started feeling better about his decision. He said his goodbyes and rumbled out of the marina on a moonless night.

Would you believe he entrusted Marco with the care of Roxanne? Rik had no idea how long he'd be away, and they were borderline friends now. The arrangement was that Marco could use Roxanne while he was away. His fingers were, of course, collateral.

Rik didn't know how long "away" was going to be —or if a visit to Fox Hill Prison was in his future. That's right, they were headed to the Bahamas. Home to freedom and one of the worst prisons on earth. One that he would personally like to avoid. There were more than a few boys there that might object to his profession.

Do you recall a recently disgraced bitcoin billionaire who thought he could stall for time in Fox Hill? He lasted two days … before begging the US Marshal Service to come save him. Now he's safe and sound in a good ol' American jail with three squares a day.

They made the passage slowly through Stiltsville. Last time they'd come through here, Carmen had enjoyed seeing the magical houses, but now she was lost in her own thoughts. This time, instead of turning south at Fowey Rocks Lighthouse, they headed southeast for Andros. It was the perfect place to disappear.

James Pinder would meet them off tiny Williams Island. Like the good friend that he was, he'd asked no questions when Rik had called. He'd simply said he'd be there.

Carmen climbed the ladder to the bridge and snuggled up to Rik in the red glow of the bridge. "We're going to be alright, aren't we, Rik?"

"Of course," he replied. He wasn't willing to share the risks involved, but knowing there might be a leak at USCG and an evil horde of South American banditos might be looking for them didn't leave many options.

"I'm glad you killed him," she said out of the blue. It was hard to see, but her eyes were glowing fiercely.

Rik hadn't seen this side of Carmen. He had no idea what that POS had done to her in Colombia and had no right to judge. But at that moment, an old Loggins and Messina song went through his head.

His lyrical thoughts were broken when Carmen offered to make a pot of coffee, which was a great idea. It was midnight, and they had a four-hour run ahead of them. While she was gone, he turned off the AIS system to help digitally camouflage their existence in the Gulf Stream. The AIS was an international identification system that helped ships recognize each other and avoid collisions. They needed no nosy neighbors tonight.

After Carmen brought him a thermos full of Colombia's finest, Rik insisted that she catch some sleep below. She argued until he quoted Jason Bourne's "Rest is a weapon" line. She smirked and withdrew down the ladder, leaving him alone with his thoughts on the dark, starry night on the Gulf Stream.

After several hours of running, Rik noticed a blip on the radar screen. It was a large vessel, ten miles away to the south and moving fast. It was clearly on an intercept course with them! It could only be the 110-foot Coast Guard cutter *Dauntless*. She would be on them soon, and they'd be no match for her armament, including the alarmingly accurate MK 75 deck gun. His mind was racing, running through options. He saw only one.

Rik turned on the autopilot and changed course to the northeast. It would now look like they were running away. He also turned the AIS back on. He wanted their undivided attention. He went below and told a sleepy Carmen his plan.

Their only hope was to escape unnoticed in the tender while the cutter chased the vacant *Exquisita* northward. The tender's low profile would certainly evade the cutter's strong radar. He launched the flats boat while she grabbed some emergency gear and provisions. The Gulf Stream was no place for a fifteen-foot boat at night, but they were desperate. And he was confident in his abilities.

They stepped carefully into the tender and cut loose from the now northbound *Exquisita*. They watched her lights dim, and they headed once again to their coordinates. A short time later, they watched the lights of the *Dauntless* go by in hot pursuit of the pilotless sportfish.

Thirty minutes later, they reached their destination, but without radar or a FLIR infrared system, Rik wasn't sure if James was in the area. He thought he could hear another small boat, but he couldn't risk hailing out loud. He remembered an old night vision trick his uncle had taught him. At night, you can see an object more clearly if you look at it from the corner of your eye. Instead of staring at what you think you see or hear, stare slightly away, and it will become clear. It had to do with rods and cones and their angles in your eye. Or something like that. He'd slept through biology.

He did as Uncle Jax had instructed, and sure enough, there was a skiff dead ahead. It had a lone figure in the bow. It was his friend James. They made it and were safe. James pulled up alongside them, and quick introductions were made. Just as the three exhaled a communal sigh of relief, they were lit up by a bright spotlight, stunned by this apparition from the dark.

The *Dauntless* must have launched a fast boat. His deception hadn't lasted long but maybe long enough. "This is the United States Coast Guard. Step away from the cockpit! I'm going to ventilate your engines!"

Rik immediately thought, *That mother stole my line!*

Rik quickly kissed Carmen and said, "I love you," then pushed her brusquely into James's skiff. He had just enough time to implore James to keep her safe. No matter what. No reply was needed from his Bahamian brother.

Then Rik ducked his head down, pinned the throttle, and headed seaward away from his beloved and James. The go-fast immediately gave chase and even fired a couple of warning shots. *What a pussy!* Rik thought. He headed seaward, hoping he could buy enough time for James to escape with Carmen into the desolate backcountry of Andros.

ELEVEN

The smaller of the two massive sentries yanked the black canvas hood off Rik's head. You know, the kind really bad guys wear in the movies? Who knew they smelled like old donkeys? Rik Mead did.

"Where the hell am I?" he asked harshly. He blinked, his eyes adjusting to the light. "Pull the wool outta your ears, sailor! Where the fuck am I?"

The larger of the massive sentries punched him in the stomach, clearly a nonverbal clue to keep his mouth shut. Crude. But effective.

The last forty-eight hours had been a sleep-deprived blur. They caught Rik fifteen miles off Nicholls Town in North Andros. He'd given the Coasties a hell of a chase, but someone had forgotten to top off the boat's gas tank. It was a real reunion at sea when the *Dauntless*, with *La Exquisita* in tow, caught up with him and his new fast-boat friends. The captain knew his Coastie crew was frustrated, so they used the flats boat for target practice. It now joined a long list of drug-running planes and boats on the floor of the Bahama Bank.

Rik was first transported to a secret base near an Everglades marsh. It was hard to conceal that sulfur smell at low tide. He was then put on board a helicopter with the aforementioned foul-smelling bag over his head, and now here he was in a sterile room with two tough guys. Heavily armed contractors, with no identifying insignias.

A door opened, and four tight-ass officers walked in. Rik took that back—the senior officer was no tight-ass. Rik could see it in his eyes: He'd seen things. Things and situations a civilian would never encounter. He was not someone to trifle with. Tall, square-jawed, salt and pepper hair. Rik liked this guy—except he suspected the man was going to put him in a concrete box for the rest of his life.

Square Jaw started pacing back and forth, deep in thought, before finally speaking. "Master Chief Meade, I am Commander Robert Eisendorf with the Special Tactical Operations Unit. You are in a safe house near the Truman Annex in Key West. We use this place from time to time for 'special' situations."

He went on. "And you, sir, are very special…and in a shit ton of trouble."

Tell me something I don't know, Rik thought. This guy was turning out to be a dick.

"Prior to last Tuesday, you had served your country well and you're one tough son of a bitch to survive a helo crash in open water. And we were all rooting for you in the International Sniper Competition. Too bad that flu took you out.

"But now you've broken seventeen sections of the Uniform Code of Military Justice and several that haven't even been written yet. Frankly, we don't know what to do with you. Put you in military prison? Discharge you? Keep you around?" That last statement brought a round of chuckles from everyone in the room. Including Rik.

"You've put the USCG in a difficult spot. You initiated a relationship with the daughter-in-law of one of the most notorious narco-terrorists on the planet. You then killed her husband and his son in a most spectacular way. We all agree he won't be missed, but the USCG is not in the business of being judge, jury, and executioner."

Rik interrupted, "Bu—"

Cutting Rik off, Eisendorf raised his voice. "Shut your pie hole! Your superior—the one who's in charge of your life—is talking! *Comprende?*" Not waiting for an answer, he continued, "You then smuggled a Colombian citizen, under US military protection, into a foreign country. And involved a decorated Bahamian service member. Do I have it right? Did I miss anything, Master Chief?"

Rik thought of a few details he'd missed but decided it was in his best interest to keep his pie hole shut.

"Here's the deal. Take it or leave it. You died two nights ago. You fired on the brave men and women of the *Dauntless*, and their Mk 75, turned you and your boat into cinders and ash."

Shit! Rik hadn't seen that coming. As I said earlier, his world was turning upside down.

"You will be given a new identity but remain in the USCG under a newly created outfit. We recognize that you possess certain skills, and having a cartel contact may benefit us. You will be able to operate discreetly in the shadows, where official Coast Guard personnel simply can't go.

"You can have a new life if you stay out of trouble. From time to time, you will be contacted by Lieutenant Jill Wright, here on my left, for your assignments. You will also receive a monthly stipend. Think of it as a pension.

"You won't be on the books, and if something should happen to you…you're just shit out of luck. Questions?"

Rik sat there, pondering all this information. He eventually said, "I want to see Carmen."

"Good luck. We found your friend James Pinder in a shack on Miskito Cay yesterday. Very cleverly hidden. He had a large bump on his head, and your precious Carmen was gone. Along with his skiff, money, and handgun."

"Huh? Why would she do that?"

"I know you're confused, Chief, but men in love do dumb things. We now believe the tip we received about the five narco boats came from Carmen herself. It's possible she wanted the USCG to bump off her husband. And who better than an angry boyfriend to pull the trigger?

"We also believe the attack on her was staged. Staged to enrage you. It worked. And wait for it…we have satellite imagery that suggests your helo was hit by a ground-to-air rocket. She went down in two thousand feet of water, so we'll never know for sure. But it suggests the cartel took out a hit on you. They can be very dramatic, in case you didn't notice."

This was too much. Rik felt pale and weak. Lieutenant Wright handed him a glass of water. He downed it in one long, loud gulp. The water helped, and his brain was regaining some elementary functions.

"What happens to *La Exquisita*?"

"She's yours if you want her. We frankly want to get rid of her. We've retitled it, but you'll need to rename it. It behooves us for you to have ocean access. We'll underwrite the costs within reason.

"I'll be leaving you now. Good luck, Master Chief. Godspeed and Semper Paratus. Lieutenant Wright has some paperwork to go over with you." And with that, the man who had just changed his life abruptly left the room.

The reserved Lieutenant Wright announced, "We are preparing a new identity for you, Chief Meade. We want you to relocate to the Florida Keys and have you adopt an island lifestyle. Blend in. Become a charter captain if you like. Whatever suits you. But you cannot give the air of 'retired Coast Guard.' Do you understand? It's essential that no one takes an interest in your life. You'll be another drifter who ends up in the Keys. You can keep your first name, but you need to select a new last name."

Her words were distant, and his mind wandered. He heard a loud rooster outside with circadian rhythm issues. Roosters were the official bird of Key West and served as wandering alarm clocks. He gazed out the window toward the crowing bird, its head held high as it patrolled the cracked sidewalk. Just beyond the rooster, partially hidden behind a spray of pink bougainvillea, was an old street sign, sun-bleached and slightly askew.

Duval Street. Rik smiled.

Duval Street was the artery of old Key West. This mile-long stretch of island chaos was more than asphalt—it was a state of mind. It ran from the Gulf to the Atlantic, like a heartbeat through the bones of old Key West. It was drag queens and dive bars, street preachers and poets, cigar smoke and steel drums. It was life. It was Fantasy Fest. It was loud, colorful, unapologetic—and somehow still charming.

It felt right. A grin began to form in his stoic smile.

He turned back as the lieutenant's voice broke through again.

"So, Chief, do you have a name in mind?"

He turned slowly; the grin fully formed now.

"Yes, I do."

A pause.

"My new name is… Rik Duval."

TWELVE

Three Months Later

For Rik, three months had passed in a blur. Rik "Duval" was settling—or, more accurately, struggling—to find a semblance of normalcy. He was growing accustomed to the Key's slower pace, but deep down, he still had one foot in the madness he'd left behind.

Rik had been trained to be a guardian. A protector. The Coast Guard salved his need to defend those who couldn't. Daily missions intercepting drugs, human cargo and saving boaters from themselves. He needed that. He was born to it. Waiting for possible *off the books* orders was tedious and boring. He needed more.

He put those thoughts aside, groaned, rolled out of his bunk, and instantly regretted it. His head felt like a cracked-open crab claw, throbbing from too many Conch Tikis at Bonefish Woody's last night. He should have paid attention to the drink's motto: "More than two—you'll forget how money works."

He stumbled into the galley of the renamed

Exquisita, reached for some aspirin, and downed three with a splash of orange juice. Through the window, he noticed Larry, the dockmaster, battling a leaf blower, and the leaf blower was winning. Every time the guy fired up that infernal machine, Rik fantasized about using a garrote to put it out of commission—along with Larry. It was just a joke, *of course*. Probably.

The Kingfisher had been playing at Bonefish Woody's last night. God, that kid could play the blues like he was born for it. Rik swore he still heard the riffs bouncing around his skull, or maybe that was just the hangover again.

Coffee was next. Having joined the Coast Guard right out of high school, quality coffee was part of Rik's life. Not froufrou crème de la crème *mochafaditos* from fancy stores but a dark, manly brew of high-quality liquid testosterone. He had spent many nights fueled by this virile ambrosia on small boats patrolling the Port of Miami and on bridges of cutters on moonless nights cruising the Gulf Stream. Even the thermoses on board the Dolphin helos were filled with good java, or joe as they said.

In went the perfectly ground beans from his favorite coffee-growing land, Jamaican Blue Mountain. You can talk all day about your Kenyan, your Peruvian, or even your Honduran bean, but nothing beats the golden-brown Blue Mountain. Next, he added a pinch of salt and a broken eggshell. Don't ask. It's a naval military secret.

With caffeine settling his nerves, he remembered his appointment that day. A mandatory check-in with his new shrink, Dr. Marconius Krakatopolis. The Coast Guard wanted to make sure he wasn't going to flip out one day and go full Michael Douglas in *Falling Down*—a distinct possibility given the right (or wrong) provocation.

Previously Rik had been the patient of Dr. Paige Turner, but she couldn't handle the Keys life. Before arriving in Rum Key, she had had no idea she suffered from tikiphobia, the irrational fear of tiki bars and bamboo decor. And, well, they are rather prevalent in the Keys. So, back to Minnesota she went.

Rik pulled into the parking lot of the new doctor's office—a rickety space crammed between a tackle shop and a dive center. He couldn't decide whether to laugh or worry. "Dr. Krak Patients Only," read the sign by his designated spot. He shook his head, the irony not lost on him.

Inside, he was greeted by several talking bass on the wall. Thankfully, all had dead batteries that kept them from singing. He leafed through a copy of *Fungus Monthly*, wondering just what sort of clients this guy saw. A voice from around the corner yelled, "C'mon in," and he came face-to-face with his new therapist.

Dr. Krak looked like a cross between an unmade bed and Albert Einstein—wild whiteish hair around a surprisingly calm face. He wore a wool turtleneck, despite the stifling heat outside, and looked up from a pile of paperwork as Rik took a seat.

"Mr. Duval," Dr. Krak started in a tone so flat it could double as a carpenter's level. "Why do you think you're here?"

Rik stifled a sigh. He wasn't in the mood for psych games, but he knew the drill. "I killed a guy. Slept with the wrong girl. Possibly have authority issues," he offered vaguely. "The usual story."

Dr. Krak's eyebrow twitched ever so slightly. "Usual?"

"Sure, Doc." His shrug was barely a twitch. "Usual for someone who's seen too much, felt too little."

The therapist nodded slowly, pen scratching across his notepad. "And this… 'guy'—did he deserve it?"

Rik hesitated. "Deserve's got nothing to do with it. He was the son of Chi-Chi Allende, head of the Tabasco cartel. Also known as El Cojón. You may know him by his English name. One Ball."

With that, they both chuckled. Although El Cojón was a maniacal killer and overall horrible person, he was stuck with a nickname that had dubious origins.

The story was that in his misspent youth, the young ladies of Sonora had no interest in young Chi-Chi and his pockmarked puss and stick figure body. So, one lonely night, at his abuelo's farm, he made the moves on a female donkey named Antoinette. Even an old donkey like Antoinette has standards and she put two hooves on his unripe avocados and *bada bing*, only one survived. It was alleged that if anyone used the term El Cojón in his presence, he got *Antoinetted* with a rusty knife. Ouch!

"And this brings you… to Rum Key?"

"Look, Doc, I needed a place to blend in. Conchs don't ask too many questions. Everyone here has a past." He leaned forward, gesturing around the small office. "This place is a black hole for people like me. You fall in and hope no one from your old life finds you."

Dr. Krak seemed satisfied. "And you're living on a boat? Isn't that… difficult?"

"*Bum Runner*'s not just a boat. It's *home*." Rik shrugged. "As close to it as I'm going to get anyway."

"And what about *her*? Carmen, right?"

The question hung in the air like a live grenade. Rik ran his tongue over his teeth, stalling. "What about her?"

"Do you regret being with her?"

"I regret *not* shooting her when I had the chance." He meant it to sound flippant, but it came out heavier than expected. "But I loved her, Doc. That's the truth."

"And she betrayed you?"

Rik didn't answer. He looked away, feeling the familiar mix of anger, regret, and lingering affection twisting in his gut. "It's complicated," he muttered finally.

They talked for nearly an hour, Rik's voice slipping into a monotone as he recounted the last few months. He watched Dr. Krak's face, waiting for some hint of surprise or horror at his stories of murder, deception, and betrayal. But the man's expression remained infuriatingly neutral.

Finally, at the end of the session, Dr. Krak leaned back in his chair and announced, "I've come to a diagnosis."

Rik braced himself.

"You suffer from *Sanitas mentis*."

Rik gulped, "Is that bad?"

"It's Latin for 'You're too sane for your own good.'"

Rik laughed. This guy was more than just a shrink—he was a character straight out of a Carl Hiaasen novel. "So, what's the treatment?"

Dr. Krak opened a small drawer and said, "Well,

we can't be too careful in these situations. Lucky for you a lovely young rep from Big Pharma with big hooters and a Saran Wrap skirt left a sample of their latest miracle drug. I'm going to give you a two-week supply."

With that, the doctor opened a gel pack, popped a couple of pills into his mouth, swallowed them dry, leaned back, burped, and said, "If they work, I'll let you know."

Rik stared at him in disbelief, then slowly rose from his chair. "You're one weird dude, Doc."

Dr. Krak just smiled. "And you, Mr. Duval, are my new favorite patient."

As Rik walked out of the office, he was torn between amusement and skepticism. Was this man the most eccentric con artist in the Keys, or a therapist with unorthodox brilliance? The ambiguity lingered, but it was swiftly overshadowed by more urgent priorities. Now, he faced the formidable task of navigating his "new" life, a daunting endeavor that demanded immediate attention and strategy.

THIRTEEN

Lieutenant Wright made a call to the newly christened Rik Duval, her tone laced with a blend of urgency and secrecy. "I need to see you in person," she insisted. "There's something important we need to discuss, but it's not safe over the phone." Her words hung heavy, hinting at the gravity of the news she bore.

Rik suggested Bonefish Woody's Bar—and *occasional* strip joint as well. The strip joint technically wasn't licensed by the authorities on Rum Key, but whenever it "popped up," the city fathers were always in the front row, pockets stuffed with ones and fives.

Bonefish Woody's was legendary because of its weekend party band, Billy and the Debauched. Their leader and frontman was Billy Tiger. Billy was a good friend, though Rik didn't see him often; their lifestyles didn't exactly mesh well. While Rik preferred a quieter existence, Billy thrived on smoking, drinking, women of suspect morals, and the occasional bar fight—they were his Botox. They did wonders for him.

Billy stood six feet, seven inches tall, strong as an ox, with long black hair frequently adorned with sea shells. He was a member of the Pahokee tribe, who inhabited the southern end of the Everglades—a sovereign nation within the United States.

This hadn't always been the case. To establish their sovereignty, tribal leaders visited Fidel (El Pendejo) in 1959, who in turn recognized their nation. This act embarrassed the Eisenhower administration, who promptly granted the Pahokee nation status. After all, what did the federal government care about twelve square miles of gator-infested swamp?

Billy had been a card-carrying member of the Pahokee tribe until an elder had found him in bed with his daughters—that's right, plural. Billy always had a big appetite. After that, he was kicked off the reservation and wandered the back roads and estuaries of Florida until he washed up on Rum Key.

Billy started as a bouncer at Bonefish Woody's but soon discovered he had a knack for singing and mayhem. His shows were infamous, breaking the moral codes of most Florida counties—but not Monroe County. If Caligula had a house band, it would have been led by Billy. His shows were a combination of standup comedy, rock 'n' roll, and bacchanalia. He even used a giant sex toy as his maestro's wand. If you weren't getting into the "scene," he would smack you in the head with it.

Bonefish Woody's was a half mile down on A1A from Rik's waterfront home, Sailfish Bay Marina. So, he simply walked down to meet Lieutenant Wright. Billy was already there, so they chewed the fat for a while, snacking on some golden fried conch fritters, while Rik waited for the lieutenant. For all his crazy antics, Billy was an old soul and never asked about the whole new identity thing. But he knew Rik's safety, and his own depended on it.

Around noon, Lieutenant Wright walked through the beat-up front door and almost stumbled into the bar counter. She was dressed in the standard USCG female uniform—a funny cap, a white blouse, a navy skirt over the knees, and black pumps. She was an attractive woman, but let's just say Ralph Lauren was not on the Coast Guard's payroll.

She was then greeted by a loud screech.

"Raawk! Attention! Officer on deck. Officer on deck!

Lieutenant Wright had just been greeted by Left Eye Louie, the fifty percent owner of Bonefish Woody's. Confused? This will take a while…you see Left Eye Louie is an African grey parrot who belonged to Woody, the bar's original owner. Woody left everything to Louie after he was shish kabobbed in an unsanctioned, jet ski jousting accident. The Rum Key coroner, after sobering up, said alcohol may have been a contributing factor to his demise.

Now Louie was a pretty good proprietor, aside from his proclivity to cheat the IRS. But he did have a gambling problem. A big one. He was always looking for some action. I mean he tried to launch an underground key deer racing circuit on Big Pine Key! It might have worked but the capuchin monkey jockeys refused to wear silks. Sadly, late one night, in Woody's smoky back room, Louie went all in with a full house and lost half the bar to a Yankee with no tells and a straight flush.

Lieutenant Wright turned to the voice and said, "At ease sailor." As her eyes adjusted to the dark she saw Louie wore a tiny pirate hat and had a patch over his right eye. She approached and Louie squawked, "Give us a kiss. Give us a kiss."

She leaned to kiss his cute. little beak and he squawked. "Raawk. Lower honey. Lower."

She didn't know how to slap a parrot so she turned around abruptly and bumped into Rik.

"I see you met Left Eye Louie. He's quite a charmer isn't he?"

"He's a pervert is what he is!"

"Probably. Tomorrow he'll blame it on the bourbon. Or the scotch. I'm not sure what he's drinking this week. Anyhow come on over and meet my friend Billy."

Her eyes still hadn't fully adjusted so it took her a moment to take in Billy. Her expression was the same as most people's the first time they laid eyes on Rik's larger-than-life friend—shock and awe. Rik made introductions, and Billy excused himself to go raise a little hell somewhere else.

"Well…he seems interesting," Lieutenant Wright said.

"Yep," Rik replied. "I've known him forever. I'd trust him with my life."

"You may have to," she replied curtly. "Seeing as he knows your former identity."

"You said you had news, Lieutenant?"

"I do. We have information on Carmen. Our DEA contacts have traced her back to Colombia, where she appears to be working with her father-in-law, Chi-Chi Allende. Our best guess is that he's grooming her to take over the operation one day."

Rik's head still spun when he thought of her. He had slept with a narco-terrorist. How could he have been so stupid? It had cost him his career. But what doesn't kill you makes you stronger—or some BS like that.

They continued talking about the precautions Rik was taking and the possibility of future missions for him. The USCG was contemplating a joint task force with their Bahamian neighbors, and James Pinder and Rik would liaise together. It would be good to see Pinder again. Rik wondered how many Goombay Smashes he'd have to buy to make up for the bump on the head Carmen had given him.

Lieutenant Wright reached into her noticeably nondesigner purse and handed Rik a very high-tech-looking phone. "Here, you need to keep this sat phone with you at all times. It has the latest NSA encryption software, and please don't use it for personal calls. Those satellites cost the taxpayers a ton of money."

Rik pocketed the device, and they continued talking. At one point, the formal-looking and bookish Lieutenant Wright crossed and uncrossed her legs, and the standard-issue skirt rose a bit. Suddenly, Lieutenant Wright was an attractive woman. Rik put that thought on hold. He was in enough trouble with the USCG.

They snacked on delicious smoked wahoo dip, and eventually, she asked, "Rik, how do you know Billy? Have you been friends long?"

"It's kind of a long story."

"I'm on the Coast Guard's dime."

"I grew up in West Miami. In my teens I lived with my Uncle Jax—he's a story for another time—but he left me to my own devices. It was a blue-collar area, and about twenty or thirty miles west of us lived the Pahokee tribe. We didn't see them very often.

"One of the popular things for us at the time was go-karting. We were teenagers, building our own go-karts using Briggs and Stratton lawn mower engines. We reeked of oil and gas and, yeah, we got into a little trouble—but nothing too serious.

"I was working on a new cart and had my heart set on a 1967 Mustang steering wheel. Wood grain. Would you believe I found one? I spotted it at Sammy the Scrap King's junkyard, which was kind of an institution in the world of South Florida junk.

"Now, Sammy was a big ol' boy and one of the most cantankerous men in Miami—meaner than a junkyard dog, if you know what I mean. Anyhow, I went there with ten dollars to purchase my dream steering wheel, and he told me, 'Sure, son. Just put another zero after it,' then laughed.

"He could've done a kid a favor, but no—he had to make fun of me. I was tall and skinny, and my jeans were too short. He even added, 'Where's the flood, sonny?' But I was determined to get that steering wheel. I knew exactly where it was in the yard. So, right or wrong, I went back that night to get it.

"He had an old Rottweiler named Bella, but she liked me—I always brought her treats. That night, I snuck in, found the pile of steering wheels, and as I was stealthily walking out with my prize, I heard Sammy's voice. 'Who the hell is out there? Is it one of you nasty Pahokees stealing from me again? I'll shoot you; I swear!'

"Well, I did the obvious thing. I ran. Fast. And practically knocked over this huge kid in the back of the yard. He was a Pahokee boy. He stared at me and said, 'Who the hell are you?'

"'I'm Rik. Rik Meade.'

"'I'm Billy Tiger.' Billy looked around and said, 'Well, Rik Meade, if I were you, I'd get the hell out of here. He's gonna shoot someone tonight for sure.'

"We stood there for a minute, and then I realized if we split up, we'd have a better chance. Billy went one way, and I went the other. As I was about to hop a fence I heard a big commotion back in the junk yard. Sammy had caught Billy."

"I turned around and I saw Sammy standing over Billy pointing a shotgun at his heart. Billy was bleeding from his mouth and nose. I didn't know what to do. Then I heard the voice of my Uncle Jax saying, "Rik, you stand up to bullies. Always help those in need.'

"What did you do?"

"I climbed back down the fence and grabbed a muffler and hit Sammy in the head from behind. It barely stunned him but he dropped the gun and then me and Billy were wrestling for our lives. Sammy was swinging and gouging and outweighed us by hundred pounds. I finally ended the fight when I swung a crankshaft like a baseball bat and knocked him out cold.

"Billy and I ran till we were out of breath. When we finally stopped I asked him if he and his friends really stole from Sammy. He said, 'Absolutely not.' He told me that Sammy was a blatant racist, and they would sneak in at night and rearrange his junk to make him crazy. But they never stole. That was against their way.

"When I finally made it home, my uncle saw me and asked what happened. I thought he was going to beat me, but Sammy had already done that job. After I told him the story, Uncle Jax disappeared for a couple of hours. When he came back, his knuckles were raw and bloody, but he never said a word. I never saw Sammy again.

"The next time I saw Billy, we were racing and he bumped into me on turn three at Michelle's Go Karts. After the race, we were starving, so we went to the Pit barbecue joint. He turned out to be a really good guy. I liked him. We came from different worlds, but as kids, we had stuff in common. We liked adventure, being outdoors, and we were just starting to get interested in girls—but not quite yet. We didn't see each other often, but we became like brothers. Blood brothers, in fact. I'll always have his back, and he'll always have mine. That kind of bond is rare, but in the end, it's all that matters."

Rik looked at Lieutenant Wright. "So, that's how we met. Are you still awake?"

"That's sweet, although your uncle sounds kind of scary."

"Yes and no. I'll tell you about him another time."

They wrapped up their conversation, and Lieutenant Wright headed back to Miami. After she left, Billy came back. "She seems like *a lot* of fun," he said sarcastically.

Rik didn't answer, but Billy continued, "I just hung up with my nephew, Kenny Osceola. Wanna go on an airboat ride? He's going python hunting and could use a good shot like you."

Rik thought it over for a moment and said, "Sure, I could use a change of scenery."

FOURTEEN

Several days later, Rik headed up A1A and then turned westward onto Tamiami Trail. In the 1920s, this modern road was built to connect Tampa with Miami, hence the name. It now cut through the Everglades and the Pahokee nation. Lining both sides of the road were airboat concessions, restaurants with all-you-can-eat fried frog legs, and several swamp ape museums. You know…the usual Florida stuff.

The sun was setting when he reached the boat ramp where Kenny was waiting with his airboat. Kenny Osceola, who appeared to be in his early twenties, was dressed for the part: a baseball cap with a battery-powered headlamp, camo T-shirt, jeans with a big boy knife, and well-worn boots. Rik, however, looked less like the part. But he did have an AR-15 and professional training behind him. He was looking forward to brushing up on his hard-earned marksman skills and ridding the Everglades of the horrible scourge known as the Burmese python.

These snakes were an invasive species and had

flourished in the last fifteen years. Originally released as out-of-control pets, they could grow to sixteen feet and two hundred pounds. Sadly, they had practically wiped out many of the native animals, such as raccoons, otters, and even deer.

After exchanging greetings, Rik asked how long Kenny had been piloting airboats.

"Since I was five," he said with a smile. "My grandfather, Toby Cypress, would sit me on his lap and let me work the rudder stick. He would tell me over the headset that it was the closest thing to flying he could imagine. He taught me all he knew about the Glades. I love it out here. I can't imagine working anywhere else."

"You work out here?"

"Yep. I'm a licensed trapper for the State of Florida. My specialty is the Burmese python. My ancestors wouldn't believe the damage they've done. And, no offense, but the white man caused this."

"None taken. You're right."

With that Kenny gave Rik a brief overview of how an airboat worked. The flat-bottomed boat was pushed by a large propeller driven by a five-hundred-horsepower gas engine. The boat was steered by a control lever that turned twin rudders located behind the surprisingly large wooden aircraft propeller. Oh, and they were loud! So loud that Kenny handed Rik an intercom headset so they could communicate.

Rik placed his AR-15 in a scarab alongside the front seat, and they were off. It had been a long time since he was flying with a headset on and a rifle at his side. He was loving life!

They flew over moonlit rivers of grass, through shallow channels known as sloughs, and past dry hammocks where deer and other critters congregate during high waters. But their prey was Burmese pythons.

Rik liked Kenny. He was a quiet and determined young man. He didn't speak much and let his actions do the talking. *Kinda like me.*

Eventually, they found their quarry slithering along levees and old trails, and Rik started picking them off one by one. The boat was piling up with carcasses and looking very macabre. He began to think there might be some python boots in his future. Like the rock stars wear.

After midnight, they agreed it was time to head back. As they were heading through the Shark River Slough, Kenny suddenly said, "Shit, the rudder stick is acting funny." With that, the control cable snapped, the rudders twisted hard right, and they went into an uncontrolled turn. While spinning, the airboat hit a stump broadside and flipped upside down. Luckily, Rik went flying free, but his head hit something hard. He was dazed and unconscious for a minute. When he came to, he could hear moaning from underneath the flipped airboat.

"Kenny!" he yelled. "Hang on! I'm coming." He waded through the dark water, now filled with gasoline and oil, to the overturned airboat. He dove underneath and found Kenny semiconscious. Rik knew Kenny was in pain but would drown if he left him there. He dragged him out and pushed him roughly on top of the airboat. Kenny yelled in pain and then passed out. Rik searched for injuries and found the source of his agony; Kenny had a compound fracture of the femur. It was a ghastly injury, and the broken bone had nicked his femoral artery. He was losing blood fast. Kenny didn't have much time.

Rik knew he would bleed out if he didn't do something fast. He took his belt off and used it as a makeshift tourniquet. Doing this could be a risky procedure, but Rik had no choice. He also had no pen, so using Kenny's own blood, he wrote TQ 1:00 AM on his forehead. This way trauma personnel would know how long the belt had been restricting blood flow to his leg. Next he stabilized the leg using his rifle scarab and some dock lines.

At this point, Kenny came to and started mumbling about the radio. Rik caught his drift. There was no cell phone reception this far out in the Everglades, but Kenny's radio was smashed. Rik reached in his back pocket for the sat phone. Thank goodness it was okay. *Semper Paratus*. He turned it on and found he had a good signal. He immediately called Miami-Dade County 911.

Miami-Dade County has one of the best emergency services in America and access to two Life Flight helicopters. When the operator picked up, Rik tried to calmly explain the situation. She understood their predicament quickly and informed him that one of the emergency helicopters was outbound to Miami Beach and the other was down for maintenance. The earliest he would see a chopper was in one hour. Airboats would take at least an hour and a half. "He doesn't have that long," Rik said. "Here are our coordinates. I'm gonna make another phone call."

He then rang the mission desk at Air Base Opa Locka. Tony, who happened to be walking by, picked up. The connection was terrible, so Rik quickly said, "Tony, this is Rik Duval. I mean Rik Meade. I have an emergency, and I need your help." Click. The phone went dead.

Rik hit redial, and Tony again picked up and said, "Look, buddy, it's a federal offense to crank call a military installation!"

Before he hung up again, Rik yelled into the sat phone, "Tony, your sister dates an out-of-work musician, and you hate pumpkin pie."

Silence, then, "Who the fuck is this?"

"Tony, it's me, Rik Meade. I'm not dead, and I need your help. I'm in the Everglades with a kid who's bleeding out. Spin up the helo! Please!"

Tony hesitated for a minute and said, "The *Dauntless* blew you to bits off Andros. I attended your memorial."

"I owe you a hundred and twenty-seven bucks from the poker game at Stu's!"

"Rik, is it really you?"

"Yes, you stupid fuck. Now fire up the Dolphin, find a medic, grab a trauma kit, and get your ass in the air. Here's the lat-lon."

He hung up. His guys were the best in the business, and Tony would be there ASAP, but he needed to focus on Kenny. He had to keep him alive until the air cavalry arrived.

Kenny was moaning, slipping further into a fog, and Rik crouched beside him, gripping his shoulder. "Stay with me, buddy. Just a little longer. My guys are coming and they're the best there is!"

Then—a sound. Not the wind. Not a bird. It came from the sawgrass.

At first, it was subtle. A low, rasping rustle, like dry reeds brushing together. But then it deepened—a steady deliberate crunch. The kind of sound you only hear when something big is forcing its way through brush that was never meant to part.

Rik froze.

The sawgrass cracked, each blade folding and

snapping with the slow, awful patience of a predator that knew it had time.

He couldn't see it. But he didn't need to. There was blood in the water, and whatever was out there had found them. Not a panther. Not a wild boar. No flapping, no snort—just weight and purpose and silence between the steps. It could only be a big bull gator.

He reached for his AR-15 with the smooth, automatic motion of someone trained for nightmares but never pictured this one.

Safety off. Finger ready. Heart thudding in his throat. Whatever it was, it was close. And it wasn't stopping.

He grabbed Kenny's headlamp and pointed it in the direction of the would-be gator. There it was: two large, glowing red eyes moving fast toward them. Rik knew there was only one spot on a gator that was a kill shot, and it was a quarter-sized area behind the eyes. *Slow is smooth. Smooth is fast.* He centered himself, took a breath, and squeezed off a round: boom…bull's-eye. Or *gator* eye. The gator exploded at his feet, thrashing furiously, but was soon silent.

He exhaled deeply and started calculating time estimates in his head. They'd crashed some thirty miles west of Opa Locka Air Base, which should be a flight time of ten minutes. The crew needed ten minutes to spin up the helo and grab their equipment, which meant they should be here in twenty minutes. "Hold on, Kenny," he implored. "Hold on."

Kenny moaned again. He started rambling and saying crazy things. Rik figured the pain and the blood loss had resulted in hallucinations, but this was more. He appeared oddly focused. He listened intently to Kenny's words.

"I see it. I see the path!" Kenny exclaimed over and over.

To calm him down, Rik finally said, "What do you see, Kenny? What path?"

"The path my ancestors created for you." And with that he passed out again.

Rik had no time to process Kenny's strange words as he heard the distinct sound of the Dolphin's rotors approaching from the east. To make their location more visible, Rik grabbed Kenny's headlamp once again and flashed it repeatedly at the incoming sound.

This helped, and Tony was soon hovering over them. The lifesaving basket descended through the hurricane-like prop wash. He picked up the unconscious Kenny and strapped him in. The hoist operator, staring down intently, began to hoist immediately. Once Kenny was safely on board, he began to make a second drop for Rik. But Rik waved him off. Every second counted, and they didn't need to waste an additional minute hoisting a passenger. Tony understood, so he spun the helo east and headed immediately for Jackson Hospital's trauma center, the best place in South Florida to save Kenny's life.

Rik climbed back on top of the airboat with his AR-15 and kept a wary eye out for hungry gators as he waited for the airboats to find him. *What a night. It was good to hear Tony's voice, and it was good to reconnect with his team.* They meant the world to him, and he hated being isolated from them. He wasn't sure how this was going to play out now with Lieutenant Wright and Commander Eisendorf, but he had no regrets.

His thoughts then drifted back to Kenny's ramblings, strange and scattered as they were. Rik knew just enough about Native traditions to hesitate before dismissing them. Among the Plains tribes, there was a sacred rite called the Sun Dance—a ceremony steeped in pain and purpose. Skewers were pierced through flesh, binding the dancer to a central pole. Through suffering came visions—glimpses of the spirit world, communion with the Creator.

Was it possible that Kenny, broken and bleeding, had stumbled into that space between worlds? Was that what was happening now? Had Kenny's agony torn something open? Because Rik could feel it too. A subtle pull. Something ancient... watching. And waiting.

Two hours later, a Miami-Dade Fire Rescue airboat team showed up with lights ablaze. The team leader stood up and slowly took in the apocalyptic scene: twenty dead pythons scattered about, a large alligator with a very large hole in its head, and a very tired hombre sitting atop an upside-down airboat cradling an AR. All he could do was whistle and say, "What the hell happened here?"

After giving Rik a once-over, the paramedics insisted on taking him to a nearby hospital. But he needed to see Kenny. He downed a thermos of coffee at the fire station and finally found Kenny around noon the next day, asleep after lifesaving surgery. His room was filled with men and women in multicolored jackets and skirts, all obviously from his Pahokee tribe. The oldest looked at Rik, silently shook his hand with an anvil grip, and escorted him to a room down the hall.

"Rik, my name is Toby Cypress," the old man said. "Kenny is my grandson. Thank you, my son, you saved his life. You showed great courage yesterday. That kind of courage deserves recognition. Therefore, we wish to give you this." He extended a leather bag toward Rik.

Curiosity piqued, Rik accepted the bag and carefully opened it. Inside, nestled within the soft fabric, was a very old wooden rod intricately carved with symbols he didn't recognize. "What is this?" Rik asked, his fingers tracing the surface.

"This is an artifact of my people. It was entrusted to our family for generations. We believed it was meant for a brave heart—a protector. You are now its keeper. There are stories, powers, within it that you must discover for yourself."

Rik felt a shiver run down his spine. He had no idea what the artifact might mean for him or what responsibilities came with it. But as he held it, he sensed a deep connection to the land and the history of the Pahokee people.

"I will guard it," he vowed, looking up at Toby. "And honor its significance."

"Good," Toby said, his gaze steady. "You will always have our support. You are one of us now."

Later that day, after receiving updates on Kenny's condition, Rik stepped outside the hospital. The sun was setting, casting a warm glow over Miami. He took a deep breath, inhaling the salty air. He heard and then saw an osprey flying overhead and thought, *Odd, he's pretty far from the Everglades*, but it was a welcome sight.

He pulled out the artifact, holding it up to the light. The intricate carvings danced in the fading sun, and he made a silent promise to uncover its secrets and honor the connection he now had with the Pahokee tribe.

FIFTEEN

It had been several days since the incident in the Everglades. Rik had heard that Kenny was doing well. He often stared at the strange scrimshaw artifact and felt the odd markings with his fingers. He swore it took him back in time. When he held it, he felt something old and mystical, as if his feet were in two different centuries.

Since the accident, he had been doing odd jobs on the *Bum Runner* but was getting a little stir-crazy. So, against his better judgment, he walked down the road for a beer.

He walked into Bonefish Woody's and was immediately greeted by Left Eye Louie who squawked, "Raawk. Where's the vig. Where's the vig?"

"I don't owe you shit Louie!"

"Raawk. Till Friday. Till Friday!"

"Bite me Feather Locklear," and Rik turned his attention to the 'proceedings.'

Even at that hour, it was a party! It was like Key

West Fantasy Fest, but louder, crazier, and drunker. There weren't many rules here… or on Rum Key for that matter.

Of course, this melodious madness was led by the ringleader of musical mayhem himself—Billy of Billy and the Debauched.

Billy's onstage persona was hard to describe. Imagine Paul Bunyan meets Steven Tyler. That night, his hair was dyed purple with a few seashells tied in. His shaggy mane was topped with a cowboy hat, and the whole ensemble was finished with a feather boa. All the while, he waved a maestro's baton, which was actually a giant sex toy. Just a normal night at Bonefish Woody's.

He gave Billy a nod as he finished the popular "Who Put the Pepper in the Vaseline." The first set of the night wound down, and shortly thereafter, Billy strode over to the bar and ordered a couple of Chuck Norris shots for the two of them. Not familiar? It's a concoction of raspberry vodka, whiskey, grenadine, energy drink, and hot sauce. Liquid testosterone. It will also roundhouse kick your liver. Billy drank them like water when he was performing and, well…when he wasn't performing, too.

Rik looked at his two shots with a sideways glance, as he always did, and Billy muttered, "Commie pussy," before downing both like a parched desert castaway.

He wiped his mouth and said, "Well, you had quite an adventure in the Glades. You saved my nephew's life. The entire tribe is talking about you."

"How did you find out? I thought you were ostracized."

"Well, I do have back channels. C'mon, they love me." They both laughed at that because he personally knew that the chief would stake him down in a fire ant pit in a heartbeat over his prior indiscretions.

"Listen," Billy continued, "I need a favor. Coconut Carl didn't show up tonight. His wife arrived unexpectedly from Texas. I hear she's mean as a rattler and a crack shot. I suspect he's on a bus headed north by now. Anyway, I need a little percussion for the next few numbers. Can you help a brother out?"

Well, this year couldn't get any stranger, so Rik found himself onstage, trying to keep in time while Billy belted out crowd favorites like "Divers Do It Deeper," "Him So Horny," and his usual closer, "Why Don't We Get Drunk and Screw."

It was fun to watch the crowd dynamic during Billy's performances. Early on, some of the female tourists were disgusted by his antics—singing dirty songs, telling filthy jokes, and swinging that pink dangly thing around. But these same women, especially after imbibing a few Panty Dropper shots, a house specialty, warmed up to the oversized, maniacal man onstage. After the closing set, Rik overheard this conversation:

Tipsy Tourist Woman: "You were great, Billy. Do you have a real name?"

Billy: "Thank you kindly. Sure do. It's Heywood."

Tipsy Tourist Woman: "Well, that's an unusual name. Does Heywood have a last name?"

Billy: "Sure. It's Jablowmi. Heywood Jablowmi."

At this point, they either slapped him, called the cops, or smiled mischievously. Rik didn't stick around for her reply. He simply moseyed down to the *Bum Runner*. He was tired and needed some rest. His current state of mind reminded him of a Jimmy Buffett song.

He sat down in the salon, poured a nightcap, and again pondered the artifact Toby Cypress had given him. It was made of hard, dark brown wood—lignum vitae, which grew around there. It was super dense wood that didn't even float. He wondered what the numerous strange carvings meant.

While he was deep in thought, the boat listed to port, and there was a knock on the salon door. Not waiting for a reply, Billy Tiger ducked in and went straight to the bar and poured himself a generous nightcap.

When he was done, Rik asked, "What, no scalps tonight?"

Billy replied dryly, "We don't do that."

"Good to know."

"We do cut nuts off, though. We make coin purses out of 'em."

"What happened to Miss Oklahoma?"

"Well, first she slapped me, then she threatened to call the cops. Then she invited me back to her room at Boca Chica Resort."

"And…?"

"I don't know, Rik. I must be getting old. My moral compass is acting up. Must be the moon phase or something. I really mean it; there's some serious juju in the air. Maybe this south wind is stirring up some spirits. Anyhow, I couldn't take advantage of her. Not tonight."

"Well, I'm proud of you, my extremely large friend."

"Hey, what are you holding?"

"Chief Toby gave that to me."

"What? He did?"

"What the hell does it mean?"

"He didn't tell you?"

"He just said it's been in the Pahokees' possession for generations. That it's very valuable. And now I'm its keeper. For me to discover its secrets. Oh, and I can't tell anyone. Well, you're not just anyone. Then he left. You know the guy is kind of scary."

"I've never seen it, but I've heard about it. There's a legend, too!"

"Get outta here!"

"First of all, it's called the Kahatee."

"Go on."

"Well, the legend says that this rod holds the key to a treasure hidden by Black Caesar. Black Caesar was a pirate who had a camp on the south end of Elliott Key. Supposedly, the Kahatee provides the directions to his treasure."

"No shit?"

"No shit."

After that last eloquent exchange, they just sat there contemplating. He couldn't speak for Billy, but numerous thoughts ran through his mind: *Where the hell is this treasure? What's it worth? Why me? I wonder if Lieutenant Wright has nice lingerie?*

Billy and he chatted for a bit, but when he was leaving, he said, "The Kahatee has some strong juju on it. Be careful, my friend. People would kill to know its secrets." With that, the boat again listed to port, and he was gone.

SIXTEEN

That night, Rik slept uneasily, all that talk about legends and pirate gold—and the Lieutenant Wright *lingerie* thing—lingering in his mind. As he was making his morning coffee, the phone rang. Coincidentally, it was her, Lieutenant Wright.

The lieutenant said bluntly, "Rik, are you ever going to take me fishing?"

"Sure, I didn't know you wanted to," he replied.

"I'm from Iowa, for God's sake!" she exclaimed. "I've dreamed about the ocean since I was a kid watching reruns of *Flipper*. The Coast Guard was my dream job, but my outfit doesn't see a lot of ocean time.

"So…what's a girl gotta do? Don't answer that! One day, will you please take me fishing? I don't care if we catch anything. I'd just love to be out on the ocean and away from land for a while—and all this crazy cartel business."

He thought about it for a minute, and frankly, her idea sounded good. *A couple of Red Stripes, fishing poles, and a pretty girl on the ocean? What's the worst that could happen?*

"I'll tell you what, Lieutenant. Meet me tomorrow morning at zero seven hundred hours, and we'll try our luck for dolphin."

"Dolphin?" she said with disgust. "You fish for dolphin?"

"No, no, you've got it all wrong. In the Keys, we call mahimahi 'dolphin' or 'dolphinfish.' Further south, they call it dorado. Old habits die hard; they'll always be dolphin to me, which is significantly different from a porpoise. Anyway, see you at dawn. Bring a hat, sunglasses, and sunscreen."

She showed up as if she were on military time. "Welcome aboard," he said. She was dressed in a cute fishing-type outfit, and once again, he noticed that the lieutenant had a really nice figure. But this was just a fishing trip—nothing more, nothing less. His plan was to go after dolphin—no, scratch that, mahimahi—out past the drop-off.

Rik loved that darn fish. Pound for pound, they provided the most excitement of any fish in the Keys and could be caught most of the year. Except on a full moon. That was a whole 'nother story.

They idled out of the marina and turned the corner, and he gunned the *Bum Runner* towards a small beacon called Bug Light. This was where they could find Sandy the Bait Man most mornings for some live bait and a few stories.

He saw Sandy and yelled over the engines, "Hey, man, got any lively pilchards?"

"Sure do. How many do you need?"

"About three dozen."

Rik idled up next to Sandy's boat, and Sandy handed him net after net of live pilchards, which went straight into the transom live well. This setup was nice because the side of the live well was plexiglass, so they could see their bait much like an aquarium.

Loaded with bait, they headed south for blue water and, hopefully, mahi. The lieutenant climbed up to the bridge. "What are you looking for?"

"Now, there are two ways to fish for mahimahi. One, you can troll, which means dragging your baits out behind the boat hoping to find a fish or two. This works but can be kinda boring. Or you can sight fish and look for signs."

"Signs?"

"The first thing I look for are birds. Several kinds of seagoing birds feed on fish, and dolphin feed on those same fish. So, usually where there are birds, there are dolphin. We can look for them with binoculars or on the radar. But one of my favorite ways is to find frigate birds."

"What are those?" the lieutenant asked.

"Frigates are really cool. They're large, soaring birds with really impressive eyesight. They can see the dolphin deep in the water. So, when you find the frigates, they are usually near mahimahi. When they start diving towards the surface, that's when it gets crazy.

One of the coolest sights you'll ever see is the combination of a frigate diving for the surface and, underneath, a big bull dolphin chasing a flying fish. The bull dolphin will erupt out of the water, the flying fish is entirely out of the water, and the frigate and the bull are both vying to catch their airborne meal. It really is an incredible sight."

"So, it sounds like you're hunting, huh?" she said.

"That's a good way to put it. And that's how I tend to look for my mahi."

He was using the radar to locate flocks of birds and binoculars to scan for anything else. And there they were—two high-flying frigates four miles away. He pointed the boat in their direction, and as they got closer, the birds descended as if they were on the hunt.

As they approached, he climbed back down to the cockpit and put out two of his favorite trolling lures: blue-and-white Islanders with a ballyhoo behind them, and for good luck, a trusty black-and-red feather. His plan was to troll near the diving frigates and, if they hooked up, use the pilchards to catch any other mahi that might be hanging around.

The frigates were now close to the water, diving and whirling as they sought their prey. Then, bam—

the port rod went off screaming. They had a big bull on. A few seconds later, the other rod went off, and they had the cow. The big ones traveled in pairs.

"This is going to be fun," he said. He put the boat in neutral, put a fighting belt on the lieutenant, and had her fight the larger fish, which was now headed for Cuba. She looked at him in shock, but he just told her to hang on.

He addressed the other bent-over rod while assisting her. He boated his fish quickly and placed it in the fish box that already had ice in it. Now, they addressed her fish. It was a fifty-pounder, not easy for an accomplished angler, much less a novice.

Her fish made run after run, and she stuck with it. After thirty minutes, he thought she was going to give up. He wiped her brow and gave her a cola. She looked at him longingly, or so he thought. Eventually, she got the fish close to the boat, and he told her to back up. He grabbed a gaff, caught the fish right behind the head, and lifted it quickly into the fish box. The dolphin slammed about, which shocked the lieutenant. But eventually, the fish calmed down.

He was so caught up in the excitement that he forgot to see if any others were hanging around. So, he cast out a few pilchards on spinning rods, and sure enough, zip, zip, zip—they were hooked up to three more in no time. It continued like this, catching smaller schoolie dolphin. In the spirit of sustainability, they released most.

After an hour and a half in the hot sun, the lieutenant was exhausted. He sat her down in the teak fighting chair and gave her a nice cool towel for her head and a beverage.

"This sure is exciting," she said. "Now I see why you love fishing so much."

"Well, it's not always like this. Remember, I've been doing this all my life, so I've learned a few tricks along the way."

He brought out some sandwiches and they climbed back up to the bridge to enjoy the breeze, the clean salt air, and the beautiful day.

They were silent for a bit then the lieutenant said, "When I met you and Billy at Woody's you mentioned your uncle Jax. I assume he taught you how to fish?"

Rik was always reluctant to talk about his upbringing. But with Jill it was different. So, he replied, "Yep. We spent weekends on a rundown houseboat docked near Alabama Jacks. But to me it was heaven. He taught me every aspect of hunting. On land and water."

"So, he taught you how to shoot too?"

"Yes. We would go into the Everglades with his M40 sniper rifle. He wouldn't talk much about why he had one but it certainly had seen some use. Anyhow, he would set up shooting scenarios since I was six or so. I loved every aspect of it and he said I'd eventually be better than him.

"But there was more to it. He taught me more than just the mechanics of shooting. He taught me to feel the entire scene before pulling the trigger or releasing a spear underwater. In the Everglades I'd watch how the lily pads bent, how the water moved. I'd see the motion of dragonflies. And in the ocean how schools of baitfish moved or the sounds or even lack of sound. It was kind of heavy to think that way but it was also peaceful. It allowed me to focus on the shooter's mantra. *Slow is smooth. Smooth is fast.*"

"That is kind of heavy. Your uncle seems very interesting. And complicated."

"He is. Was. I haven't heard from him in a while. Let's change the topic for now. I don't see any point in catching more fish, so why don't we head in?"

It was noon, and the sun was high overhead. They passed Alligator Reef and its gorgeous blue waters, waved to a couple of people in center-consoles, and even a few crazies on paddleboards.

They next approached Hawk Channel, which meandered parallel to most of the Keys. It was a deep-water channel, used by boats like the *Bum Runner* and marked by the occasional navigational marker.

He hadn't been aware they were in the area, but he noticed a Coast Guard barge replacing the buoys in Hawk Channel. One of the Black Hull fleet as they were called. As they neared the barge, a Coastie was hopping up and down, waving his arms. Rik slowed the *Bum Runner* down and pulled up next to the vessel.

"Hey, fella…you okay?"

The young Coastie yelled back, "Man, I'm glad you stopped. My wife just went into labor. She's a month early. She's at Fisherman's Hospital, and I'm stuck out here. Radio's down, and now I have no cell phone reception. Can you give me a lift to shore?"

"We can do better than that. Fisherman's has a dock behind it. I'll get you there as fast as possible. Jump on, brother." With that, the Coastie hopped on board, and Rik spun the *Bum Runner* around and gunned it!

On the way in, they learned a little about their expectant father. His name was Dale and like the lieutenant, he also he also hailed from Iowa. What was with all these Midwest people in the Keys? Also like the lieutenant, he'd dreamed of living somewhere, one day, with saltwater vistas.

This wasn't necessarily his dream job, but he was content. Due to budget cuts, Dale was a one-man operation, replacing and repairing navigational buoys from Key Largo to the Dry Tortugas, his ultimate destination, with a refueling and resupply stop in Key West. His boat wasn't pretty, but she was stable and could carry a lot of gear. He affectionately called her *Lil' Annie* as the USCG didn't name boats that small. He was a relative newlywed, and Rik guessed all the fresh salt air was conducive to starting a family. And, well, here they were.

Rik brought the *Bum Runner* off plane, then steered her cautiously down Fisherman's tiny channel and pulled up to the hospital dock. They didn't even tie up. Dale started to hop off, then froze. Rik yelled down from the bridge, "What's wrong?"

"The *Lil' Annie*. I can't leave her out there!"

Rik replied, "I'll tow her to Sailfish Bay Marina. You can get her in a couple of days. She's in good hands. I used to be a—"

Before he could finish, Lieutenant Wright kicked him in the shin.

"I mean, I know a few Coasties. They'll help me tow her in."

With that assurance, Dale hopped off, yelling, "Thanks," but before Rik could say anything, the lieutenant hopped on the dock too. She gave Rik the universal sign that she'd call him. He thought, *What a nice gesture*. Dale was far from home and could use some Coastie backup right now.

Rik got on the radio, and a few marina buddies met him back at the *Lil' Annie*. It wasn't easy, but they eventually got her squared away on a vacant dock back at Sailfish Marina.

His next task was to clean the *Bum Runner* and fillet the fish. While filleting the last mahi, Lieutenant Wright showed up in an Uber.

"So, feeling maternal?" Rik asked.

"Shut up, Rik," she replied playfully. "It was beautiful. I was there. His wife, Brenda, was alone and scared and asked me to stay. It was wonderful!"

"Tell me all about it—but remember, I'm a guy," Rik smiled.

"Well, when we got there, Brenda was surrounded by machines and beeping monitors. She looked up as we entered the room, and you could see how relieved she was to see Dale. He introduced me and she thanked me profusely for finding her husband. I told her it was really you. She asked me to stay for the delivery.

"Dale grabbed her hand, and they talked softly for a bit. Then she closed her eyes, exhaling in gratitude. The doctor and nurses were busy, but they were glad Dale was there.

"The doctor finally said, 'It's time, Brenda.

"With a final push, I saw the baby come out. And Dale was there to see it! It was so beautiful, I started crying.

"I started to leave, but Dale said, 'Wait.' He was all teared up, too. 'Thank you,' he said, 'for helping me get here. And thank Rik. You two are amazing!'

"It was beautiful. I was there. It was wonderful!"

Rik raised an eyebrow, clearly moved despite his usual guarded demeanor. "Well, you did a good thing, Lieutenant."

She smiled back, feeling a warmth and bond she

hadn't expected. "You did, too! Dale kept saying thank you! He said you guys are friends for life. And if you ever need anything, he's your guy."

Hearing this, Rik smiled inwardly, thinking at the moment he had enough "guys." But it was a crazy life, and you could never have too many friends.

The day wound down, and the lieutenant and he shared a beer. She eventually headed home with twenty pounds of fillets for her and her friends. Rik was left alone in the cockpit with a beer and confusing thoughts regarding the lieutenant. And the mystery surrounding the Kahatee.

SEVENTEEN

Billy looked over at Rik and said, "Is that all she's got?"

Rik grinned and pinned the throttles, and the *Bum Runner* topped out at forty-three knots, burning a wallet-busting two hundred gallons per hour. They were headed northbound in Hawk Channel to a small island called Porgy Key. Billy knew an old loner who lived there named Gemini Jones who could possibly help them in their quixotic quest.

Gemini had lived on Porgy Key for most of his life. His father had purchased the barren island around 1900. He and his sons had grown limes and harvested sponges for the mainland. Several years ago, the State had bought the property, but Gemini was allowed to live out his life in the only house he had ever known. After the Key lime industry was undercut and the sponges died off, he'd guided for a living at the Coco Lobo Fishing lodge across Caesar Creek on Adam's Key. There he'd guided several presidents searching the flats for the elusive bonefish. They were world class in these parts. It was also said that he'd become a treasure hunter and knew many of the secrets related to the pirate Black Caesar, who lived in these parts.

They were enjoying the ride and were almost halfway to Porgy Key when the VHF came to life on channel 16. "Ahoy, *Bum Runner*. This is the United States Coast Guard. Is there a hot bite somewhere?"

Huh? Rik scanned the horizon quickly and didn't see any Coast Guard vessels. Then, out of the corner of his eye, he saw a fast-moving orange Dolphin helicopter approaching fifty feet off the water. It was his former pilot and good friend Tony at the controls.

Rik grabbed the mike and said, "What are you doing down this way? Let's switch to channel twenty-two." These were public frequencies, so their conversation had to be somewhat guarded.

"We just flew a mission to the Featherbed Banks. Two boaters forgot the whole red-right-returning thing and played bumper cars with their boats. Thank goodness the only serious injuries were to their wallets. Where are you headed?" Tony asked.

"We're headed over to see a friend of Billy's on Porgy Key. He needs checking on every now and then," Rik said. There was no need for anyone else to know about their real mission.

"Well, safe travels, see you around."

"Hey, why don't you bring Erica down one day, and we'll take the *Bum* out for some yellowtail fishing?" Rik suggested.

"Wow, Rik, that's a great idea. I'd like that. I'll give you a ring," Tony replied. With that, he increased the power, and soon, the rescue helicopter was out of sight.

"Who was that?" Billy asked. He had a right to know since they didn't exactly want to broadcast their mission.

"That was my former pilot, Tony. He's a great guy, and I miss him. This whole new identity thing has put a cramp in my prior friendships, but I trust him with my life. Just as I trust you. He's had a tough row—he lost his wife to cancer several years ago. Now he's saddled with debt and has to raise a teenage daughter on his own."

"Man, that sucks. Maybe after you take them fishing, you can bring 'em by Bonefish Woody's and take in a show?" Billy suggested. They both laughed at that horrible thought.

They soon approached the entrance to Caesar Creek Channel and began the short, twisting journey to Gemini's ramshackle dock. While they were tying up the boat, Billy mentioned that Gemini didn't see or hear too well, and they should tread lightly.

As they approached his shack, they heard an old voice yell out, "Who's out there? Get off my island, or I'll blow your fuckin' heads off!"

Well, his hearing was just fine. At that moment,

they both heard the distinctive sound of a shotgun being racked. Rik yelled to Billy, "Duck!"

Boom! The top of the sea grape tree behind them disappeared in a hail of what he hoped was birdshot.

Billy yelled out, "Gemini! Gemini! It's Billy Tiger…with a friend!"

"Go away, you nasty Injun, you're not welcome here!" came the crusty reply.

Billy turned to Rik and said, "We may have had an issue in the past." Through cupped hands, he yelled, "Gemini, forgive and forget! I brought gifts! We're walking in—don't shoot, I repeat, don't shoot. I've got a friend with me!"

They walked in stooped over and somewhat reluctantly. There sat Gemini in an old chair with an even older shotgun resting on his knees. He might have been past his expiration date, but Rik could tell he meant business.

Billy slowly reached into a canvas bag and pulled out a large bottle of Maker's Mark Bourbon, two boxes of Berger cookies, and a large can of high-quality peanut oil. These gifts soothed the old man's anger management issues, and the tension on the island began to subside. But Rik noticed the Remington was never far away.

"Alright, alright," the old man said. "I'm too old to hold a grudge. What brings you here, Billy? And who the hell is this?"

"This is Rik Duval," Billy replied. "He's a good friend of mine."

"Rik Duval? That's a made-up name if I ever heard one. Who the hell are you *really*?" Gemini asked.

"I'd tell you," Rik replied, "but then you'd be in danger. And we wouldn't want that."

"Okay, I can buy that. Unlike your king-size friend here, I know when to mind my own business. Hey, Rik Duval, do you know the difference between Billy and Fat Albert flying over Cudjoe Key?"

"No."

"Nothing," he shouted, and then Gemini erupted in laughter. Oh, ho, ho! Rik smiled but also felt bad for Billy. After savoring his mean joke, Gemini finally said, "What do you want, Billy?"

"We want to know about Black Caesar. Can you tell us anything?"

"Why should I tell you anything?"

"Cuz there's another bottle of Maker's Mark on the boat."

"Okay, okay. Well, I can tell you he was real and lived across the channel just north of here."

"Really? How can you be so sure?" Rik asked.

With that, Gemini unbuttoned the top button of his raggedy shirt, revealing a gold piece hanging from a lanyard. "Because over the years, I've found a bunch of these here doubloons. They were his alright. Black

Caesar was real, and the treasure stories are real—so real, in fact, that someone already found half of it."

"What?" Rik and Billy both exclaimed together.

"That's right. Several years ago, a fellow named Will Honliban, or something like that, found the famed blue turtle and a hidden scrimshaw stick, solved the puzzle, and found a boatload of gold."

Rik pulled out the scrimshaw stick and asked, "Did it look like this?"

"That's it, that's it! How did you get that?" Gemini asked.

"A Pahokee elder gave it to me after I helped his grandson in the Everglades."

"Well, that thing holds the clue to the second treasure."

"Do you know how to decode it?" Rik asked.

"Not exactly, but I do know that the clues involve compass headings."

They chatted for another hour, sharing old stories. Before they left, Rik asked if the old man needed anything. He said no, but he did look thin, so Rik went back to the *Bum Runner* and put together a bag of groceries for him. And the promised bottle of bourbon.

As Rik was walking down the coral path, he was joined by a grizzled mutt of a dog. The mutt had a spring in his step and took a liking to Rik. Probably because his shoes were a bit fishy.

When Rik handed Gemini the groceries, he said,

"Who's this fella?"

Gemini said, "Well, that there hound is Jimmy Legs. He showed up here a couple of years ago. God knows how he got here cuz it's an island after all. Anyhow, he's good company and catches most of his food at low tide. Got one crazy trait, though. Never, I mean never, say the word *mango* around him." Gemini whispered the word as if it were the Fort Knox password.

"Well, who knows who taught it to him, but when he hears that word, he'll bite the balls off the guy who says it. My friend Snapper Dan was the unfortunate one to find out. He no longer comes around here, and I don't blame him. He sings soprano in the church choir now. I hear he's very good. Anyhow, thanks for the vittles."

As they were walking back down the rickety dock, Gemini stuck his head out and yelled, "Oh! One more thing, boys—think backwards!"

"Backwards?" Rik asked.

Gemini slammed his old, weather-beaten door without another word.

They left the desolate island, and as they headed back down Hawk Channel to Rum Key, Billy and Rik talked about how to solve the scrimshaw mystery.

Billy said, "Well, we're no closer to solving the Kahatee, that's for sure."

"Yes, but did you see his doubloon? There was a

pirate back there. And where there's a pirate, there's gold. We can figure this out."

"Man, I'm thirsty. All this pirate talk makes me want a beer." Billy descended the bridge and returned with a six-pack of Evil Lager beer. He downed the first in one gulp and offered the next one to Rik, who declined. By the time they arrived at Sailfish Bay, Billy had downed them all.

"Ya know, Rik," Billy said, feeling no pain, "this a fine beer. Maybe I had too many, but it's funny… their name backward is Live Regal. I could live regal man. Regal Billy. That's me. Funny how some things make sense if you look at them backwards."

Backwards!

Well, if two lightbulbs could appear above their heads like in a cartoon…

After quickly tying up the *Bum Runner*, they both went inside. Rik grabbed the Kahatee but Billy inexplicably went to the galley.

Rik yelled, "Are you drunk?"

"Not yet, I'm decipherin'."

He went to his pantry, grabbed some flour, a packet of yeast, some oil, and sugar, and threw it all into a bowl, mixing it up. Rik asked, "What the hell are you doing?"

"Patience, white man," Billy said. Rik sat back and watched him work, knowing there might be some method for his madness. Eventually, Billy produced a big ball of dough and said, "Now we let that sit for an hour."

They shot the breeze for an hour, and then Billy rolled out the dough ball with a rolling pin—making quite a mess. Billy then took the artifact and rolled it across the dough, producing the scrimshaw markings but in reverse. Now, they were more intelligible—like some type of language and various numbers.

"Now what?" Rik asked.

Billy took a picture of the markings and said, "I know a guy."

Now, that phrase could have very different meanings for different people. Sometimes it meant, "I know a guy who can help the situation and will save our asses." Other times, "I know a guy" could lead to making a screwed-up situation much worse. But Rik had to trust Billy. He said he'd reach out to a researcher friend at the University of Miami.

Billy went back to his fridge and started grabbing onions, tomatoes, and various other ingredients. Rik asked, "Now what the hell are you doing?"

"I'm hungry," Billy said. "I'm making a pizza."

It took several days, but the photo of the strange markings finally got results from the UM researcher. When Billy got the findings, he asked Rik to meet him after hours at Bonefish Woody's.

Rik was excited when he walked in the door. "What did they say, Billy?"

"Want a drink?"

"No, what did they say?"

"You sure? This Pirate Punch of Regret is real good. Three of these and you'll be wearing body paint by morning!"

"Listen, Wayne Regretzky. What did they say?"

"Alright. Alright. The figures were a language used by the Tuareg people of North Africa. It was an ancient script called Tifinagh. This all made sense as it was rumored that Black Caesar was a Tuareg. And they identified an area in the Keys and provided compass headings."

"Whoa, we need a chart."

Billy said, "Got one right here."

The translated message seemed to triangulate a certain spot—80 degrees off Matecumbe Key and 110 degrees off the southern tip of Islamorada. Bang—there it was. Indian Key!

"The treasure has to be at Indian Key," Billy said.

"Damn, Billy, you're good."

"I know."

"We need a plan," Rik said.

EIGHTEEN

One night, after an after-hours planning session at Bonefish Woody's, Rik walked wearily down the docks to the *Bum Runner* and noticed something amiss. There were lights on in the forward cabin, and he was certain he had turned them all off. He boarded quietly and silently entered through the salon door and grabbed one of the many Glocks hidden on the Bum Runner. This one was in a hidden drawer underneath the electric panel.

He moved forward, then down the steps to the staterooms. The government had trained him for situations like this, but never solo. There should be four or five guys behind him now.

His stateroom had been ransacked, and that was when he saw the intruder.

"Hands up, dickhead!" Rik yelled.

The startled intruder, dressed all in black with a ski mask, charged at Rik before he could fire a round. They were now engaged in a life-and-death struggle. The intruder was much bigger than Rik and pushed him backwards down the companionway back into the salon. They rolled and tumbled, breaking lamps, chairs, and mementos. Rik's Glock went flying under a chair. This was no crackhead burglar looking for something to sell. He had skills. And right now, Rik regretted every shot of booze and dollar draft he shared with Billy these past months.

They were back on their feet now, panting and sweating. The intruder was reaching for the Cordova pistol strapped to his leg. Rik knew it was the official handgun of the Colombian Army—a thought-provoking choice for a sidearm. It was made in Colombia and named for the "Lion of Ayacucho" himself, General José María Cordova Muñoz. But now was certainly not the time for weaponry comparisons.

Rik countered the move with a knife hand to the throat, allowing him to knock the gun down the hallway. The intruder grabbed his throat with one hand, but the other produced a knife. He lunged with a quick slash across Rik's chest, blood now flowing slow but freely.

It was a Mexican standoff. Rik was panting and bleeding more than he cared for. They circled like Oddjob and James Bond in the closing scene from *Goldfinger*. Rik was now next to the settee where he stored fishing gear. He raised the seat, never taking his eyes off the intruder. He was organized, and he knew exactly what he wanted. Rik pulled out an eight-foot gaff that he used for king mackerel fishing.

The intruder clearly wasn't a fisherman and stared at the implement, confused. Rik lunged at him, and when he missed, the intruder seemed amused, as if he had Rik at a disadvantage. But now, Rik pulled back hard, and the gaff embedded in the intruder's hamstring, causing him to go down with a loud thud. Rik was on him in an instant, putting the muzzle of his gun in the intruder's mouth.

"How do you like me now!" Rik said. He knew it wasn't the line he'd been expecting either. Unsure what to do next, he bashed the intruder in the head with the Glock's butt and Ninja Boy was out like a light.

Rik searched the burglar, and as expected, he carried no identification. Rik was at a loss for what to do next. He wanted to call the cops but knew he wouldn't learn a thing if he did. So he did the next best thing—he called Billy.

Billy was there in a flash, and when he came on board, all he could say was, "What the hell happened here?" His eyes scanned the busted-up boat, and then his bloody friend, and what looked like a Latin ninja tie-wrapped to a chair. A ninja with a very big knot on his head and a stinky old fish rag in his mouth.

"Thanks for coming, Billy," Rik said wearily. "I found this guy ransacking the boat. He was looking for something."

Rik had barely finished speaking when Billy

moved like lightning and smashed the guy in the face so hard his nose exploded. "What are you doing here?" Billy hissed through gritted teeth. Rik was terrified of his friend at that moment, and he wasn't the one tied to a chair.

The ninja mumbled something, and Billy pulled the rag out. "Talk," Billy yelled, spraying the man's face with spit. The ninja's words were measured and spoken in a thick Latin accent, but because his nose was obviously broken, he sounded like Elmer Fudd with a Latin accent.

"Futh you, *pendejo*. You hit wike a whittle girl. I'm not tellwing you theet."

Billy then hit him so hard he knocked Ninja Boy and the chair over. The ninja wasn't going anywhere, so Billy motioned for Rik to join him in the cockpit, out of earshot.

Billy spoke first. "You know, he sounds like a Latin Elmer Fudd. And man, he can take a punch."

"I know. He's no amateur. I don't think we're going to get anywhere with him tonight. Maybe we should just call the cops?"

"I know a guy who can get answers out of this prick." There it was again—Billy knew a guy. Well, Billy was on a roll, so Rik went along with his latest plan.

Thirty minutes later, a tall, thin elderly man, dressed in stiff black preacher's garb, strolled down the dock. He handed Rik his business card: *Preacher Peter Payne—No Pain, No Gain.*

The preacher was a defrocked Pentecostal priest from Oklahoma, the kind who held lethal snakes like bridal bouquets and occasionally spoke in tongues. He'd fallen into trouble with a militant Christian yoga coven, and now he was a one-man evangelical road show, preaching the gospel of pain.

He came aboard, assessed the situation, and, seeing the intruder, said, "You, my good man, should tell these men what they want to know."

The ninja shouted back, "Fudd you, padre. I'll bet you hit wike a whittle girl too. You skinny gwingo!"

"Oh, my brother, such sweet words! You fill my heart with joy. The Good Book says that those who are crushed in spirit will be saved. Yes, brother, I intend on crushing your spirit so that ye will be saved! Hallelujah! Can I get an amen?"

Silence.

Preacher Payne looked back, coughed and said louder, "Hallelujah! Can I get an amen?"

This time Billy and Rik chimed in with a loud, "Amen, Brother Payne!"

The preacher then turned to his latest parishioner and said, "My son, that's fine with me. 'Tis a joyous day and hallelujah—I welcome all my new parishioners. We will pray together soon. Wait here, please. I'll be right back with some of my acolytes.

You are just going to love their fellowship!"

Preacher Payne joined Rik and Billy in the cockpit and said in his Midwestern drawl, "Is it just me, or does he sound like a Latin Elmer Fudd? Anyhow, I'll be right back. I just need a few things from my van. Oh, and trust me, he'll be singing like Taylor Swift in no time."

Preacher Payne strode in long, lanky, happy steps to the top of the docks, where he disappeared into a beat-up old white van—the kind favored by perverts and deviants. The van bounced around a bit like it was attending Burning Man, and then the preacher slowly emerged, carrying one big-ass snake. The thing was at least ten feet long.

The preacher stumbled under the weight of the reptile and stepped precariously into the cockpit. After his recent Everglades outing, Rik was a little wary of big, slithery things.

"Fellas, I'd like you to meet Julieta. She is a South African anaconda, hungry, and well, let's just say she's very, very good at her job."

Rik opened the salon door for the preacher but didn't venture inside. The last thing he saw as the door closed was the ninja's saucer-sized eyes. After thirty minutes, the preacher opened the door and sarcastically said, "Let me introduce you to the very loquacious Mr. Ricardo Santos of Villeta, Colombia."

Rik and Billy walked into the salon and each saw

something they hoped never to see again. Julieta's massive head had clamped down on the back of Ricardo's noggin, which served as an anchor point for the rest of her body. She was coiled around his diminished torso, terminating at his waist. His head was a lot bigger than Rik remembered, and his eyes were definitely bulging out of their sockets. Like Marty Feldman but way worse.

In addition to being in obvious pain, he could not catch his breath. Exactly what Julieta intended. All of this, was a prelude to her unhinging her jaws and swallowing him whole just like a deer or capybara in her native land.

Ricardo tried to talk, but now his voice sounded not only like a Latin Elmer Fudd but an underwater Elmer. "I'll talwk! I'll talwk! I'll twell you anything. Get this theeng off of me. It's keeling me." Or at least that was what they thought he said. It was really hard to be eloquent when an anaconda was eating you alive.

The preacher, who was used to this speech pattern, replied, "Sure, Mr. Santos, as soon as you tell my benefactors everything they want to know."

"Athk! Athk!"

Preacher Payne adjourned to the cockpit, and Rik and Billy started their "investigation."

Rik asked rapid-fire questions: "Who are you? Who sent you? What were you looking for?"

"She thent me," Ricardo stammered. "Carmen

thent me."

"*Carmen?*" Rik pressed.

"*Thee Thee*. She knows everything."

Huh? "What does she know? How does she know?"

"She knows about the thick. The artifact. She knows it leads to tweasure."

"How does she know?"

"The boat is bugged, señor. There are eyeth and eerth everywhere."

Rik was shocked and needed time to think, but he also needed to get this guy off his boat.

The good preacher read Rik's mind and said, "Would you like this here fella to disappear for a while? I have a nice spot where I could put him on ice for a week or so."

"That would be great. By the way, what does your service cost?"

"Oh no, no, no. I do all this for the greater glory. But if you'd like to donate to the Church of Payne, we can continue our struggle."

Rik grinned at his pretzel logic and paid him a cash donation, and they collectively hustled Elmerito up the dock and into the old van. Rik couldn't help his curiosity, so he stuck his head in the back. There were jars, boxes, and aquariums with neat little signs. Lionfish, baby gators, black widows—you name the exotic, pain-filled creature, Preacher Payne had it. Rik even saw a gerbil sign. Don't ask.

Since the boat was bugged, Billy and Rik talked on the dock, out of electronic earshot. Rik told him he was going to call Lieutenant Wright and tell her what happened. She could then call in an anti-surveillance unit to rid the boat of all the bugs. He would probably omit the part about the artifact. That was on a need-to-know basis.

Now that Carmen knew their plans, it was time to speed up the operation.

NINETEEN

Rik slept horribly that night. Tossing and turning, thinking, and dreaming about legends, gold, and eventually Carmen. He couldn't keep her out of his mind. He was unable to find even a few minutes of peace. So, when the phone rang at dawn, it was a welcome distraction.

"Rik…it's Tony. Did I wake you?" Tony's voice came through the line, hesitant but hopeful.

"No, I've been up," Rik responded, his voice low. "What's going on?"

"Hey, were you serious about taking me and Erica fishing? I mentioned it to her, and she's hasn't stopped talking about it. She's been going stir-crazy at home. Frankly, we both could use some time on the water."

Rik could hear the tension in Tony's voice, and he knew that feeling all too well. "Yeah, Tony. Let's do it. Can you make it today?"

"Sure! What should we bring?"

"Just some snacks. I've got everything else covered."

As Rik lay back in his bunk, he felt a rare smile spread across his face. This trip could be a good distraction, not only for Tony and Erica but for him as well. Seeing Erica's excitement and spending time with Tony would be a nice break. He was all too aware of what they'd both been through lately. And truth be told, he could use a day of fishing just as much as they could.

With a lot to do, he finally rolled out of bed, his muscles stiff from the sleepless night. He began making provisions for the trip, checking the gear, and packing essentials. The day was just beginning, and the morning air held a promise of something like hope.

Tony and his daughter arrived around 10 a.m., with Erica's eyes widening in wonder at the sight of Uncle Rik's new boat. They all settled on the bridge, and Rik navigated the boat south, heading towards Alligator Light. He had a spot in sixty feet of water that was always productive, and he knew it would be a perfect place to target yellowtail.

When taking kids fishing, Rik liked to keep it simple and fun. Yellowtail provided plenty of action without requiring a long journey, and the unexpected piscatorial surprises that might show up were always a bonus.

After anchoring, Rik dropped two chum bags into the water, watching the oily scent drift back behind the boat. He rigged up some light spinners and gave Erica a quick rundown of how to use the gear. Her enthusiasm was infectious as she listened attentively.

"The key is building a good chum line," he explained, watching the first ballyhoo appear—a good sign. They quickly used hair hooks to catch several, tossing them into the live well. It wasn't long before Rik knew it was time to shift their focus to the main event—yellowtail.

"Alright, Erica, here's the deal. You have to open the bail and keep feeding line to the yellowtail. If you stop, the bait will spin, and that's *no bueno*. Yellowtails are smart and won't bite a spinning bait," Rik instructed with a grin.

Erica took it all in, her small fingers working the reel carefully. Within minutes, they had some decent-sized fish on the line, including several flags, the nickname given to large yellowtail. She was having the time of her life, her laughter echoing across the water as she pulled in fish after fish, even getting the hang of removing hooks.

Back on the bridge, Rik and Tony cracked open a couple of cold ones, watching Erica at work.

"Rik, I really appreciate this," Tony said, a hint of emotion in his voice. "She loves being out here on the boat. I wish I could afford something like this."

Rik chuckled, taking a long sip of his beer. "Hey, I couldn't afford it either. Uncle Sam helped out. And besides, what's mine is yours, *amigo*. Just say the word and we'll go out anytime. Ya know, wahoo season is right around the corner."

Tony gave a wistful smile. "Yeah, I know, but still. I can't help being a bit jealous. Though, you definitely went through hell to get it."

Rik's eyes clouded for a moment as memories flashed through his mind. "You're right about that. I practically died to earn it." He paused before turning to Tony. "But how are you holding up?"

Tony sighed deeply. "It's been rough, man. Our insurance wasn't what I thought. I've got more bills than I know what to do with."

"How can I help?" Rik asked, his voice earnest.

Tony shook his head. "Nah, I doubt you've got that kind of cash."

Rik thought for a moment, then shrugged. "Well, the boat's debt-free, thanks to Uncle Sam. We could put some financing on it, and I could give you the cash."

"No, no, man," Tony said quickly, waving his hand. "I really appreciate it, but I'll figure something out. What's the worst that could happen, right?" He tried to sound lighthearted, but there was an edge to his words.

Rik nodded, and then Tony changed the subject. "You know, I've been training on tandem rotors over at MacDill Air Force Base on weekends. And I'll get a pay bump when I'm certified. When I eventually leave the Coast Guard, I'll have a skill the oil companies are looking for."

"How'd you snag that gig?" Rik asked, raising an eyebrow. "I heard that was a real plum assignment."

"Orders came in two months ago," Tony said, shrugging. "Those babies can lift twenty thousand pounds, you know?"

Before Rik could respond, Erica's sudden shriek cut through the conversation. She had hooked into something big—a forty-pound barracuda. The fierce, toothy fish thrashed, its silver body flashing beneath the surface.

"Oh boy, looks like Mr. Big Teeth is here!" Rik shouted, his grin widening as he and Tony rushed down the ladder to help. There was no way he was letting Erica or Tony handle that bad boy on their own.

After a tense moment, they released the barracuda back into the water, and Rik decided it was time to move on to phase two. With all the commotion behind the boat, it was the perfect time to try for something bigger lurking near the bottom. He rigged up a couple of live ballyhoo on two big spinners with extra-long eighty-pound fluorocarbon leaders. He then sent them down, aiming for mutton snapper or a black grouper…Rik's favorite bottom fish.

"Erica, this is a different kind of fishing," Rik said, his voice serious. "When you feel the bite, you reel like crazy. You only get one shot—these fish will run for the rocks, and if they get there, it's over."

She nodded, her eyes wide with focus, and they waited. About half an hour later, both rods bent over.

"Doubleheader!" Rik shouted, adrenaline pumping as Erica and Tony each grabbed a rod, reeling as if their lives depended on it. Their determination paid off—soon they had a fifteen-pound red grouper and a twelve-pound mutton snapper in the boat. Rik whooped with excitement.

"As my old friend Captain Ken from Key West used to say, 'There ain't nuttin' like a mutton!'"

They fished for a while longer, but as the sun slowly set for the evening, the action slowed down. On the way back, the hunger from a long day on the water hit them hard. Rik offered to cook up a traditional Keys smorgasbord for dinner.

"Rik, you don't have to do that," Tony hesitated. "I'm sure you've got plans."

"Nah, man. It'll be fun. Besides, there's nothing better than fresh fish," Rik replied with a smile.

Erica, worn out from the excitement, fell asleep on the stateroom bunk. Rik filleted their catch while Tony played sous chef. In the galley, Rik put together a simple egg wash, cut the fish into chunks, and coated them in Italian bread crumbs before frying them up in peanut oil. He even used his trick of putting the bread crumbs in the blender first for a finer grind. Then he whipped up a dipping sauce—half mayo, half spicy brown mustard, just the way he liked it.

The smell of fresh fish cooking brought Erica out of her deep sleep, her nose twitching. Soon, they were all sitting down to feast of fried fish, salad, rice, and a slice of Key lime pie Rik had made the day before. As they ate, Rik told them stories about growing up with a Key lime tree in his backyard. And how squeezing the limes for pie always seemed to take forever, but of course, was worth it.

As Rik was walking his tired guests up to their car, a lightbulb went off in his head. All the talk about food and limes made him recall his youth manning a mango stand. The stand had earned him spending money in the summers. Maybe Erica could manage one and, with Uncle Rik's help, produce a real profit. Even earn some college money and take the heat off Tony?

He mentioned all this to Tony, who was cautious but eventually embraced the idea.

"Great," Rik said. "I'll get on it!" And with that, he waved goodbye to his tired, sunburned but happy guests.

The fishing trip had been a great distraction, but now, as he watched the last rays of the sun disappear, Rik redirected his focus to the Kahatee. *How are Billy and I ever going to figure out what the hell is going on?*

TWENTY

After the incident with their stuttering ninja and the reemergence of Carmen, the pressure was on. Rik and Billy had to stay two steps ahead of her, whatever she was up to.

They believed the treasure was somewhere on Indian Key. This small island had once been a bustling maritime community with a focus on wrecking. Its ghostly remains were now overseen by the State Park Service.

A scouting trip was in order, and the logical starting point was from the nearby world-famous Robby's Marina and Tarpon Sanctuary. Robbie's was a Keys legend. Its waters were patrolled by large, hungry tarpon that tourists fortified with bait. The two went there and joined the visitors for the daily run to Indian Key.

It was a short boat ride, and when they landed, they joined the delightful Mayra Williams on her park ranger tour, trying to blend in with the sunburned, suntan-lotion-scented vacationers. It was easier for Rik than for Billy, whose undercover disguise consisted of wearing an XXXL Miami Dolphins retro football jersey with the number 54. Rik overheard several people ask if Billy played for the Dolphins, and one even asked if he was Zach Thomas, the beloved All Pro middle linebacker.

Rik eventually asked, "Number 54—I didn't know you were a Zach Thomas fan?"

"Oh no, my uninformed friend, this is not a Zach Thomas jersey. Zach was a great linebacker, but it was also Wahoo McDaniel's number."

"Who the heck was Wahoo McDaniel?"

"Who was Wahoo McDaniel?" Billy, dismayed, palmed his forehead. "Only the greatest Miami Dolphins middle linebacker in 1968! He was a Choctaw-Chickasaw tribal member, and after his football career, he became a legendary—nay, world-class pro wrestler!"

Rik wasn't sure if Billy was truly upset, but he eventually said, "Okay, okay, I understand."

"And you call yourself a fan. You really do need to bone up on your Dolphins history." Their diatribe was interrupted by the ranger's speech. They listened intently.

"Folks, I know it doesn't look like much, but would you believe this island was actually a small town and a bustling community? In the early 1800s, people made their living salvaging boats that ran aground on the local reefs. At this time, wrecking, as it was called, was both legal and extremely lucrative. If the legends are to be believed, the locals aided the wrecking of ships by relocating navigational aids and occasionally planting false ones."

Billy and Rik glanced at each other, thinking the same thing. What a perfect place for a pirate to store his gold, knowing that one day it would be surrounded by people with an equal penchant for relieving others of their valuables.

The ranger continued, "The mayor of this community was Jacob Houseman. Houseman's empire included a store, hotel, dwellings, cisterns, warehouses, and wharves. Known for his shady business practices, he constantly feuded with the other salvagers."

The ranger moved on with her pale and sweating audience in tow, but Billy and Rik broke away from the group. They scouted around for potential treasure locations or clues, but nothing really made sense. Like most of the Keys' islands, it was formed out of hard coral and was difficult to dig holes in or create hiding places.

All the buildings had been razed, but in one corner of the town square there was an odd cellar-like formation with a sign identifying it as "Mystery Feature" whose purpose remained unknown. In the far corner, there was a hole, possibly a drain.

They were discussing the possibilities that this may be an important clue to Caesar's treasure when Ranger Willams appeared out of nowhere, startling both of them. "You boys seem interested in this site," she said. "You know there are several legends associated with this ruin."

"Really? Please go on," they uttered simultaneously.

"Well, once a year, a ghost orchid appears here. The legend is that it commemorates the date Black Caesar was hung. Have you ever heard of him?"

Rik and Billy played dumb, but the ranger's expression signaled she didn't believe them.

She continued, "Well, Caesar was a local pirate who amassed and hid a fortune in gold in the Keys. Want to know my theory? I think this feature is connected somehow to the treasure. I can feel it. The legend also says that his gold was always marked with the symbol of a ghost orchid."

They both mumbled and stuttered until she finally said she must round up her group. Before she disappeared into one of the low-hanging canopy trails, she turned and said softly to Rik, "Grab the bottom. You'll thank me later."

Grab the bottom? What the hell did that mean? Maybe the ranger had been on Indian Key a little too long. Rik and Billy ignored her last words and were both now baffled and excited at the same time.

"Did you hear that? A ghost orchid every year. Damn, that's cool."

They walked the probable path of the drain hole to the shoreline. It was difficult to see because of the mangroves, but it looked like there was a sort of outflow pipe. The water was clear, and they estimated it to be about ten feet deep. It looked large enough for a person to explore.

Billy looked at Rik and said, "Don't look at me. I'm not fitting in that damn thing. Besides, I'm claustrophobic." Rik smiled, and they decided to come back later that night with scuba gear to see what was inside.

Rik also knew the tidal currents were vicious here and so he planned his exploratory visit during slack tide, which wouldn't give him much time.

That night, they returned with Rik's flats boat that sat on the bow of the Bum Runner. They had to constantly shift the weight around because of Billy's three hundred and fifty pounds, but eventually, they anchored near the suspicious outflow pipe. Billy helped Rik put on his gear and said, "Listen, brother, I don't know anything about scuba diving, but maybe I should tie a rope to one of your feet so I can pull you out if you get in trouble?"

Rik smiled. His first reaction was to give a sarcastic reply, but as he got older, he had learned that when people offered help, no matter how crazy, you didn't chide them for it. In fact, you frequently accepted it. But in this case, he said, "Thanks, brother, next time."

With that, Rik spit in his mask, placed it over his head, and slipped over the side, swimming to the outflow pipe. He wiggled his way through the mangroves and found it covered with a rusty grate. Trying not to damage any roots, he managed to yank the grate off and pull himself inside.

He squeezed through the narrow passage, noting that it wasn't a pipe at all. It was a carved passage, or perhaps even a naturally formed conduit. Either way, the rough limestone was rubbing his shoulders raw. He regretted not wearing a wetsuit but didn't want the added buoyancy.

His dive light illuminated the walls as they started to narrow, barely large enough for him and his tank. It became clear that he would have to leave it behind if he wanted to move further in. He slipped off his BC and tank, took a breath, and moved inward.

After fifty feet, Rik reached a section that angled upwards—clearly leading to the hole they had seen above ground. But there were no sightings of any clues. He pushed himself backward, feeling a bit claustrophobic, and reached for a quick shot of air.

Rik did another look around, and seeing nothing, grabbed his gear and returned to the boat. He told Billy there was nothing there, and he was a little surprised at

Billy's reaction.

"Listen," Billy said sternly, "you get your ass back in the water and scour that pipe. Don't you dare come back empty-handed! There's something there. I know it! Don't make me get in there with you!"

That last remark was kind of funny because Rik had never seen Billy in the water. He was sure he would look like a giant Goliath grouper floundering around in the shallows. But, you know, there's nothing like a bit of positive reinforcement and uplifting coaching to move you out of your comfort zone. Tonight, Billy was Rik's own personal Tony Robbins.

So, back he went, amped up. This time, Rik examined every square inch, and Billy was right—he did see something unusual. There was a piece of limestone that appeared to be cemented in place. He returned to the boat to get some tools.

Rik dove back in and began picking at a mortar seam, eventually removing a roughly ten-by-ten-inch section of the wall. He shined his dive light inside the opening and saw a small wooden tablet. He grabbed it, turned around, and retraced his path back to the boat.

As soon as he left the safety of the mangrove roots, the current grabbed him. Rik had lost track of time and the tide had turned. Viciously. He was a strong swimmer, but never in his life had he experienced anything like this. Black Caesar's ghost was hanging on to the clues with ghostlike abandon.

He was moving seaward away from the boat. He regretted not having a whistle. Or a wetsuit. *This isn't how his story was supposed to end*, he thought. Lost at sea, succumbing to hypothermia—or worse, the man in the gray suit. As he tumbled over and over, the mysterious ranger's words came to mind. *Grab the bottom.*

The current was always less fierce at the bottom, so he kicked downward. It was sandy with eel grass but there were small rocks, almost like handholds. He grabbed onto one to stop his backward motion and took a minute to regain his composure.

He then began pulling himself back to the boat. This was no easy task, but doable. The ranger's strange words might have saved his life. *How the hell did she know?*

As Rik climbed breathlessly over the gunwale, he handed Billy the tablet. Billy stared at him; his heavy arms crossed over his chest. He leaned over and said, "See, was that so hard? Geez, do I have to do everything around here?" The glint in his eye, however, told Rik that Billy was just as anxious about the tablet as he was.

Rik just smiled, and they both sat down and shined a light on the wooden tablet. Just like the scrimshaw stick, it was likely made of lignum vitae wood. But it was blank! Rik turned it over and over. Nothing!

They sat there, staring at the blank tablet in

disbelief. Billy's scowl deepened as he let out a frustrated grunt, kicking the boat's cooler. "What the hell? We came all this way for a frickin' piece of wood?"

Was the Kahatee wrong? Had the UM researcher let them down? Had Rik almost been swept out to sea for nothing?'

They stared at the blank tablet. Disappointed. Frustrated. But something told Rik this wasn't a dead end. No, this was just the beginning.

TWENTY-ONE

Billy and Rik's nerves were getting the best of them. Paranoia was creeping in. Neither trusted an open line, and their conversations quickly devolved into coded messages.

Rik called Billy and his voice came over the line, cautious but with an edge of urgency. "Any new thoughts on the Conundrum?"

"No, but the Monarchs are in Mexico."

Rik paused, glancing around, as if someone might be eavesdropping. "Perhaps Robinson Crusoe can be of assistance?"

Billy hesitated, then spoke, his words layered with hidden meaning. "Yeah, but he may be pulling a Cherry Garcia."

Rik frowned, growing impatient. "Is the Covenant of the Ark safe?"

Billy's voice grew low, almost a whisper. "Leave the gun, take the cannoli."

That was it. Rik had enough. "Billy, cut the crap and get over here."

Within moments, Billy was there. Standing in the

Bum Runner's galley, leaning over the counter, staring at the blank wooden tablet before them. The supposed key to their mystery. A tablet of lignum vitae wood stared back at them. Mocking them. Challenging them. As if Caesar was saying, "Let's see you what ya got, Rik, and your plus-sized friend too!"

The anticipation of finding something remarkable, a secret worth all the effort and secrecy, was rapidly giving way to disappointment.

"Blank? This can't be it," Billy muttered, a harsh edge to his voice as he fought to contain his irritation.

Rik was equally frustrated. It didn't make sense. After all the effort—tracking down the Kahatee's cryptic information, diving through that treacherous, narrow conduit in pitch-black water—there had to be something more. Lignumvitae wasn't just any wood; it was one of the hardest, most durable woods out there. It was chosen to protect something, to preserve it.

"Don't you know a guy?" Rik asked, throwing his hands in the air. "You always know a guy."

Billy shrugged, his shoulders slumping slightly. "Not this time, man. I'm at a loss here, boss. Got nothing. Blank. Dead in the head. What about you?"

Rik sighed, pacing the small space as he thought aloud. "Well, I'd say we ask either Chief Cypress or Gemini Jones. They're the only two people I know who have any experience with… wooden clues."

Billy shook his head. "Chief Cypress is out of the

question. I heard he's in Arizona, learning to fly planes."

Rik stopped pacing, staring at Billy incredulously. "Flying planes? Weird hobby at his age."

Billy laughed. "Would you believe the tribe bought three firefighting airplanes? They're like those old flying boats—they skim lakes and scoop up a thousand gallons of water, then drop it on fires. Been using them out West for years. The Pahokee elders thought it would be smart to have them to safeguard the reservation in case of a wildfire. And guess who's going to be lead pilot? Yep, Chief Toby Cypress."

Rik couldn't help but grin. "Well, I want to be like him when I grow up," he said, a glint of admiration in his eyes.

Billy returned the grin but soon turned serious again. "Alright, back to business. Looks like we're heading back to see Gemini. Porgy Key it is."

Half an hour later, they were blasting north, the rumble of the Bum Runner's engines cutting through the wind and waves. They decided to take the longer route offshore, hoping to get lucky and hook a mahi or two while they cleared their minds. But Poseidon frowned on them today. After an hour of trolling in two hundred feet of water with no luck, they turned back west, heading in toward Caesar Creek Channel.

As they tied up to the weathered dock near Gemini's shack, an uneasy feeling settled over Rik.

Something was off. The spot was strangely quiet—no barking from the old stray dog that normally hung around, no smoke rising from Gemini's fire pit.

Billy called out a few times, his voice echoing off the thick mangroves that lined the shoreline. No answer. They exchanged a glance. Something wasn't right.

Rik nodded toward the door. They approached cautiously. The ramshackle door creaked open, revealing the small, cluttered space of Gemini's home—or what was left of it. The room was in disarray; chairs were overturned, papers scattered across the floor, and a shattered lamp lay in pieces near the corner. Signs of a struggle were everywhere.

"Damn it," Billy muttered under his breath, his eyes scanning the mess.

It didn't take them long to search the shack—it wasn't big enough for much hiding. But there were no signs of Gemini, no clues as to what had happened or why he was gone. Rik clenched his jaw, a storm of anger brewing within him. This was just another complication, another roadblock in an already twisted journey.

"If the cartel or someone else hurt that old man, they'll have to answer to me," Rik said, his voice cold, anger dripping from every word. He thought of his conversation with the Painter, how he'd threatened to gut him like a pig. That same rage boiled up now, fiercely, but without a target. He felt powerless, and that feeling was worse than the anger itself.

Billy looked over at Rik, seeing the tension etched across his face. He placed a hand on his friend's shoulder, a gesture meant to ground him. "We'll figure this out, Rik. One way or another, we'll get to the bottom of this."

Rik exhaled, forcing himself to take a deep breath. "Yeah," he said, though his voice lacked conviction. He looked around the chaos of Gemini's home once more before scribbling a quick note—just in case Gemini returned. They propped it up on the one unbroken chair, weighed down by a half-empty bottle of Maker's Mark.

With nothing else to be done, they returned to the Bum Runner. As they untied the lines and pushed off from the dock, Rik cast one last glance at the shack, the uneasy feeling settling deeper in his gut.

That was when they heard a rustling in the bushes. Each pivoted, ready for a fight. But it was Jimmy Legs, Gemini's dog. According to Gemini, he was a real survivor and didn't look any worse for wear. But they couldn't leave him here all alone. So, with a quick whistle from Rik, he jumped on board like he'd been an ocean dog all his life.

The ride back to Sailfish Bay Marina was quiet. Even Billy, usually full of jokes, was lost in thought, staring at the horizon as they cut through the waves.

The sun was beginning to set, painting the sky in hues of pink and gold, but Rik found no comfort in its beauty. His mind was on Gemini—what had happened to him, where he might be, and whether he was even still alive.

Back at Sailfish Bay they docked the Bum Runner, securing her to the pilings as the sky darkened overhead. After making a makeshift bed for Jimmy Legs, Rik looked at Billy, his friend's face barely visible in the dim evening light. Rik half expected Billy to come up with some poignant advice. And he did.

"Let's snap out of it, man! It's pop-up strip club night at Bonefish Woody's. Let's check it out!"

Rik replied, "I don't know. I'm not really feeling up to it."

"C'mon, the girls are hot, and they've got a new light show that I hear is pretty cool."

Not wanting to be a drag, Rik agreed but said, "I'm bringing the tablet for safekeeping. I want to keep my eyes on it."

"Whatever floats your boat."

They walked into Woody's and noticed Louie's perch was moved next to the dance floor. His pirate hat was askew, he held a wad of singles in his right claw and was loudly squawking, "Raawk. Walk nasty for Louie. Nasty for Louie. Raawk. I saw better landing strips in 'Nam baby."

They found themselves a table and ordered a

couple of Drunken Macaws. Billy looked longingly at his drink and stated, "Man, the last time I was overserved these babies I woke up in Bimini." With that he downed the first in one long gulp and loudly said, "Now that's the ticket!"

It was bizarre how Woody's could turn into a strip club, but Rik wasn't about to argue. The girls were hot, the drinks were cold, and the music was great. He loosened up after a while, and again Billy was right—the lights were awesome.

Occasionally, Platinum and her friends, Silver, and Aluminum, would stop by to discuss physics. Also, dark matter theory and the potential of interdimensional time travel. I'm kidding. They were on a mission to relieve Rik and Billy of their cash. Rik made a mental note, however, to help Aluminum with her stage name.

After an hour or so, something caught Rik's eye. When the black lights came on, he saw a shimmer on the tablet. "Billy, look at that!" Billy saw it too, and they both jumped up. They ran to the nearest black light, held the tablet underneath, and sure enough, there was writing on it.

"Holy moly," they both muttered.

"You see that?" Rik asked, his voice tense.

Billy squinted, then his eyes widened. "I knew it. There's something there."

There was writing. It was faint and glowed blue-green. It appeared to be a riddle:

Have you sins for which you must atone?
Will you end up in a pile of bone?
Reverse your fortune if you dare,
Fortune awaits those who finds me lair.

This was huge. Caesar was communicating with them through his version of invisible ink. Jellyfish in the Keys used bioluminescence, and Caesar apparently figured out a way to synthesize and write with it. It was mind-boggling, but now they had to figure out the clue.

They sat back at their table, relieved that the secret was temporarily safe. The writing was only visible under black light, so they were the only ones who could read it. For now. They pondered the riddle, getting nowhere until after the bar closed. Billy, who practically co-owned the place, locked up, and put on a pot of coffee.

"Pile of bone" could only mean one thing around there. Numerous Native American burial mounds existed in the Everglades and the Keys. They were considered sacred. Bad juju to disturb them, according to Billy.

They set that thought aside and focused on the line "reverse your fortune."

"What's there for us to reverse?" Billy wondered aloud.

Suddenly, Rik's eyes lit up. "I've got it!"
"What?"

"The compass headings! We need to reverse them."

"Do you remember them?" Billy asked.

"Yeah, they were 80° and 110°. So, if we reverse course, we add 180°, making them 260° and 290°."

Billy grabbed an old chart from the bar wall, and they applied the reversed headings from Matecumbe Key and the southern tip of Islamorada. They converged on Shell Key—an unpopulated island with an Indian burial mound. Like Indian Key, it was part of the State Park system but was closed to the public for the majority of the year.

Billy shook his head. "Hell no, I'm not goin' within five miles of Shell Key. You don't mess with ancient stuff, man—that's how you end up cursed or eaten by raccoons with glowing eyes. Look at the fellas who opened King Tut's tomb—*bada bing, bada boom, body bags.* Every single one of 'em!"

"Billy, we have to check it out!"

Billy snorted, but his eyes darted like he was checking for shadows. "No way, man. I'm afraid of no man—but ghosts? Spirits? Duppies? That's where I draw the line. I'll fight a gator with a pocketknife before I poke a dead man's resting place."

"C'mon, man! You don't believe in all that hoodoo voodoo, do ya?"

"Really? Then explain this. I was layin' low in Cayman Brac and I met a woman with indigo eyes. We danced and later kissed on a secluded beach. Then she evaporated in my arms and floated into the sea. She was a sea spirit. I collapsed and woke up the next day naked in a crab trap with a conch shell duct-taped to my ear. I ain't been the same since."

"Really, Billy? You were always a few shrimp short of a boil."

"To this day when I think of her I start talkin' backwards. So, yeah, you're on your own!"

"Billy, I can't do it alone," Rik pleaded, and after some convincing, Billy sighed.

"I might know a guy who can look after me. I mean us."

"Get outta here. Who would help in this situation?"

"You'll see. Give me some time to make the arrangements. Then we'll take the tender over for a brief exploration. And I mean really brief!"

TWENTY-TWO

Rik's mind was a storm of thoughts and worries. Chasing pirate gold felt like the kind of outrageous adventure that would make for a good story someday, but that wasn't what disturbed him. What kept gnawing at him was Tony and Erica. They weren't just any family—they were his family, forged not by blood but by bonds built over time. On land, water, and in the air.

Tony had been the guy who always had his back, the one who stood between Rik and danger time and time again. And now, life had turned on Tony. A decorated veteran, a man who had given everything to serve his country, reduced to struggling to provide for his little girl. Rik couldn't let that stand—not when he could do something about it.

The idea of a smoothie stand wasn't grand, but it was a start. A way for Erica to shine, to feel proud, to hold onto her childhood a little longer. Rik wasn't exactly an entrepreneur, but he knew one thing: He'd do whatever it took to give that kid a chance. So, he turned to Billy.

Billy Tiger had a knack for making things happen. He suggested they talk to Bob, of Bob Is Here fruit stand fame. If anyone could get them the fresh produce they needed, it was him. Rik had heard the legend before—a kid selling a single cucumber on a forgotten roadside, turned into a Miami icon by sheer grit and a giant sign. It was the kind of bootstrap story everyone loved.

The three of them met at Shriver's BBQ. As Rik laid out Tony and Erica's story, the emotion in his voice silenced even the usually tough-as-nails Billy. Bob didn't hesitate. "Let's make it happen," he said, promising to source the best mangos South Florida could offer.

Rik threw himself into the project. He built the stand with his own hands, piecing it together from repurposed shipping pallets. Every hammer strike felt like a vow—to Tony, to Erica, to himself. Billy came through with three industrial blenders, claiming they were "rescued" from a bankrupt restaurant. Rik wasn't fooled; he found the brand-new boxes in a dumpster, still gleaming with the sheen of newness. It was a small reminder of Billy's big heart, buried under layers of whiskey barrel bravado.

Tony's neighborhood was known for its sprawling lots and horse farms, but not exactly bustling with foot traffic, so Rik knew Erica needed more than a stand.

She needed customers. And Rik wasn't about to let her sit outside in the South Florida sun, waiting for a miracle. So, he called in the Coast Guard network, the brothers and sisters who understood what it meant to look out for your own.

They showed up in droves, car after car lining up for Erica's mango smoothies. The sight brought a lump to Rik's throat. Erica, beaming as she handed out drinks, didn't just look happy—she looked alive, like she was finally seeing the world as something full of possibility.

The buzz grew. Local news stations picked up the story, calling it a testament to community spirit. But Rik wasn't satisfied. He made a few more calls, using a fictitious name, stirring up a rivalry between SouthComm and Homestead Air Force Base. The result was magical. Week after week, uniformed men, and women from every branch of service packed the block, their laughter and camaraderie filling the air.

But not everyone was charmed. Tony's neighbor Karen, who epitomized the worst kind of suburban entitlement, began complaining about the "inconvenience." Rik was ready to lose his temper, but Commander Eisendorf—one of Erica's biggest fans—handled it instead.

"Would Taylor Swift tickets solve your problem?" he asked Karen, deadpan.

Karen paused, suspicious but intrigued.

"Possibly."

"Here you go," Eisendorf said, handing over the tickets. "Now, not another peep. *Comprende?*"

"Yes, sir," Karen mumbled, slinking back to her house, where she promptly bragged to her daughter about "the great sacrifice she'd made to obtain the tickets."

Things were looking up for Erica. But, as with all good things, trouble wasn't far behind. A sour-faced county food inspector named Yancy showed up, flashing his silly badge and demanding to see licenses, permits and insurance. Items that Erica couldn't possibly have. The poor girl looked up at him, confused, and meekly offered him a smoothie.

Tony stepped in, thinking it was all a prank. But as the inspector's tone grew more severe, Tony realized this wasn't a joke—it was bureaucracy at its worst, targeting a kid trying to make an honest buck.

The conversation was also overheard by Erica's unofficial but highly effective security detail—Leatherface and Grizzles. These men, once infamous in their Warlock motorcycle gang days, had softened over time, but their distaste for bullies never ended.

"What seems to be the problem here, Officer?" Leatherface asked, his voice low and dangerous.

"This minor is violating every health code in the book," the inspector replied smugly. "Chapters 474.12 and 612-B1, to be exact," he added as he waved an official-looking booklet around.

"Hmm. Let's not discuss this in front of the kid," Leatherface said as he and Grizzles gently guided the inspector behind a nearby and absurdly large pickup truck.

"That's funny," Leatherface said, stepping in closer. "Because Section XIX.50 of the Desert Eagle handbook says kids can sell anything they want as long as it's 'cool and delicious.' You know this code section, right?"

"I've…I've…never seen it," Yancy stammered.

Leatherface leaned in closer to the inspector's noggin and, in one fluid motion, pressed the barrel of his massive Deagle pistol into Yancy's left eye socket. "Can you see it now?" he growled.

The inspector's voice shot up an octave. "Yes. Yes, I can."

"Good," Leatherface said. "Now, you're gonna buy three smoothies—one for me, one for Grizzles, and one for yourself. Then we're gonna have a chat about manners."

"And if I don't?" the inspector croaked.

"Well, there's a sweet gator hole five miles west of here," Leatherface said, his tone cold. "Me and Grizzles here are gonna tie you waist-deep to a cypress tree, dip your feet and hands in pig blood and watch Ol' Snappers twist your limbs off one by one. It's a slow process you'll likely regret."

Grizzles grinned, a wicked glint from his one good eye. "Ya know, mister, it's been a while since we had a good taffy pull."

The inspector gulped, his bravado dissolving quickly. "I think … I might have misinterpreted the rules," he stammered, reaching for his wallet. He bought three smoothies, his hands trembling as he handed over the cash. Erica, ever polite, thanked him and smiled, her innocence a stark contrast to the surrounding tension.

The stand became more than just a business. It was becoming community hub. Neighbors who'd barely spoken before now shared stories over smoothies. Military personnel from every branch made it a point to stop by; their camaraderie was a testament to what could be achieved when people came together. Even Karen, now a proud owner of Taylor Swift tickets, softened, waving at Erica each morning from her porch.

For Tony, the stand wasn't just a way to make ends meet—it was a reminder that no matter how tough life got, there were people who cared, people who showed up when it mattered. One evening, as the sun dipped below the horizon, he pulled Rik aside.

"You didn't have to do all this," Tony said, his voice thick with emotion. "But you did. And I'll never forget it."

Rik looked at him, a small smile playing at his

lips. "You kept me alive out there, Tony. This? This is nothing compared to what you've done for me."

One quiet evening, after the last car had pulled away and the street was bathed in the soft glow of string lights, Erica handed Rik a smoothie she'd made herself. "This one's for you," she said.

Rik took a sip and grinned. "Yum—perfect."

As Erica ran off to join her dad, Rik leaned back against the stand, watching the two of them laugh together. The air was filled with the sweet scent of mangoes and the hum of cicadas, and for the first time in a long while, Rik felt a deep peace. He'd started this journey thinking he was helping them, but in the end, he was the one who had gained.

TWENTY-THREE

Just like Freddie Mercury said, *The show must go on!* Fortified by three Smugglers' Delights (three of those and you'll be running down A1A in someone else's flip-flops), Rik found himself back onstage with Billy and the Debauched. He was banging away on the bongos, trying to keep up with Billy's new set list. His mind was occasionally elsewhere, but the rhythm and the music offered a great escape from their latest exploits.

Rik had always loved music but had never played in a band before. He greatly appreciated the teamwork involved and likened it to his Coast Guard days. Every mission was dependent upon numerous people doing their jobs and working in concert with one another. Everyone had each other's back, and he missed that camaraderie. But Billy's band, no matter how crazy it got, gave him a similar feeling.

He also enjoyed watching Billy work the crowd. He was a natural entertainer, and his antics—like whacking people with his "toy"—as the audience roared. His favorite routine was "knighting" random drunks, who would then bow in mock reverence. It never failed to make Rik chuckle, no matter how many times he saw it.

Tonight, Bonefish Woody's was packed, the music loud, and Rik was several drinks in when he caught a glimpse of someone. A flash of auburn hair, the same exotic beauty he hadn't been able to forget. Carmen? No. That was impossible. She was in Colombia. Rik blinked hard, trying to focus, but the phantasm was gone as quickly as it appeared. The club was crowded, a bit smoky and the spotlights blinding, so it was very hard to see deep into the crowd.

Twice more that night, he thought he saw her. Each time, his pulse quickened, but then the apparition vanished into the crowd. He shook his head, rubbing his eyes. He really needed some sleep. Lately, he felt like he was being haunted by more than just his past.

After the final set, Rik headed back to the boat, hoping to find some peace in the rocking of the waves. As he was nodding off to sleep, he felt the boat shift, not from the wind or current, but from something—or someone—else. His instincts flared. Reaching for his Glock, he moved toward the salon from his cabin.

"Who's there?" he called out, voice steady, though his pulse raced.

"It's me, *mi amor*."

Rik froze. That voice. Soft, purring, familiar.

Carmen.

The salon door slid open, and there she was. As real as the moonlit night. For a moment, Rik didn't know whether to pull the trigger or pull her into his arms. Against every screaming instinct, he chose the latter.

He embraced her, but after the warmth of the moment faded, his guard snapped back into place. He gently pushed her into a seat, eyes narrowing. "What the hell is going on? Why are you here? Why now?"

Carmen's eyes gleamed with something between fear and desperation. "You don't understand, Rik. I had to protect us. I love you. I never stopped. I've been trying to keep you safe."

"Safe? By running? By disappearing without a word? Why did you leave Pinder? Do you know what you put me through?"

"I didn't have a choice!" she said, voice trembling. "I had to vanish, even from Pinder. He couldn't know where I was, or they would've found me. I didn't want to hurt him, but it was the only way."

"Where did you go?"

"I made my way to Nassau, where I have friends. Dangerous friends. They got me to Colombia. I had to smooth things over with my father-in-law. I blamed everything on you and the government. It wasn't true, but it kept us alive."

Rik's mind churned, trying to digest the words.

"So, he believed you?"

"Yes. I convinced him. Now we can be together again. I can help you. I can help the government. I'm done with that life. I don't ever want to go back to it!" Her voice cracked, tears sliding down her cheeks. "Rik, they bugged the boat. Remember, I was attacked too."

Rik's mind whirled. "Who was behind it? You expect me to believe it wasn't you?"

Carmen shook her head violently, her expression raw. "No! I would never do that to you. It must have been El Cojón. He's been following me ever since. Why would I bug my own boat, Rik? You've got to believe me."

Before he could respond, she threw her arms around him, her lips pressing against his with a sudden, fiery urgency. It was a kiss that broke through his walls, a kiss that could burn the doubts away. But in the back of his mind, something gnawed at him. *Could this really be the truth? Could everything have been some terrible misunderstanding?* His heart begged him to say yes, but his instincts whispered otherwise.

They ended up in his stateroom. It was familiar. Dangerous, even. For a few hours, the past slipped back into place. She kissed his temple and whispered, "I'll never leave you, Rik."

He stared at the ceiling, unsure if he was hearing a promise… or a warning.

But when Rik woke in the early hours of the morning, Carmen was gone. And so was the Kahatee.

Billy didn't ask any questions when Rik called him early the next day. He never did.

"Can you meet me?" Rik asked, pacing as he spoke.

"Of course."

"Where are you now?"

"Third and Marlin Lane."

Rik knew that location. It was a vacant lot. Billy never stayed in the same place for long. He lived out of a shipping container—a deluxe, solar-powered, air-conditioned unit with all the comforts of home. A moving fortress. Billy preferred to stay off the grid, shifting his container to vacant land owned by friends to avoid unwanted attention. Especially from jealous husbands, possessive boyfriends, and the occasional maniacal stripper.

When Rik arrived, he banged on the secret entrance and heard Billy yell, "*Entrez-vous.*" Billy was sprawled in a hammock, looking as relaxed as ever. "What's up?" he asked, eyes scanning Rik with a knowing smirk.

Before he answered, Rik looked around and noticed some new "decorations." "Are those scalps hanging over there?" he asked incredulously.

Billy smirked again. "They're crazy looking, right? No, they're a bunch of old squirrel pelts that I bought at an estate sale. Sure look like scalps, right? The ladies really love the stories I make up about 'em."

Rik shrugged. He was used to this kind of thing. He then proceeded to tell Billy everything about Carmen's sudden appearance, her tearful confessions, and the missing Kahatee. When he got to that part, Billy just shook his head and grinned.

"How can you be so damn stupid?" Billy said. "I thought I was the impaired one around here, but you, man—you've got me beat by a mile."

Rik frowned, feeling a knot tighten in his stomach. "What do you mean?"

Billy stretched lazily. "Didn't you notice anything different about the Kahatee?"

"No… why? What are you getting at?"

"Because I swapped it."

"You what?"

Billy chuckled. "Yeah, I had Larry at Barry's Woodworking carve a replica. With a few extra details. I figured something like this might happen, so I switched them out."

Rik blinked, stunned. "You replaced it? When?"

"A while back, before all this craziness started. Just had a feeling you might need a backup plan. You're welcome, by the way. I suggest you call

Lieutenant Wright and tell her about all this. And, as for where the real Kahatee is…" Billy paused with a sly grin. "Well, I think it's best you don't know. Trust me, it's in a safe place."

Rik let out a long breath, nodding slowly. "Thanks, Billy. I owe you one."

"You owe me a lot more than one."

TWENTY-FOUR

Whack! Slap! "Goddamn mosquitoes. Gordito, get your fast ass in here!"

A weeble-wobble of a man appeared in the doorway, moving with the caution of someone approaching a rattlesnake, his entire body glistening with moisture. Not the kind that comes from a single exertion—this was layer upon layer of perspiration, like someone had been varnishing him in sweat for years.

"Yes, Carmen," he stammered, his voice matched his quaking knees.

"Did you visit this…this dump before you brought me here? Perhaps even go online *and do some research*? You know I hate mosquitoes! Do you have any idea how much I pay for this skin? A fortune. A *damn fortune.*" She punctuated the words by swatting another mosquito into oblivion.

"Yes, Jefa, but you said to find something out of the way…"

"I meant a Motel 6, you *idiota*!" Her eyes

narrowed, laser-focused on him like a cat sizing up a cornered mouse. "Manuel! Feed Gordito to the *cocodrilo* in the canal."

"No, Miss Carmen! No!" Gordito's hands flew up, his soft jowls wobbling with panic.

"Oh, lighten up, Francis." She rolled her eyes and gave an exasperated sigh. "I'm kidding. Can no one take a joke around here?"

Before Gordito could relax, Carmen whipped out her pistol and, with a casualness garnered by experience, put a small-caliber bullet through the center of his shiny forehead.

For this trip, Carmen had chosen a Miami Beach–themed aqua CCP M2 Walther pistol for her up-close work. As she was admiring the smoking little gun, Gordito's oversized, *pastalito*-fueled body hit the broken concrete floor with a comically soft whump! But nobody laughed. Carmen didn't inspire that kind of mirth.

"Now… *will you please feed him to the croc?*" she said, her voice cool and detached.

The surrounding men scurried into action, hauling Gordito's lifeless body toward the dark water nearby. Somewhere in the murky depths, the massive Jolene eagerly awaited her next meal.

What Gordito had found for Carmen—before his termination as operations manager—was an abandoned Nike missile base in the Upper Keys. Back in the '60s, these places were cutting-edge military deterrents against nuclear bombers out of Cuba. But this one was the black sheep of missile sites, a forgotten bastard child of the Cold War.

Time and Florida's relentless nature had reclaimed it. The missiles were long gone; the buildings were hollowed-out ruins, and the mangroves had smothered the structures in green, giving them an almost mythical jungle ambiance. For men like Gordito, growing up navigating jungles in Central and South America, it was practically paradise. Carmen, however, did not share that sentiment.

"Flaco! Get your skinny ass in here!"

A man shaped like a human toothpick appeared in the doorway, moving just as cautiously as Gordito had. He, too, glistened in that sticky South Florida way, though his sweat wasn't nearly as impressive as his late colleague's.

"Yes, Carmen," he croaked, his voice barely above a whisper.

"How did that *estúpido* Ricardo get caught?" she demanded. Carmen, with her normal icy demeanor, glared sharp enough to draw blood. "You're the new ops manager! Do you want to be demoted like Gordito over there?"

On cue, the men froze at the sound of crunching bones coming from the canal. The massive crocodile, now thoroughly engaged with Gordito's remains, was working its jaws with terrifying efficiency. The reptile wolfed down Carmen's recently sacked employee in a welcome alternative to her typical meal of anhingas and gar. The marbling was superb and overall, it was quite a delicious and unexpected meal. Although the gaudy oversized cowboy belt buckle that many of Carmen's guys wore did not go down so easily and would present the croc with an unusual digestive challenge in a few days.

Soon after inhaling this new type of meal, the crocodile started feeling tingly and euphoric. These feelings were not typical for an American saltwater croc. But clearly, the amount of cocaine in her meal had a positive effect on her, and her small brain now associated large silver buckles not only with good nutrition but with feeling good and high.

A large cowboy buckle was a status symbol among narco cowboys. This was one thing they would never give up. It made Carmen crazy, as she wanted her guys to blend in like all the other invasive species, but there were only so many fights she could pick.

Carmen stared at Flaco, one perfectly sculpted eyebrow arched. "Do I have to do everything around here? Take this!" And with that, she handed him the replica Kahatee. "Unlock that UM research nerd and get him working on this. That shithead Coastie has a line on a fortune of gold, and we need it! Now bring me my car! And find me a civilized hideout. And if there's so much as *one* mosquito, Flaco… you're next on the menu."

TWENTY-FIVE

It was finally time to explore Shell Key. Rik braced himself for whatever his friend might have concocted to shield him from imaginary spirits. But even he couldn't have predicted this ensemble. Billy stood at the dock, grinning in the moonlight, dressed in a tattered black trench coat that looked like it had been dragged from the bottom of the sea.

The coat was a patchwork of trinkets and charms: seashells, bells, rusted coins, a couple of gongs, and what looked suspiciously like a mummified iguana dangling from one sleeve. Every step sent a chorus of clinks, clangs, and rattles through the night air, echoing over the water like a ghostly parade.

To top it off, he wore what appeared to be a large crocodile skull as a helmet.

Rik pointed at the improvised helmet. "What the hell is on your head? Is that a crocodile skull?"

"It's a headdress. Something wrong with your eyes?"

"You know that's a protected species, right?"

"Exactly! It's protecting me!"

"What the hell else are you wearing?"

Billy shot him a serious look, glancing over his shoulder, checking for eavesdroppers. "Listen, Rik. In matters of the spirit world, you don't take chances. My shaman friend from Peru told me we need protection out here. *Real protection*. These charms"—he touched a small, worn amulet hanging over his heart—"they're like armor. The vibrations will keep us safe. And if we run into anything… otherworldly, I'll handle it. We touch nothing unless I say it's safe. Got it?"

Rik rolled his eyes, but a thrill of curiosity kept him from questioning it. "Fine. Just…try not to sink the boat with all that clanking armor of yours."

They climbed into the skiff, and Rik adjusted his weight to keep the boat from tipping. Billy's charms jingled and clanged, making every movement sound like a ghostly wind chime. As they set off, the moon cast a cold silver light over the water, illuminating the thick, swirling mist that drifted in and cloaked the shorelines like a veil. Rik shivered; the air felt colder than usual for a Florida night, carrying a damp, earthy smell, as if the islands themselves were breathing.

When they arrived at Shell Key, they beached the boat quietly, both of them moving cautiously as they stepped onto the soft, powdery sand. The silence was broken only by the rhythmic lapping of the waves and the occasional cry of a distant bird. Shadows loomed from twisted mangroves and palmetto fronds, and as they pushed deeper into the trees, the dense foliage swallowed the moonlight, plunging them into a murky, greenish darkness.

Billy paused, closing his eyes, and muttered something under his breath, shaking his beads. He took a small glass bottle of what looked like salt from his pocket and sprinkled it in a circle around them. "For protection," he whispered, his voice barely louder than a breath. The back of Rik's neck pricked as he sensed they were being watched.

They had barely ventured a few yards in when a bright beam of light cut through the trees. A park ranger, flashlight in hand, was striding toward them with a sharp, no-nonsense look on his face. "Shell Key is closed after sunset," he called out. "You two need to leave. Now!"

Before Rik could respond, Billy crouched down, his eyes wide and glassy. He mumbled in a mix of nonsense syllables and vaguely Mayan-esque phrases, waving his arms in slow, jerking movements. Rik realized he was creating the illusion of a trance. He quickly joined in. "Ranger! Please stop talking! Kahlua Motunga is entering an altered state. Didn't anyone tell you about tonight's ceremony?"

The ranger frowned. "Ceremony? What ceremony?"

Rik gestured to Billy, who rocked back and forth,

a low hum rising from his throat. "The Night of the Anhinga," he said, his voice low and serious. "Only an accredited shaman such as Kahlua can walk Shell Key tonight to commune with the ancient spirits. It's… an ancient ritual. We must not be disturbed."

Billy let out a high-pitched wail that sounded unnervingly like a mix between a wolf howl and Yoko Ono. The ranger's flashlight wavered, and he took a half-step back. "No one mentioned this to me… Alright. Just… be careful," he mumbled, glancing nervously at Billy before retreating into the darkness.

Once the ranger was gone, Billy stood up, dusted off his coat, and smirked. "Works every time," he said.

They pushed deeper into the island, and the air thickened, laden with the smell of damp earth, decaying leaves, and a faint metallic tang that made Rik's stomach twist. They followed the narrow trail of sand that led to the old shell mound, the object of their expedition. The mound was barely visible under a blanket of thick undergrowth, but the moonlight painted it with a silvery glow, casting long shadows that rippled in the breeze.

Billy held up a hand. "Wait." He reached into his coat and pulled out a bundle of beads, muttered a soft, rhythmic chant as he scattered them around the mound. Rik's pulse raced with a mixture of anticipation and dread.

Rik took a deep breath, kneeled beside the mound,

and started digging with a small shovel. The sand was cool and slightly damp under his hands, giving way with each scoop. Every time his shovel scraped against something solid, he felt his heart lurch, expecting to hit bone, metal, or something worse. Finally, he brushed aside a layer of sand to reveal a bone—white and gleaming in the moonlight.

Billy gasped, taking several quick steps back, his charms jangling. "That's it! We're dead. It's been an honor, Rik!"

Billy was halfway to the boat, clanking the whole way, before Rik caught up to him. "Billy, wait!" Rik showed him the bone, examining it carefully. "It's not human. Look at the shape—it's from a cow. Caesar probably put it here to keep people from digging any further." He held it up for Billy to see. The bone cast eerie shadows over their faces.

Billy hesitated, his eyes flicking from the bone to the mound. "You're sure?"

"Positive. Now let's keep going."

They resumed digging, and soon Rik's shovel struck something wooden. He pulled it out carefully, revealing a small chest, its hinges rusted and covered in green patina. Both men stared at it, their breaths coming fast and shallow. Rik reached out and slowly lifted the lid. Inside, glinting faintly under the moonlight, lay a pile of small ingots, tarnished but unmistakably valuable. Each bearing the likeness of the ghost orchid. Just like Gemini had said.

They exchanged a look, disbelief and excitement mingled in their eyes. Rik's flashlight illuminated the edges of other chests nestled deeper within the mound, partially obscured by sand and shell fragments. They frankly didn't have a plan for this discovery. And they certainly weren't going to try and haul it away now.

So, without exchanging a word between them, they sealed the mound back up as best they could. The return trip was equally silent, both of them too shaken to speak as a mist thickened around them, swirling like ghostly fingers over the water.

As the lights of the mainland came into view, Billy finally spoke, his voice barely above a whisper. "What now?" Rik looked at him, "I don't know."

Slicing through the silence, they heard it—a wail that came from another world. Haunting, the sound followed them across the water. It was loud, long, and drawn-out like a cry from the depths of despair. They both recognized it as the call of a limpkin, a long-legged water bird.

But perhaps it was Caesar's ghost, reminding them to honor his wishes.

TWENTY-SIX

Now that they discovered the gold's location, it was time to meet with the Phat Man. If there was gold in the Keys or adjacent waters, he was the man to talk to. Rik had heard of him, but of course, Billy actually knew him. They arranged a rendezvous in Key West.

The next morning Rik hit the road. Roxanne and he could use some fresh air, and the drive down to Key West never disappointed. A few hours alone with his thoughts would give him the time he needed to process all the recent crazy events. Plus, there were always some quirky spots along the way that never failed to make him smile.

It wasn't long before Rik passed by Betsy, the Giant Lobster. She was a famous roadside attraction in Islamorada. Back in the '80s, a local restaurant owner had hired a sculptor to create her. The restaurant hadn't survived, but Betsy sure did. Standing thirty feet high and forty feet long, she was made of fiberglass and impressively detailed. Betsy had moved a few times— as lobsters tended to do—but now she stood tall in front of an artist's village. She was one of the most photographed landmarks in the Keys.

Further down the road, Rik spotted stacks of stone crab traps piled high. Stone crab season was going to start soon, but until then you'd see the traps stored by the roadside. The thought of stone crabs had Rik's stomach growling. Out of all the great food in the Keys, stone crabs were his favorite. His buddy Rob caught them by hand, but Rik wasn't that bold. Reaching into holes you couldn't see and trying to grab a crab without getting pinched? No, thanks.

When Rik was a kid, his family had their own traps. They'd bait them with all sorts of nasty stuff from the slaughterhouses in West Miami. Rik would never forget the first time he'd pulled a trap. There was only one crab, but it was massive, and he had no clue what to do. You were supposed to remove a claw and toss them back—they'd grow it again, believe it or not. If the size was right, you could legally take both claws, but that seemed cruel. When both claws were removed, they turned from scavengers to filter feeders, but Rik could never bring himself to take both.

That first crab was a tough one. Rik couldn't twist the claw off, so he grabbed a big pair of pliers, said, "Sorry, buddy," and—you guessed it—the crab spun around and latched onto his forearm, pinching him like he had the pliers. Rik screamed, and if the crab could have screamed, it would have, too. The pliers and the crab went overboard, nearly taking Rik with them.

Over the next few weeks, Rik got better at catching stone crabs and removing their claws. And like any responsible fisherman, he immediately put them on ice. After his first really big haul, and boiling and chilling the claws, he proudly served them up, only to find the meat stuck to the shell. They tasted great but were a nightmare to eat.

A few days later, Rik was talking to an old-timer at the dock, and he mentioned his problem. The old salt laughed and said, "That's what happens when you put 'em on ice. Don't do that. It makes the meat stick to the shell." *Who knew?* On his next trip, Rik followed the advice: no ice. When he got home, he boiled and chilled them again, and this time, the old-timer was right. Perfection. Want to know his dipping sauce recipe? It was the same as what he used for fish: half golden-brown mustard, half mayo. Simple, but perfect.

Most people used a hammer or a nutcracker to open the claws, but Rik found the best tool was an old metal soup spoon. Sounds odd, right? But it worked. Hold the claw in your hand and give it three firm whacks with the back of the spoon. Listen carefully, and on that third hit, the sound will change—a dull thud. That means there's a hairline crack. Pry it open, and voilà, the best-tasting seafood in the world.

Rik was getting hungry just thinking about it. *Maybe I'll invite the lieutenant down for a stone crab feast*, he thought.

Rik was soon on the Seven Mile Bridge, gazing at the countless shades of aquamarine stretching out to the horizon. No roadside attractions here, just the Key's beauty on full display.

Right on cue, he spotted Fred the Tree. Fred was a local celebrity, of sorts. Running parallel to the Seven Mile Bridge was a section of the old railroad track built in 1912, which was now crumbling and dilapidated. Yet somehow, an Australian pine had sprouted right in the middle of it. Named Fred.

Fred was a survivor—a true Conch. He'd withstood hurricanes and storms, standing proud and resilient. Around him, the waters teemed with tarpon, and occasionally, a giant hammerhead showed up. But Fred? He kept standing tall, a symbol of the hardiness of the Keys.

Thump! Thump! Roxanne rolled over the Cow Key Channel Bridge, the bumpy threshold to Key West. There was no turning back now. Once you crossed into Key West, you couldn't leave until something notable happened. That was just a rule here, as sure as the sun rose over the Atlantic to the East and set in the Gulf, west of Mallory Square.

For some, "notable" meant a tequila-drenched night on Duval Street, where reggae rhythms and Jimmy Buffett wannabes helped blur the line between dusk and dawn. For others, it might mean an encounter with a leather-clad performer in towering platform shoes, doling out discipline to tourists with curious appetites. For Rik, though, today was about a different adventure. He was here to meet a shady character in a shady place.

Key West was more than beaches and sunburnt visitors. It was an odd, eccentric world where Ernest Hemingway downed daiquiris, ghosts and rumors lingered, and an underground crowd that harbored a passion for treasure.

Mel Fisher, the most famous of these treasure hunters, would have made a fine pirate if he'd lived in another era. In this one, he was a wrecker, a man who recovered the lost Spanish treasure ship *Atocha* and claimed a fortune worth four hundred and fifty million dollars in gold and silver. But Fisher wasn't alone; there were others, lurking in shadowy bars and smoky back rooms, whose fingers were equally twitchy for gold. One of them was the Phat Man.

The Phat Man's reputation preceded him. He was a whisper in the world of black-market gold—a transporter, a shadowy broker, a man who would've made Auric Goldfinger look like a petty thief. He moved gold quietly, out of sight of prying eyes. Be they the IRS, the State of Florida, or criminals? Hard to tell the difference these days. The Phat Man was who you called if you wanted to keep your precious metals private and safe.

"Don't stare at the Phat Man," Billy had warned. Rik had assumed the Phat Man was, well, a large individual. When Rik finally saw him, he realized "large" didn't cover it. The Phat Man was a mountain of a man, medium height but weighing in at an easy four hundred pounds. His bald head gleamed like a polished bowling ball, and his perfectly slick round dome added to his imposing presence.

The Phat Man's "office" was in the back of an Asian massage parlor. Rik wrinkled his nose as he was led through dimly lit hallways, the air thick with cheap perfume, incense and the faint, unsettling scent of bleach. He wished he had brought some hand sanitizer. Copious amounts.

They reached a small room furnished with bamboo and rattan, and Rik found himself seated across from the Phat Man. He was settled in an oversized chair like a Caribbean governor surveying his sugar fields. Dressed in a white suit that strained at the seams, the Phat Man dabbed at the sweat beading his forehead, eyeing Rik with what might have been amusement or calculation.

After a bit of preliminary chitchat, Rik eased into the real topic. They had talked little on the phone, for obvious reasons, but he'd been told the Phat Man was the best in the business.

"I understand you're the man to talk to about

gold," Rik ventured.

The Phat Man grinned, his voice silky smooth and unhurried, tinged with a hint of Barry White. "Yes, yes, I am."

Rik leaned forward slightly. "Well, let's start with some hypothetical questions. Say I knew someone. A guy who found a lot of gold … and he wants to get it out of the country. Could you help?"

"Help?" the Phat Man repeated, his eyes gleaming. "That's what I do. Trust me, everyone—from Uncle Sam to the folks at the Florida Department of Revenue—wants a piece of that pie."

"And what exactly do you bring to the table?"

The Phat Man settled back in his groaning chair. "I bring thirty years of navigating the seamy underbelly of the gold business. From Alaska to Africa. From South America to Asia. My clients are a who's who of people averse to paper currency, taxes, and authorities. My reputation speaks for itself. Your bullion will be safe with me."

"How will you move it?"

"In this kind of situation, I'd suggest a shrimp boat for transport. Low-key, lots of capacity, and no one questions a shrimp boat moving through these waters."

He leaned in and continued, a conspiratorial glint in his eye. "You deliver the goods to me and I'll take it from there. Just tell me where it needs to go."

"For now, let's say somewhere probably south of

the border. A shrimp boat's a solid idea, but… is it fast enough?"

The Phat Man let out a deep, rumbling laugh. "Oh, you're in for a surprise, *amigo*. My latest shrimp boat, the *Ensenada*, has been upgraded. Twin two-thousand-horsepower Cats and hydrofoils. She'll cruise at fifty miles an hour, easy, day and night. If I had to guess your final destination—and I usually have a good guess—she could be there in under twenty-four hours after loading."

Rik nodded. This guy wasn't just a middleman; he planned every detail, and it was clear his reputation wasn't just talk.

"So," the Phat Man continued, his voice dropping. "Can you get the 'cargo' to Fort Jefferson the first week of November? It's closed for repairs, and it's about as desolate as it gets. Perfect for a little, shall we say, off-the-books activity?"

Rik considered it. "I think so. Let me call my partners, and I'll confirm with you."

"And my fee?" The Phat Man's eyes gleamed.

"How do you charge?" Rik asked.

"Five percent of the market value," the Phat Man said smoothly. "And I only get paid once the delivery is confirmed. Fair enough?"

"How negotiable is that?" Rik asked, already knowing the answer.

"Not at all."

Just then, the phones on the Phat Man's desk started ringing, one after another. His face darkened, and he muttered, "Time to go." He pressed a button beneath the desk, and a section of the rear wall slid back to reveal a narrow corridor. "Hurry," he urged, his voice low.

Rik followed as the Phat Man led him through a small passageway. Key West had always been a place for people who didn't want to be found, and old buildings like this often had hidden exits. As they emerged around the corner, Rik found himself in the back room of a familiar bar—Hemingway's.

In a shadowed corner, Rik spotted a few Coasties from the Key West base, laughing over drinks. He doubted any would remember him, but it served as a reminder. He had to keep a low profile here.

The Phat Man, looking more relaxed now, sidled up to Rik. "So, your last name's Duval, like the street?"

Rik gave him an amiable smile. "Yeah. It's an old family name. I've got ties down here."

The Phat Man chuckled. "Well, I like to seal deals over a good bottle of Papa's Pilar rum. Do you know why the bottle is shaped the way it is?"

"No, why?"

"It's patterned after a World War II canteen. Clever, huh?"

For the next two hours, they traded stories and shots, rum flowing as easily as their conversation. Rik could feel the Phat Man sizing him up with each toast, each laugh, each clink of their glasses.

"You know," the Phat Man said, after another long swig, "there's always more to a job like this. Someone else after that gold? I've been hearing stories—rumors about Indian gold in the Upper Keys for years now."

Rik shrugged, playing it cool. "I just know my guy found a lot of gold, and he wants it somewhere it won't be found again."

As the Phat Man was contemplating this last statement, his cell phone rang excitedly. He glanced at it nervously and then said to Rik, "Listen, we need to separate ASAP. Go tell the manager over there in the Panama hat that *the crow sings at midnight*, and he'll tell you what to do. He's a friend. Goodbye for now. *Vaya con Dios, mi amigo*." And he was gone in a large flash.

Rik was confused and didn't like being in situations that he didn't control. But he went up to the manager and whispered those exact words. The manager smiled and said, "The manatee swims upstream in the fall. Ah, the Phat Man's just messing with you. He must have a hot date. But *señor*…my advice to you is…if you have an appointment with the Phat Man…don't be late."

Rik left the bar and couldn't help but reflect on the old Key West adage: *you don't leave this place without something significant happening*. And cutting a deal with the Phat Man to smuggle millions in gold, well that certainly counted.

TWENTY-SEVEN

Saturday night at Bonefish Woody's had a certain rhythm to it—a slow, easy start that could lull you into thinking it would stay mellow. But regulars knew better. There was an undercurrent, like the slow climb of a roller coaster, and tonight that "click-click-clack" was palpable.

Rik wasn't needed tonight on bongos, so he settled in at his usual place at the bar, listening to Billy and the band as the bar filled with the sounds of laughter, clinking glasses, and the murmur of conversations.

After the first set, Billy came over and had a drink with Rik. "Hey, Carri," he said to the bartender, "let me have a Key West Zombie. Make it a double, will ya?"

"What the heck is that?" Rik asked.

"It's Carri's secret. But I'll tell ya, Rik. A couple of those and you'll end with a tattoo that says *No Regrots*."

Billy downed the concoction, then drew Rik closer and said, "Have you been to the john and seen the new artwork?"

"Nope. And why do you have artwork in the bathroom?"

"At first, I wanted to class the place up a bit. Maybe a nice painting of dogs playing poker where the bulldog is hiding an ace in his rear paw. Ya know. Something sophisticated. But then I found this nude painting at Zelda's antiques, so I hung it in the restroom. Then a bolt of inspiration hit me."

Rik knew that was always trouble!

"What if I covered her cooch with a tiny door? A tiny door that when opened triggered a light and bell over the bar. So, when any goombah takes a peek, the whole bar knows!"

Rik immediately said, "Billy, you truly are certifiable. But that's kind of funny. Now I don't know where to look. The stage or the bathroom door?"

Billy slapped him on the back, knocking the wind out of him, and said, "Gotta go; my devotees await!"

Billy stared at the bell and stage like a chameleon. Left. Right. Left. Right. But no one took the bait. Yet.

The Key West Zombie put Billy in rare form, his booming laugh rising above the music. He was a force of nature, singing songs he barely knew, inventing lyrics and hitting notes that had the crowd cracking up mid-song. Rik leaned back, nursing his beer, watching his friend cut loose with a grin. It was a familiar sight—Billy on a Saturday night, a grin full of sin and a pocket full of bad ideas.

In the middle of the set, the front door swung open, and in strolled a group of frat boys wearing college logos from the University of South Northern Florida. Delta Upsilon Mu fraternity, to be exact, not the brightest bulbs, and they looked ready to party. At first, they blended in, ordering rounds of shots and beers, but Rik could see the rowdiness brewing, a bit like a storm on the horizon.

Billy noticed them too, casting them a wary glance before focusing back on the band. He kept up his good-natured banter with the musicians and the crowd, but his eyes would flick back to the Delta boys every so often. After a while, one of them, the clear leader of the pack with a thick neck and a louder-than-necessary voice, yelled over the crowd, "Hey, Cochise, sing 'Seminole Wind'!"

Billy froze, his broad grin faltering. Rik could see the subtle change in his posture. But Billy was used to shrugging off nonsense, especially from out-of-towners. He ignored the comment, downed a beer, and picked up the chorus of another song the band was playing. The moment passed, and for a while, the frat boys settled back into their corner, caught up in their own jokes and jabs.

Eventually, the leader had to make room for more beer. Drain the dragon. Release the Kraken. Shake hands with the president. You get the idea. So, he entered Billy's version of an art gallery and those in the know waited expectantly. Mr. Big Balls didn't disappoint. Ding. Ding. Blink. Blink. It sounded like the SAR horn at a Coast Guard base.

Well, Frat Boy eventually emerged, and Billy couldn't help himself. He quieted the band and said into his mike. "See anything interesting, Junior?"

Now Frat Boy might be a member of the DUM fraternity, but he figured out pretty quickly what had happened.

"So," he shouted out, "How about playing 'A Boy Named Sioux'? Get it? Sioux, like the tribe? S...O...O..." Spelling was not his strong suit, but he laughed, looking around to make sure his buddies were joining in. They were drunker and bolder than before, egging each other on.

Billy set his drink down slowly on one of the amplifiers, rolling his shoulders like a boxer stepping into the ring. He could let one slur go unpunished, but not two. Rik leaned forward, tensing, but Billy raised a hand, signaling him to stay put. He climbed down off the stage and made his way through the crowd, his eyes locked on the frat boy. The kid, still smiling, looked up at Billy and froze, only now realizing how large the man towering over him was. But then, as if emboldened by the liquor, he gave Billy a challenging look and, to everyone's surprise, threw a punch straight at Billy's gut.

Billy didn't flinch. He looked down at the frat boy, then gave a slow, dangerous smile. Rik could feel the shift in the air, a buzz of anticipation rippling through the crowd. The kid had no idea what he'd just started. In one swift motion, Billy grabbed him by the shoulders, lifted him off his feet, and launched him a good ten feet through the air. The kid hit the floor with a loud thud, and for a moment, the bar was dead silent.

The silence shattered as the rest of the DUM boys jumped in, roaring as they rushed Billy. Rik was up in an instant, pushing through the crowd to back up his friend, and that was when Lieutenant Wright appeared at the entrance. She stopped just inside, hands on her hips, taking in the scene with an expression that was equal parts exasperated and amused.

"Billy, what on earth are you doing?" she called out, her voice carrying through the noise.

Billy paused mid-punch, turning to her with a grin. "Just teaching some manners, Lieutenant. These boys need a little schooling."

Lieutenant Wright smirked, shaking her head as she watched him dodge another punch with surprising grace. Before moving deeper into the bar, she noticed Left Eye Louie bobbing and weaving on his perch like he was shadow boxing. He was giving boxing advice like Angleo Dundee in the Fifth Street Gym on Miami Beach.

"Raawk. Time to rumble! Time to rumble!"

"How you doing Louie?"

"Wings up! Wings up!"

"Louie, what is that? Is that... a tattoo?"

"Raawk! Yep! No regrots. No regrots!"

The Lieutenant was getting nowhere with Louie as he was heavily involved in the fight. *He must have some action on it,* she thought.

She turned and moved through the crowd, positioning herself where she could intervene if things went too far, but was content to let Billy handle it his way.

The fight now erupted in full force. Rik threw himself into the mix, dodging elbows and blocking punches, but Billy was the star of this WWF show. He picked up a barstool, wielding it like a makeshift shield as he fended off two frat boys trying to back him into a corner. And then, as if things couldn't get more surreal, Billy grabbed his infamous "pink weapon"— that odd, dangly rubbery item he always kept nearby. It wasn't much to look at, but in his hands, it became a weapon of chaos. Every time one of the frat boys charged at him, Billy swung the absurdly long pink sex toy, whacking them square in the head and sending them stumbling back, dazed.

Lieutenant Wright burst out laughing as she watched Billy fend off the attackers with his unusual choice of weapon. "Billy, need a hand?" she called out while tripping one of the frat boys. Billy started a smart aleck reply, but he had to pay attention to a beer bottle being aimed at his head.

For the next few minutes, it was an all-out fray. Rik took a couple of hits but held his ground, and Lieutenant Wright helped keep the crowd back, making sure things didn't spiral out of control. By the time it ended, all the frat boys were sprawled on the floor, some nursing bruises and others looking dazed. The bar was littered with overturned chairs and spilled drinks, the air filled with the scent of sweat, alcohol, and adrenaline.

An extremely happy Left Eye Louie was handing out ice-filled Ziploc bags from the bar, like party favors. You see, as soon as the brawl unfolded, he placed a parlay bet, including insurance, with his bookie Frankie Long Legs, a nefarious flamingo who hung out day and night at the Organ Grinder down the street. His instincts were right on and he won big.

As Louie strutted around yelling, "Raawk, pay the man, pay the man," the Lieutenant asked Rik how Louie lost his eye?

Rik looked at her incredulously and said, "His eye is fine. He just thinks chicks love the pirate look."

The frat boys were starting to come around, mumbled thanks to a degenerate parrot, and rubbed their heads and faces where Billy's "pink weapon" had left marks. Lieutenant Wright helped Rik patch up a cut on Billy's forehead, using a bar napkin and some superglue she'd pulled from her pocket.

Both Billy and Rik looked at the superglue suspiciously. The lieutenant then said, "I never told you I was team medic in the Girl Scouts? This stuff is a real lifesaver." Without waiting for a reply, she applied a judicious amount to Billy's wound, thus avoiding a few stitches at the ER.

"Impressive choice of weapons there, Billy," she smirked, pressing the napkin to his cut.

"Hey, it worked, didn't it?" he chuckled. "Never underestimate the power of a good, improvised weapon."

Just then, Deputy O'Malley, Rum Key's version of Barney Fife, appeared. It was rumored he was allotted one bullet while on patrol, just like Barney. He strolled in, his eyebrows lifting as he took in the disarray. "Everything alright, boys?"

"No trouble here, Deputy," Rik said, his voice casual. "Just a few, uh, slip-and-falls."

O'Malley raised an eyebrow, clearly unconvinced but too used to this crowd to ask further. "Uh-huh. Seems like every Saturday night, Bonefish Woody's has an unusual number of slip-and-falls. Well, carry on, but keep the slips to a minimum, alright?"

With a shake of his head, he turned and left. As the deputy's footsteps faded, Rik tossed beers to the frat boys, and soon enough, laughter replaced the tension. Billy settled next to the DUM leader, the two of them laughing like old friends.

"Look, man," Billy was saying, taking a swig of beer, "if you're gonna punch someone, don't lead with your chin. Keep your right hand up, cover your face. Otherwise, you're gonna end up on the floor every time."

The frat boy nodded, wincing as he touched a fresh bruise. "Thanks, Billy. And, uh… sorry about that 'Cochise' thing. I can be an ass."

As the chaos finally died down, Rik glanced at the pink weapon Billy was still holding. "You really kept that thing handy, huh?"

Billy grinned, holding it up proudly. "Oh, it's got its uses." Then, with a wink, he unscrewed the base and revealed a hidden compartment. From inside, he withdrew the Kahatee he'd kept hidden for safekeeping. "Better with me than in some box somewhere."

Around 2:00 a.m., as the bar cleared out, Rik, Billy, and Lieutenant Wright were the last ones left, the three of them nursing beers and laughing about the night's events. Billy leaned back, letting out a satisfied sigh. When Rik wasn't looking, he handed two small metal objects to Lieutenant Wright.

"What's this?" she asked as she stared down at the pair of brass knuckles.

"They'll even out a fight when you're against the odds. Hopefully, you never need to use them."

She looked at him slyly, then placed them in her purse.

After a brief pause, Billy broke the silence with a hearty laugh. "Damn, I needed that," he exclaimed, stretching his arms above his head. "Shook out all the cobwebs and got my blood pumping. Now I'm fired up for whatever comes next."

Rik and Lieutenant Wright exchanged amused glances, each knowing that as long as Billy was around, there'd never be a dull moment. Like Billy said, whatever came next, they'd all be ready. Semper Paratus.

TWENTY-EIGHT

"Rik?"

"Yes, Lieutenant?"

"I have new information regarding Carmen that you need to hear. I need to come down tomorrow morning. I can't discuss it over the satellite phone."

Rik paused for a second. He felt like a cheater, having been with Carmen several days ago. It wasn't like he and the lieutenant were an item, but she was creeping into an area that he was unfamiliar with. An area of caring with a pinch of carnal lust.

Back to Carmen, though. Just the mention of her name sent chills through him. But he eventually said, "Sure, c'mon down. Oh, and do me a favor—on your way down, can you stop by Knaus Berry Farm and pick up some cinnamon buns?"

She sighed. "Sure, because I have nothing better to do…"

"Trust me, Lieutenant. You'll thank me."

The good folks at Knaus Berry Farm made the best cinnamon buns in the world. And definitely not keto!

In fact, it had been said that South Florida had only two seasons: when Knaus Berry Farm was open in the winter, and when it was closed in the summer. Their cinnamon buns were soft, sticky, and dripping with goodness.

The next morning Rik waited in the parking lot, squinting in the harsh sunlight, as the white government-issue Impala pulled in. Lieutenant Wright wasn't in uniform, which meant she intended to keep this visit low-key. She wore a pair of stylish jeans and a gray T-shirt, her hair pulled back. As she opened the passenger door, the sweet smell of Knaus Berry Farm buns wafted downwind right into Rik's olfactory system. His mouth watered instantly, and he could see she'd already taken advantage of the delights.

"Rik," she said, holding up a half-eaten bun, "you weren't kidding. These are ridiculous. I've had two of them on the drive and stopped twice for coffee. Oh my God, I'm wired. Let's talk, but first, I need to come down from this sugar high."

They settled in the Bum Runner's salon, a spread of cinnamon buns on the coffee table. Rik devoured two in quick succession, savoring the sugary warmth as he prepared for whatever news the lieutenant was bringing. She finally set aside her own half-eaten roll, wiped her hands, and looked at him, her eyes focused, all traces of good humor now gone.

"Rik, I've been in a series of meetings the last few

days with the DEA's intel branch. We've got some disturbing news about Carmen."

Rik felt a prickle of dread. He knew Carmen had secrets, but somehow, hearing it from Lieutenant Wright made it worse. Rik's stomach tightened, but he kept his expression neutral, his face blank. He'd spent enough time under pressure to know that giving anything away would only raise suspicions. He wasn't ready to reveal his recent involvement with Carmen.

"Go on."

"Well, for starters, we believe she's starting a new series of operations for her father-in-law, El Cojón."

"What kind of operations?" Rik asked, his tone casual, feigning surprise. He didn't like lying to Lieutenant Wright—he respected her too much. She was a straight shooter, reliable, and one of the few people he could actually trust. But today, he was playing his cards close.

Rik leaned forward, listening as she detailed Carmen's three-pronged ruthless strategy.

"First, they're going to exploit natural resources. The rainforests of South America, particularly in Brazil, are rich in valuable reserves—gold, hardwoods, lithium. These resources can be extracted and laundered through legitimate channels, turning dirty money into clean funds. And with minimal regulations, they've got a competitive edge. Think conflict diamonds, but legal."

Rik's jaw tightened. This was more than just a shift in cartel operations; it was an assault on an entire ecosystem and the Indigenous communities within it.

"Second, she's planning a complete overhaul of their drug transportation system. She's worked with nautical engineers to develop a new kind of submarine, more like an underwater tractor-trailer. Picture mass-produced waterproof containers that can withstand depths of one hundred feet. Then they're towed by the tractor submarine to their destination. After a run, the tractor-subs detach the 'cargo' and return for more. It's efficient and incredibly hard to detect."

Rik's stomach churned. He'd heard stories of the cartels' ingenuity, but this was next level. The current version of a narco sub was semisubmersible, which meant they traveled just below the waterline with a small portion of the structure above water. Her new method would require military-grade electronics and underwater acoustic equipment to detect—something the Coast Guard had yet to deploy. He stayed silent, nodding along as she spoke.

"Lastly, she's looking for isolated places to produce drugs. They're using rainforests, cave systems, islands, you name it. There's already evidence of drugs dumped at sea impacting marine life. Scientists have found sharks off the coast of Barranquilla with traces of cocaine in their systems. Carmen's team is looking at ecosystems as environments as resources to exploit, regardless of the damage. In fact, they're already encroaching on an Indigenous people known as the Toucano's."

Hearing this name triggered a memory within Rik. His uncle Jax had been involved with them in a training op gone bad. He tried not to let on, but he was shaken at the moment.

He tried to be cool, crossed his fingers, and said, "I've never heard of them. Who are they?"

"I did a little research. They lead a simple lifestyle and want nothing to do with the modern world. In the 1600s they were enslaved under a system called the 'Encomienda,' which translates from Spanish as 'commission' or 'charge.'

"The Spanish Crown's intention was to entrust the care and oversight of Indigenous people to a colonist. The colonist, in turn, was supposed to watch over and provide religious 'education.' But this was not the case. Colonists exploited their charges and enslaved them to work gold and silver mines."

Rik took a deep breath. Her words painted a dark picture of ruthless expansion into South America's rainforests, trampling over Indigenous people's land and ecosystems for profit. It was greed at its ugliest.

She continued, "They're expanding fast. There's a crooked governor in Cassadiegia, Brazil, auctioning off a huge tract of land for three hundred million dollars. The Tabasco cartel wants it but is strapped for cash. For some reason, Carmen thinks you might be able to help them finance this acquisition."

She fixed him with a sharp look, her voice hardening. "Why would she believe that? After all, you're on the straight and narrow… aren't you, Rik?"

Rik felt her gaze and maintained a calm expression, his tone easy. "How could I get my hands on three hundred million? I can barely keep the Bum Runner running on my pension."

She didn't smile. "That's exactly what I was wondering. But you know how these people think—they see everyone as a potential pawn. Keep your guard up."

He nodded, feeling a rush of conflicting emotions. She'd come down here to warn him, to protect him. Semper Paratus—Always Prepared. It was the Coast Guard's motto, but it was more than that.

She leaned back, her gaze softening. "Just watch yourself, Rik. You're smart enough to know that once you're in their crosshairs, getting out isn't easy."

Rik nodded, genuinely touched by her concern. "Thank you, Lieutenant. Really."

She stood, brushing crumbs from her jeans, the edge of her mouth curving into a wry smile. "Oh," she added, holding up the box of cinnamon buns, "thanks for these. You were right. Best I've ever had. I'll be buzzing for hours."

As Rik watched her drive away, he took a moment

to process everything. The lieutenant's visit wasn't just a casual heads-up; it was a veiled warning. She didn't know the extent of his connection with Carmen, but Rik could sense that she'd come with more than an official duty to brief him. There was genuine worry in her tone, something rare from the all-business lieutenant. The aroma of the cinnamon buns lingered, a sweet contrast to the bitterness building in his gut.

Once back on board the Bum Runner, Rik pulled out a notepad, his mind racing as he jotted down fragments from Lieutenant Wright's report: *the Toucano's, gold mining, drug subs, sharks with coke.* Carmen was running an operation that made the usual cartel dealings look almost tame by comparison.

But there was something else gnawing at him. Why did she need him? He couldn't imagine Carmen being so reckless as to bring him into the fold without a reason, especially with her father-in-law, El Cojón, in the background. The man's ruthlessness was infamous, and Rik had seen the lengths the family would go to defend their empire.

Hours later, as the sun dipped low, Rik's thoughts kept circling back to the submarine innovation the lieutenant had mentioned. He couldn't shake the image of those tractor-subs hauling vast quantities of drugs underwater, evading even the Coast Guard's best detection equipment. He had colleagues who'd dedicated their lives to fighting the cartels' smuggling tactics, and here was Carmen, engineering the next wave of undersea trafficking tech. It was personal now, a direct affront to his life's work. He thought of friends lost, missions that had almost cost him everything. Carmen's complicity felt like a knife in the back.

TWENTY-NINE

Rik was sitting on the gunwale of the Bum Runner, shooting the breeze with Billy, when his sat phone rang. He quickly grabbed it, seeing the number and expecting a call from Lieutenant Wright—it was a number only she had.

"Yes, Lieutenant?" he answered.

But instead of the familiar voice of the Coast Guard officer, a different voice spoke. A voice that was silky, smooth, and unsettling.

"Hello, Rik," the woman on the other end said. Rik's heart skipped a beat, and he nearly dropped the phone into the water. It was Carmen.

Billy, seeing Rik's startled face, edged closer to listen in on the call.

Rik stammered, trying to collect himself. "Carmen… how…?" His mind immediately went into overdrive. He knew she had amazing resources, but even hijacking a secure sat phone line surprised him. "Why are you calling me?"

A slow, amused laugh trickled through the sat

phone's speaker. "Oh, Rik, don't sound so surprised. You knew this would happen, eventually. We need to meet."

"Why should I meet with you?" he snapped, trying to stay composed. "The feds, the Coast Guard…they're all looking for you."

"And how was your meeting with the lovely Lieutenant Wright? Are her legs as nice as mine? How do they feel? Did she wrap them around you like I did?"

"Cut the crap, Carmen. What do you want? Why did you steal the Kahatee? It didn't do you much good, did it? By the way, where did you end up?"

"You didn't know? That wasn't your fiendish plot? I suppose it was your skunk ape of a friend, Billy Possum, or whatever his stupid name is. Remind me to kill him. You sent me to the Devil's Garden in the Everglades. Somebody's going to pay for all these mosquito bites, but that's for another day."

Rik smiled. He knew that was an awful place. He gave Billy the OK sign. They both hoped she'd caught the West Nile virus. Or a nice dose of dengue fever.

"Screw you, you parasitic bitch."

"Always so dramatic, aren't you?" Carmen said, her voice dripping with sarcasm. "I want to see you, Rik. Let's put all the games aside, at least for an afternoon."

Rik knew it was dangerous, but there was a

strange pull to her request. "Where?" he finally asked.

"Lorelei's," Carmen replied without hesitation. "It's open, public, no hiding spots. Mile marker eighty-two, bayside. You know it—great food, good vibe, and fantastic sunsets." She sounded like a five-star Yelp review.

Rik thought about the location quickly. Right off A1A, but it also had bay access. He could control the situation and maybe even capture her. He then said, "And you expect me to come alone?"

"Yes, alone." Her voice turned cold. "Or else…remember, Rik, I'm prepared to kill to get what I want. And those who crossed me have paid dearly."

Rik clenched his jaw. He couldn't trust her. He needed backup. He glanced over at Billy, who was listening intently. Rik nodded, and Billy gave him a thumbs-up. They were on the same page. The call ended abruptly, without a goodbye.

Rik and Billy sat in the cockpit for a while. It was a nice sun-kissed day in the Keys. Much too nice to worry about Carmen and her nefarious plans. They talked about the meeting, and Billy had a plan. He'd be disguised as a busboy. He knew the owner, and they would be more than willing to help. Another friend would wait in a boat nearby, ready to follow if she came by boat.

The next day, Rik arrived at Lorelei's by midafternoon. Billy was already there, dressed in his

XXXL busboy attire and carrying a small duffel bag. "What's in the bag, big boy?" Rik asked.

Rather than answer, Billy opened the olive-green canvas bag for inspection. He was proud to show off his level of preparedness. He had heard Rik mention the phrase Semper Paratus, and he wanted to be on board with the Coast Guard's motto. Especially when he thought he was on a mission.

Rik gazed in amazement. Billy was truly ready for everything. He saw Israeli Mitznefet headgear, night vison goggles, nunchucks, a prisoner hood, tie wraps, latex gloves, and lime.

"Uh, Billy…," he said. "If we need this, we are in serious trouble."

"Always prepared," was Billy's businesslike reply.

The sky was blue as blue could be, with scattered silvery clouds. He scanned the grounds, but no Carmen. Well, if she showed up, he had a plan…and some backup.

Rik sat at a waterside table and tried to relax. He went through his shooting drill to calm himself. *Breathe. Center. Relax. Feel your heartbeat.* He felt better, but also his muscle memory really wanted to pull a trigger!

As he waited impatiently, he saw a seaplane fly overhead. A de Havilland. He'd flown in them several times during training in Alaska. Bush pilots loved them. *Man*, he thought. *I'd love to fly one of those babies down to Fort Jefferson or even to the Bahamas. That would be living. Land in the lee of a deserted island, catch some yellowtail. Run the plane up on the beach and grill your catch. One day.*

The plane banked and descended. It was going to land in the basin by Lorelie's. Rik noted the landing was perfect and then the pilot expertly maneuvered the craft through the anchorage…right up to Lorelei's dock.

The pilot disembarked first and secured the plane. Next, two goonish types appeared. They appeared to give the all clear to the last passenger. It was Carmen!

She walked down the dock like it was a catwalk. Ladies and gentlemen, our next model is wearing a Dolce and Gabbana print sundress. Perfect for those warm Havana nights or ruining the lives of anyone who gets close to her.

Rik admitted to himself that she was stunning in a maniacal fashionista way. And what an entrance. The entire restaurant was staring and wondering who the hell arrived at Lorelei's by seaplane.

Carmen Allende did.

She immediately saw Rik, waved and half skipped to see him. To an outsider, it looked like long-lost lovers had rendezvoused at a romantic, out-of-the-way spot. But Rik's hackles went up, and his adrenaline pumped.

"Rik, my dear. You came! How simply fabulous to see you!" All this was said in a voice that most of the restaurant heard, including the kitchen staff.

Rik was standing now, eyeing her warily. "What do you want, Carmen?"

"Sit, Rik. Let's not make a scene," she said, her voice dripping with charm. "I just want to talk. By the way, the indent in your pocket tells me you brought your trusty little Glock. How cute. Just know there's enough firepower in that plane to take over a third-world nation. Or at least a portion of the Amazon." With that, she let out a disturbing laugh.

"Sit, *chico*; I mean it!"

Rik sat, but his hand never strayed far from his Glock. "Talk, then."

"Too bad about Gemini," she began casually, her words laced with malice. "He was stupid….thought he could hide things from me."

Rik's anger flared. "You didn't have to kill him."

Their prickly conversation halted while the server came by and introduced herself, along with her life story and the daily specials. They ordered absentmindedly, and their conversation resumed.

Carmen's eyes narrowed. "You still don't understand, do you? This isn't personal, Rik. This is survival. I'm giving you a chance—to join me."

Rik shook his head, disgusted. "Why me, Carmen? Why drag me into all of this?"

She leaned forward, her voice dropping to a whisper. "Because I could. Because you intrigued me. Because you're a survivor. Just like you survived your night swim in the Gulf Stream."

"You…you were behind that?"

"Yes, dear."

"You tried to kill me! And my friend Tony!"

"It wasn't intentional my love. Strictly business. We learned about your damned stealth helicopters and my father in law insisted we get rid of them. Ironic that a US made Stinger took you down."

"And the rescue gear? The radios?"

"There were to be no survivors. We hoped if the prototype disappeared the project would stall or fail. No stealth helo's for our adversary the Coast Guard."

"So, you have a mole?"

Carmen's response was delayed and measured. "My reach is long. You should know that by now. Join me. I will make you fabulously rich. And then at night. Oh, at night. Imagine the nights together, *mi amor*."

"And your husband?"

"Your questions are so tedious and boring! He was a stupid man with no vision. He had no bon sens. A man who uses his product is no longer a business man. Yes. Yes. I wanted you to kill him. Perhaps not so dramatically. You know El Cajon is really pissed at you. But your reputation as an excellent marksman is known throughout my world."

"It was an accident!"

"Sure, tell yourself that. You loved me and killed for me *mon cheri*."

"You're a psychopath."

She ignored the insult and continued, "Look, Rik, I'm going to get the gold. I know you found it or are going to find it very soon and I don't have time to waste. I need that gold, and you're either going to give it to me willingly or reluctantly. I prefer the former. Join me. You know we're good together…daytime and nighttime."

"Carmen, were you ever real? Did you ever have any feelings for me? Did the kiss at Fairchild Garden mean nothing to you? Did our nights together mean even less? I was willing to die for you that night off Andros!"

"Rik…of course I had feelings for you. I felt like you would do anything for me."

Rik's hand gripped the Glock that was now beneath the table. "The next time I see you, Carmen, it will be different. This needs to end."

Carmen stood, brushing her hair back. "Maybe. But for now, let's part as friends. Oh, and tell Billy Ray Virus over there that busboy top isn't very slimming." She glanced toward the dock, where the seaplane was waiting, its engine sputtering to life. "I have a plane to catch."

She started walking away, and Rik didn't stop her.

He watched as she left the restaurant, moving elegantly through the crowd, and stepped onto the dock. In the distance, Billy, in his disguise, gave a slight nod, but both knew there was no way to stop or follow her now.

Rik watched the seaplane lift off as the sun disappear beyond the horizon, leaving a darkening sky behind. Their paths had crossed, and they would cross again. But for now, she was gone, leaving behind nothing but uncertainty.

After Carmen's dramatic departure, Billy wandered over and said, "Hey, did you notice anything unusual about that pilot?

"Nope."

"He was barefoot. He flew the damn thing barefoot. Who flies barefoot? Anyhow, man, I got the tail number. Let's find that plane and pay the pilot a visit."

Rik didn't respond. He just watched the seaplane disappear into the horizon, knowing it wouldn't be the last time he saw Carmen.

Finding the seaplane was straightforward, thanks to the internet. It was owned by an Alaskan outfitter but leased through several shell companies to Krazy Keys Adventures, operated by Joe Mitchell at Marathon Airport.

The following day, Rik, accompanied by Billy and Jimmy Legs, headed to the airport. Jimmy Legs had proven to be a good companion, aside from his propensity to bite the testicles off any man who said the word…*mango*. But Rik knew he had to find a good home for him. His current '*lifestyle*' was not conducive to the welfare of dog.

No one was in the office, so they all wandered into the adjacent hangar. There they saw a barefoot guy working on an engine. Rik took the direct approach. "Hey, man. I'm looking for a client of yours," he said to the shoeless mechanic.

"And you are?" the man asked.

"Rik Duval. An old friend of Carmen Allende. We saw you land her at Lorelei's the other day."

The man's expression changed dramatically. "You know her!? That lady gave me the creeps. She showed up all crazy-eyed, demanded I fly her up there and brought a couple of goons with guns. I never want to see her again."

"She didn't leave any contact information?"

"None. Paid in cash, though. Like I said, she was scary."

After a bit of silence, Rik said, "Can your bird make it to Fort Jefferson?"

"Sure. I love that place. Know it like the back of my hand."

"You free this afternoon?"

"I am now! Let's fire up the Beaver."

"Huh?"

"Betty Beaver. I fly a de Havilland Beaver. Great plane."

Rik gave Billy a dirty look because he knew him like the back of his hand. And well…Billy's mind was like that of a fourteen-year-old boy at times.

"Can we bring the dog? This is Jimmy Legs," Billy introduced, and the dog bounded over to Joe, treating him like a long-lost friend.

"Great dog."

"He has his quirks, but yeah, he's a good dog."

"Sure. Let's do some paperwork, then we can board."

Jimmy Legs claimed the copilot's seat and growled softly when Billy tried to move him. "Well, I guess I have a new copilot," Joe chuckled.

Rik noticed a dancing hula girl mounted on the cockpit dash. "Who's that?"

"Layla, my good luck charm. Never fly without her."

As they settled in, Joe ran through a brief pre-flight check—almost nonchalant with a "smoke 'em if you got 'em" attitude. The roar of the engine meant everyone wore headphones, including Jimmy.

Joe gave basic safety instructions over the intercom, then added, "Ladies and gentlemen, sit back and relax. Joe Walsh will provide our takeoff music today." As the opening chords of "Life's Been Good" played, Rik exchanged a knowing look with Billy—this pilot was alright.

Their flight was smooth. Circling over the Marquesas, Rik scoped out anchorages for a construction barge. Rik was working on a deception that was crucial for moving gold unseen to Fort Jefferson. From there, the Phat Man would take over with his high-speed shrimp boat.

In between the Marquesas and Fort Jefferson, Barefoot Joe pointed out the wreck location of the *Atocha*. This shipwrecked galleon had yielded four hundred and fifty million dollars in treasure. The thought of this made our two nascent treasure hunters shiver.

As they approached Fort Jefferson, Joe pointed out its features amidst the stunning aquamarine waters, circling several times to ensure thorough planning. Rik's mind was making notes of landing sites, anchorages, and escape routes.

Upon landing back at Marathon, it was apparent that Jimmy Legs wouldn't leave Barefoot Joe's side. Rik noticed this and said, "Jimmy Legs seems pretty attached to you. Want a companion?"

"Ya know, I wasn't going to ask, but he would be great company at night. That's when I do a lot of maintenance on the Beaver."

"Well, it's settled. I think that old sea dog has a

new vocation—flying the skies of the Florida Keys.

All turned to see Jimmy Legs smile a big, toothy smile. Billy then said, "Man, I could eat the ass end of a rhino."

Joe suggested, "My cousin Theresa owns a pub nearby called Inn Between. They have great burgers and cold beer. Let's head over there."

At the pub, known for its nearby population of Key deer and walls decorated with dollar bills, they learned more about Barefoot Joe. His nickname was earned from his preference to fly without shoes, claiming it helped him feel the plane's responses through the pedals.

Joe had been a bush pilot in Alaska, but after facing down grizzlies on two separate occasions, he decided a change in venue was in order. So he looked at a map and saw that the Keys were far enough away. Barely.

After finishing their meal, Rik leaned back, wiping his mouth with a napkin. There was an ambient hum of chatter around them mixed with the occasional laugh and the clinking of glasses. You couldn't help but notice the old dollar bills that decorated the walls, each one a memento from a visitor long gone.

After a long silence Rik said, "Joe, me and Billy are involved in something. Something big. Really big. And we're going to need some type of aerial support. Can you help us?"

"Is it legal?"

"Define legal?"

"Will I go to jail or lose Betty the Beaver?"

Once again, Billy started to snicker but stopped when Rik's shoe hit his shinbone.

"Barely legal," Rik said. "But if the authorities get involved, I have a get-out-of-jail-free card for us in D.C. In fact, if there's any issue, call this number. Her name is Lieutenant Wright. She'll help." With that, he slid her phone number over to Barefoot Joe.

"Well, no guts, no glory. As long as there's no grizzly bears involved, I'm in."

With the clink of three bottles, they toasted their nebulous operation, each silently wondering what the future held.

THIRTY

It was time for Rik's compulsory meeting with the overly medicated Dr. Krak. Rik knew the good doctor's methods were unorthodox, but he did feel better after his last session. Who else could he talk to about his recent craziness? So, the next typically humid Keys morning, he pulled into the doc's parking lot. On the way in, he noticed a bumper sticker. It said, "Sanity is overrated."

"Hmm," he said out loud, "I wonder if that's the Doc's position or one of his patients'?"

Rik sat down in the only chair in the austere office, which was just a step above lawn furniture. Doc Krak quickly got down to business.

"Who are you really, Rik?" he inquired. "Are you a Space Cowboy? Or the Gangster of Love? Has anyone ever called you Maurice? How about the Pompatus of Love? I can totally see you being the Pompatus of Love!"

This line of questioning caught Rik off guard, but being a fan of classic rock, he retorted, "Where did you get your degree from, Doc, the School of Rock?"

"Please do not impugn my alma mater, the Tropical Breeze Caribbean Medical and Bartending School. A lot of great psychiatric minds have graduated from those hallowed tiki bars…I mean halls! Rik, it's my job to delve deep into your psyche and help free those demons that lie deep inside you!

"By the way, you know you're a hot mess, don't you? You're in love with the psychotic widow of a world-class narco—and, oh…you're the reason she's a widow. Don't you have deep-rooted psychoses about this?"

"Well, Doc I actually don't feel all that bad."

Doc Krak continued, "Interesting. Let me ask you, do you ever have the intense desire to wear ladies' clothes? You know…feel the smooth silkiness all over your body while you walk around a dark, musty bar? No? Yeah, me either.

"So, when we left off, the love of your life turned out to be a real bee-atch. Would you say you were hoodwinked, cheated, etc.?"

"Well, Doc, there's been some developments."

"Do tell?"

"She showed up on my boat two weeks ago and I slept with her."

"Interesting."

"Then she stole something she thought was valuable."

"Ah, classic Klepto-Coitus Disorder. It's imperative that you bring her in for co-counseling. We need to dig deep. Very deep!"

"There's more."

"Really? Don't you think that's enough?"

"We met for lunch."

"What did you have?"

"Yellowtail."

"Grilled or fried?"

"Fried."

"Very, very interesting. Sides?"

"Conch fritters and a salad."

"Very revealing. Go on, please."

"Well, she threatened me."

"I'm sure she didn't really mean it. You know how dramatic women can be."

"She held a gun on me, under the table, and threatened to blow my balls to Okahumpka. Oh, and she had heavily armed narco goons nearby. So, yeah, I'm pretty sure she meant it."

"Hmm…I need to think about this. Let's change direction. Tell me about your childhood."

"Well, I was raised by my uncle Jax."

"Where were your parents?"

"My parents disappeared."

"Were they magicians? Did they make a bad career move?"

"No, I was spending the week with my uncle Jax

when I was little and they never returned. It's haunted me my whole life. It's hard to open your heart, Doc, when everything you've ever loved just disappears…particularly with no closure.

"That's probably the reason why I could never love. I didn't want to suffer a loss again. But then came Carmen, who broke those walls down. And where did that get me?"

"Hmm. Tell me, do you ever have dreams where you're showering with a large group of military-age males and there's only one bar of soap?"

"No, Doc. Do you?"

"Not really."

"I want to know more about your uncle."

"He was a tough guy. Very secretive. I think he may have disappeared a guy."

"Like unfriended him on Facebook?"

"No. As in two went into the Big Cypress Swamp and only one came out."

"You have proof?"

"No. But I do have a 1967 Ford Mustang wood-grained steering wheel."

"Huh?"

"Never mind, Doc. Let's just say my life with Uncle Jax was not normal. He did teach me to shoot, and that turned into a vocation I was very good at. I nearly clinched first place in a sniper competition at Fort Benning."

"Tell me more, please."

"Not today, Doc. That, too, was a bad memory."

"Tell me about Lieutenant Wright. I understand she's very smart and attractive. Out of your league, but what the hell? Any interest?"

"Maybe. Doc, I need to ask you about a dilemma I have."

"Good. My specialty! Go on."

"Well, in a nutshell, I may come into some money. It really doesn't belong to me. But it really doesn't belong to anyone."

"Sounds like you've been reading *Treasure Island*?"

"Perhaps. But if it becomes a reality, what do I do? I'm no thief, but it's literally there for the taking. And it's not doing anybody any good now. Seems like a waste."

"How many zeros are we talking?"

"Lots."

"I'm raising my rates."

"Focus, Doc. What should I do?"

"There's been studies about lotto winners. They come into unholy sums of money and are miserable. They lose their friends, can't trust anyone. It's a rich man's hell."

"What would you do?"

"I'd give it to someone who needs it. Do something good. It's a miserable world and money could fix a lot of wrongs."

"Thanks, Doc. Good advice."

Internally Dr. Krak was thinking, *This boy's elevator is skipping a few floors*, but instead he said, "Well, once again I believe you are dealing with all these issues maturely and your sanity, for now, is on solid ground. But! And that's a big but. We cannot be too careful. In the words of Big Pharma… 'the more the merrier.'

"So, Rik, a very charismatic, curvaceous lady with enhanced ta-tas dropped off a flight of sample narcotics for my wonderfully screwy patients. That last batch, however, was no good. I took every one of them and nothing. But these are guaranteed. These enticing yellow-greeney guys. Let me do my standard quality control before I prescribe them." With that he downed a handful, then said, "Ah, that's the ticket. We are really making some progress here, my boy. My secretary will see you out."

"Doc, you don't have a secretary."

"What? Where is she?"

He opened a closet door and began muttering something about "third one this week." Rik started to interrupt but realized it was pointless. The yellow-greeney guys were starting to take effect.

Rik felt better. He'd met his monthly psych eval obligation. Passed, apparently. Now it was time to turn his attention to the gold. Or Lieutenant Wright. Not necessarily in that order.

THIRTY-ONE

Rik had been thinking more and more about Jill Wright and less and less about Lieutenant Wright. He was understandably gun-shy about new relationships. Carmen had seen to that. But deep down, it's in our DNA to move on, especially in affairs of the heart. So, after days of building interest, he grabbed his cell phone and made the call.

"Lieutenant Wright…hey, it's Rik."

"Hey, Rik. You know…you can call me Jill."

"Okay… Lieutenant," he teased. "Listen, I've got a craving for stone crabs, and they taste best when shared. Can you come down tomorrow afternoon and join me?"

"Stone crabs, huh? I've never tried them."

"What! Well, you're in for a treat."

"Let me guess—you know a guy?"

"Absolutely. Stoney McFarland. Freshest claws in the Keys."

"Well, thank you. I'd love to. What can I bring?"

"I was hoping you'd ask! Stop by Islamorada Beer

Company and pick up some Sandbar Sunday lagers. Tell Nik there for me. He'll give you some Key lime wedges to push in the bottles."

"Rik, this sounds like so much fun! See you then."

The next afternoon, Rik met Jill in the marina parking lot. She was dressed enticingly: wide-brimmed hat, silk blouse on the clingy, tightish side, and short white shorts that demanded his undivided attention. Slung over her shoulder was a small cooler packed with the Keys' finest beer—perfect for sweet stone crab claws.

They strolled side by side down the dock, occasionally bumping into each other. It might have been accidental—or not. Each light touch sent a subtle tingle through them both.

They stepped into the cockpit of the Bum Runner. A cooler sat ready, filled to the brim with colossal stone crab claws on ice. On a small makeshift table sat mustard sauce, and a skillet waited on the cockpit stove. Lemon wedges and melted butter stood at the ready.

"I hope you're hungry," Rik said, leaning in to place a light kiss on her cheek. That simple gesture sent a surge of emotion through them both, something they weren't sure how to define just yet.

Trying to regroup, Jill cleared her throat. "So, I know we're having stone crabs, but what else?"

Rik grinned, turning to the skillet. "Fried green

tomatoes. They go great with stone crabs."

He fired up the cockpit stove, breaded the tomato slices and gently placed them in the simmering oil. The enticing smell drifted across the dock, causing a few noses to sniff the air jealously. When everything was ready, Rik placed two colossal claws on Jill's plate. Her eyes went wide.

"Holy moly! I didn't think crab claws could get that big!"

Rik flashed a playful smirk. "Those are colossals and they're not good." He paused for dramatic effect. "They're delicious. Let me crack the first couple for you."

He demonstrated holding the claw in his left hand, interior side facing him, then giving several solid taps with the back of a heavy soup spoon. After the third tap, a hairline fracture appeared, and he pulled the claw apart, revealing a thick hunk of tender, pearly-white stone crab meat.

"Now comes the hard part," he joked. "Mustard sauce, hot butter, or lemon? These are serious choices."

Jill laughed at the mock seriousness. She tentatively dipped her first bite into the mustard sauce. One taste and her eyes lit up again. "Oh my God," she gasped. "Where have you been all my life?"

Rik raised an eyebrow in playful surprise, and Jill quickly added, "I meant the crabs! I meant the crabs."

They both laughed and happily dug in. Fried green tomatoes made a tart, crispy complement, and soon they found themselves leaning back in their chairs, sated and smiling.

"What's for dessert?" Jill teased; hands folded over her comfortably full stomach.

Rik disappeared into the cabin and returned triumphantly with a Key lime pie, its meringue topping lightly toasted and its crust golden.

Jill wrinkled her nose. "I've never developed a taste for that," she admitted.

"Ah, but this is my recipe," Rik insisted, cutting a generous forkful. "Take one bite."

She obliged, and within seconds she was hooked. "That's amazing—tart and sweet. And that crust…what's in it?"

He gave her a secretive smile. "Old Conch recipe. You've got to earn that kind of knowledge," he joked.

They rinsed their hands over the side of the boat with the cockpit hose and some lemon slices. One advantage of living on a boat is that cleanups are easy. After stowing away the dishes, they settled on the settee.

Now here was where Rik pulled out all the stops. "Sambuca?" he said.

"Sounds good."

Rik handed her a tulip glass with two fingers of Sambuca and something else.

"Rik…what's floating in my glass?"

"Three coffee beans. It's an Italian tradition. *Con la mosca*. They symbolize health, happiness, and prosperity. Salute!"

Sambuca in hand. They sat close, though not too close, letting the warm ocean breeze and the soft lapping of waves speak for them. Jill was beginning to think there was more to Rik Duval than she'd thought that fateful day in Key West.

Eventually, Jill broke the silence. "Can I ask you something?"

Rik's first reaction was to say skivvies…but instead he nodded and said, "Within reason."

She hesitated, then said, "Tell me about the sniper competition."

"That came out of nowhere. Why?"

"Well, it's part of my job to know everything about you. I read your file, but I sensed there was more to the story."

Rik took a slow breath. He'd packed away a lot of his past—put it in a box, hoping never to revisit it. Yet Jill was different. He felt she deserved some trust; she'd earned it by simply being there, genuinely interested, especially after what he'd been through with Carmen.

"Well," he began, swirling the Sambuca in his glass. "Every spring at Fort Benning, Georgia, they hold a competition to determine who's the best sniper in the world. Teams come from all branches of the US military—Army, Marines, Navy, Air Force, Coast Guard—plus law enforcement agencies and international squads. It's not just about bull's-eyes. They set up real-world sniper scenarios: unknown distances, hostage-rescue precision, rapid target acquisition … all under tough physical and mental conditions. Pretty grueling stuff."

Jill leaned forward, interest glinting in her eyes. "And the Coast Guard was invited?"

He nodded. "We're smaller, sure, and we don't get as many precision-marksmanship billets as the others. But we hold our own. That year I was feeling really good, making every shot count."

Rik paused, thinking back to a figure that loomed large in those memories. "One of the top competitors that year was a SEAL Team guy. Reaper was his operator name. Total hotshot. He'd spent time in some of the worst hot zones in the world. If half the stories are true, he saved a lot of lives. But man, did he have an ego. We were neck and neck through the stages, each of us leading in different categories. We barely acknowledged each other beyond a nod or a glare. I was riding high, shooting lights out. I couldn't miss."

Jill watched him closely. "So, what happened?"

Rik sighed. "The night before the final stage, all the shooters were stir-crazy. An impromptu get-together was organized across the state line in

Alabama. We all headed to a beer and burger joint called Bun Appétit—name sounds fancy, but it's a total dive." He smirked at the memory.

"Anyway, after a few drinks, a fight broke out in the parking lot with some locals. Reaper was in the thick of it. Five against one. He may be a SEAL, but tire irons and axe handles even the odds. I'm not sure why, but something made me step in. We were rivals, but we were still on the same side, you know."

He flexed his hand, ghost pains echoing from that night. "Long story short, I busted two fingers on my shooting hand. Needed surgery and that was that. My last stage was toast. No way I could shoot with broken fingers."

"When we met in Key West, Eisenberg said the flu knocked you out of the competition. Even he didn't know?"

"That's what I told the competition director and his people. If the brass found out we were fighting, Reaper would have been busted out of the competition. So, I kept my mouth shut."

Jill frowned sympathetically. "That's rough. Were you bitter?"

"I was for a bit. Reaper never acknowledged me having his back. He went on to win the competition and I headed home. But honestly, it was my choice to get involved. Maybe I saved him from a beating—maybe not. I guess part of me is just wired to step in when I saw a teammate, or even a rival, cornered. It ended up costing me the chance to take first. After that, I decided I was done chasing competitions."

They sat quietly for a moment, the gentle slosh of water against the hull filling the silence. Jill reached out and laid a hand gently on his arm. The contact was warm, reassuring.

Rik was wrestling internally and eventually said hesitantly, "My turn?"

"Sure Rik."

"Remember when you were briefing me about Carmen and their expansion plans and the Toucano tribe?"

"Yes, of course."

"Well, that wasn't the first time I had heard of the Toucano people."

"Really? From what I researched they've have no modern contact since the Spanish in the 1600's. Few people, even the Brazilian government, are aware of their existence. "

"That's not entirely true. What I'm about to tell you was told to me in secret by my uncle Jax. He made me promise to never tell a soul but the times have changed. And I need your advice. But first you must promise this stays between us?"

The lieutenant was surprised by Rik's intensity. And directness. But she nodded her agreement.

"Let me start at the beginning. I know you'll have

lots of questions but I won't have any answers. First, my uncle Jax was involved in one of the many shadow operations during the Vietnam War. One of his assignments was to enlist and train the Montagnard people for counter insurgency operations. They were known for bravery, survival skills, and deep jungle knowledge—ideal allies in covert operations.

"But when the war ended we abandoned them. Some were saved and relocated to North Carolina but those who remained were horribly persecuted by the Communists. I'll spare you the details but my uncle was wracked with guilt for abandoning his brothers in arms. He drilled into me from an early age you protect those who can't protect themselves. They were a fearsome people but they needed Uncle Sam's help. And we turned a blind eye."

"I had no idea. That's terrible."

"There's more. Since we got our ass kicked over there, some very secretive branches of the military began training in the deep forests of Brazil. Oh, and without their government's knowledge. That was all part of the training. Conduct training ops in the most difficult jungle in the world while not being detected by a foreign government. And my uncle, of course, was in the middle of it.

"He didn't like it but he obeyed orders. But his guys went rogue. The leader lost control and they killed everything they saw and ate very little of what they killed. They cut down large swaths for their camps. They desecrated the pristine jungle. And my uncle was powerless to stop them.

"Near the end of the operation, he came down with a terrible fever and ended up delirious in a hammock. At the peak of his fever, he saw a group of indigenous warriors sneak into the camp. He thought he was hallucinating. The were small with thick jet-black hair, topped by a small headdress in the shape of a crown. They were made of colorful bird feathers. Their foreheads and eyes were covered in bright orange face paint. All carried long lengths of bamboo. They were blowguns - silent, deadly accurate, and perfect for stalking animals—or people. It's a weapon of patience, stealth, and botanical genius.

"In seconds seven top tier operators were felled by curare. The poison of choice used by indigenous people of South America. My uncle thought he was next but instead of killing him they wrapped him in his hammock and transported him miles to their encampment. There he was cared for by a shaman and eventually recovered completely. They spared him because they had been watching and knew he was different than the seven they killed.

"He stayed with the Toucano for six months. He learned their ways, a little of their language and forged life long bonds. He knew there was no rescue mission being mounted for him and his non-existent team. If he wanted his life back, and to shield the Toucano people from the outside world, he would have to concoct a wild survival story.

"With the Toucano's help he built a crude raft and floated hundreds of miles down the Juruá River away from the ancient tribe until he reached a missionary encampment. With their help he eventually returned to civilization. The agencies he worked for, of course, disavowed him but he struck a deal. He received a cushy pension in exchange for his silence on the failed operation. And he never said a word to anyone about the Toucano. Except me."

"He told me one day they would need help. From boyhood uncle Jax trained me to be a protector, so I feel a calling to help these people. If Jax knew they were in trouble he would help too."

"So, what are you going to do? It's noble you want to help but you need resources. Frankly, you need a ton of gold."

Rick was caught off guard by that statement but he continued, "What if there was a way to help them? The Toucano. It's not exactly a fair fight. Stone Age people against the Tabasco cartel. I mean, who's got their back?"

"Go on."

"What if I…I mean, what if Billy knows a guy? A really rich guy." Stuttering a little, he continued. "Do you think he should help?"

Jill was silent for a minute, then said, "They need all the help they can get. I'm sure they would accept any assistance…no matter the source."

Rik continued with a small, sly smile, "Thanks for the advice. That crazy Billy has a wide reach. I'll keep you posted."

Jill turned her attention back to the little fragrant glass, wondering what the hell Rik was up to. But she trusted him to do the right thing. No matter how unorthodox.

The sound of evening gulls drifted through the open cockpit. The sun dipped lower, painting the sky in swirls of pink and orange. Stone crabs, Key lime pie, and impromptu confessionals about the past—an unlikely but meaningful combination. They remained there for a long while, letting unspoken possibilities hang in the humid Keys air.

Rik hoped there would be more to discover about each other, more stories to share.

For him, a new door had cracked open… like a good claw.

THIRTY-TWO

The last few days had been a blur of late nights, energy drinks, and wild plans. It wasn't every day you arranged an operation to recover pirate gold. There was no playbook. No instruction manual. They were going to have to bend a few rules. Check that. They were going to bend a lot of rules.

The old adage "fail to plan; plan to fail" was in full effect. Rik had never counted on being partners with a crazy friend like Billy, but Billy had turned out to be quite capable. Sometimes a little scary too.

It was time to recover the gold. They waited for a cloudy night, for obvious reasons, as the moon was starting to make her monthly appearance. They did, however, need a cover story in case they were stopped. Billy and Rik decided that using a lobster boat would be a great cover. They were big and could carry a lot of weight, but the drawback was they were pretty slow.

To pull this off, they enlisted the help of two old Conch friends, Salty Simpson and Wahoo Walter. They had to entrust these guys with knowledge that could cost them their lives. But these two, like their names implied, were salt of the earth.

The two lobstermen picked up the duo at Sailfish Bay, and they puttered the ten-mile trek to Shell Key. On the way, they had plenty of time to reflect on their pursuit.

Rik asked Billy, "Do you think we're doing the right thing, grabbing all this gold? I mean, what the heck are we going to do with it?"

"It's up to you, man, really," Billy replied. "Toby Cyprus entrusted the Kahatee to you for a reason. He's a wise man, and he wouldn't interfere with a legend involving the ancients. So, I'll help you get the gold, and you do whatever you think is right. But I don't see you keeping it. First, you'd get caught, and second, there are bigger forces at work here."

"I know what you mean, Billy. I feel it in my soul that we need to get the gold before Carmen does. And I have an idea what to do with it."

"One thing at a time," Billy said.

The lobster boat motored slowly up to the soft sandy beach, where they anchored in a foot of water. This was done to reduce the distance between the heavy gold and the boat. It was going to be arduous work to move the treasure, but they devised a system. As soon as they landed, they all got to work, rigging up a cable zip line. They anchored one end to a tall coconut tree near the burial mound and the other to a large cleat at the stern of the lobster boat.

When they dragged the gold crates from the mound, they hung them in a canvas sleeve and zipped them down to the boat, where they were unloaded.

During this process, Billy's big noggin managed to get in the way of a casket of gold zipping straight to the boat. Not much could drop him, but high-speed gold certainly did the trick. He stood up and staggered around.

Rik went up to him and asked, "Are you okay?"

He didn't look so good, but being a trouper, he replied, "I think so."

"What's your name?"

"November."

"Ah, you'll be fine."

Billy took a short break but was soon back in action. The process took four hours, and by the end, they were all exhausted. They used lobster traps to hide the treasure pile and started their journey home.

That was when they discovered a flaw in their plan. The extra weight had caused them to sink into the soft sand beach. They had, in effect, run aground. Thankfully, they were in sand, but the boat wasn't going anywhere. They all stood there staring at each other, until Rik said, "Let's kedge this heavy bastard off!"

Kedging is the process of putting an anchor out in deeper water and using the boat's winches to pull it out. It's not easy, but it works. Seeing no volunteers, Rik stripped down to his shorts, took the anchor, and told them to attach a bunch of buoys to it.

He swam out as far as the anchor line would allow, then cut the buoys loose, letting the anchor sink. Swimming back, he instructed them to spin up the bow winch. At first, nothing happened, but slowly, the boat began to move. They wanted to cheer but kept quiet. Eventually, the boat was in deeper water, and they could start the engines without the risk of sucking in mud and sand.

They began their trek home, grinning like pirates, with Billy's maniacal grin the widest. He could have been Blackbeard himself. Hell, in Rik's eyes, he was Blackbeard reincarnated.

They were three miles from home when they heard something over the rumble of the old diesel. A fast-moving boat with no lights. That was never a good sign. *They better know their way around,* Rik thought, *because the channels are deep, and the flats are not.*

They were on the Gulf side of the Keys, in Florida Bay, an area littered with hundreds of little islands and unmarked flats. Difficult to navigate during the day and damn near impossible at night. These guys knew their way, though—they hadn't run aground yet and were approaching fast. This couldn't be good. Wahoo and Salty Bob looked at Rik for direction. He wished he had some.

They could be Carmen's men, but who knew?

The fast boat was on them now, and Rik could make out the outlines of people. The boat looked like a center-console with three large engines, easily hitting sixty miles per hour versus their fifteen, and that was if they were empty—which they were not. A hailer called out in a Latin accent, "Stop the boat! Stop the boat!"

Salty, who was driving, looked at Rik. Rik said, "Don't. If you stop, we're dead."

Inwardly, he wished he had his Barrett. *That would even the score.* But now he had to use his brains and guile. Then Rik had an idea. He hadn't been there in years, but he knew a spot. And he was pretty sure the bad guys didn't. But he had to buy time, so he yelled out, "We need to pull a Paul Watson. Now!"

Billy said, "Who?"

Salty said, "Huh?"

Walter said nothing, as his hearing wasn't what it used to be.

Rik repeated, "A Paul Watson. You know...*Whale Wars*! The Animal Planet show?"

Billy said, "Nope, never heard of it? You, Salty?"

"Nah. I don't watch much TV. Rots your mind, you know."

Rik quickly explained. "Paul Watson was the admiral of the Whale Wars flotilla, who certainly had a little pirate in him. He and his wayward crew would rig floating lengths of chain and rope to foul the propellors of the whalers."

"Well, goddammit, we need a prop fouler now."

"Billy, grab the anchor line! Wahoo, tie all the lobster buoys you can on it."

They did this with surprising speed, so now they had a three-hundred-foot length of rope that would float.

"Salty, do you have a spool of poly? You know, for the lobster traps?"

"Sure, there's a two hundred-foot spool in that hatch."

"Grab it now. Okay, when I say the word, you guys feed those two warps into the prop wash. Try to be discreet. If they see you, it'll ruin the plan."

Billy started to say something about how his discretion was known throughout the Keys but decided this was not the time. Or the place.

They began zigging and zagging the boat, acting like they were trying to get away. But Rik was actually laying out lengths of rope that should get caught in the chasing boat's propellors. At minimum, the bad guys would have to stop and cut the line from the props. This just might buy them enough time for the second half of Rik's plan.

Sure enough, they heard the boat slow down and all manner of Spanish cursing came across the water. These guys really knew some crazy curses. It was amazing how sound travels at night, and it made all the guys laugh. Temporarily.

Back to reality. "Bob, give me the wheel," Rik said, standing behind the GPS plotter. What he wanted wasn't officially marked, but he had to know exactly where they were.

The narco boat was able to cut the lines off their props and was again at full speed. They began firing short, nasty bursts from machine guns. Everyone ducked under the gunnels, some behind the gold, knowing it could stop bullets. The enemy boat got closer and closer. Just when the whole crew thought the end was near, Rik threw the old boat hard to starboard. They were now in the tiniest of channels: Toilet Seat Cut.

Toilet Seat Cut wasn't an official channel. It had been created decades earlier by an impatient boater who wanted to get to his favorite bar faster. He'd used a small outboard to dredge his own channel—a move that would get you twenty years in jail today. Back then, though, there were no rules. The channel wasn't on navigational charts, but it was marked by sticks. Over time, for no apparent reason, people had started placing old toilet seats on the sticks, hence the name.

The bad guys saw their sudden turn and tried to follow. Wham! Bam! Hard ground on an oyster bar. All three lower units came off and two guys went flying over the bow. The rest were lying on top of each other in a jumble of broken arms and bleeding heads. The budding pirates had made it—for now.

The unloading of the gold took place on a rickety dock near a dusty construction site. This new residential development was based on shipping containers. Apparently, luxury shipping containers were a thing now. Who knew Billy was ahead of his time? Billy was in charge of transportation, and, well, he knew a guy. So, imagine Rik's shock when Billy showed up behind the wheel of a…

"Cement mixer? Are you crazy, Billy? Wait … don't answer that question."

"I'm not crazy! Think about it," Billy shot back. "This thing can carry ten tons. And who would suspect us to be carrying gold in this? No way Carmen or her goons will find us."

Billy opened up the side hatch of the mixing drum, and in went the small cases of gold. The operation took longer than expected, and the sun was rising as they wrapped up.

As Rik climbed into the cab, Billy handed him a plastic grocery bag with clothing in it. "Here's your disguise."

Rik opened the bag, looked at the outfit and groaned. The first part was a Rasta hat with real-looking dreadlocks hanging down. Next was a T-shirt that read, "All I need are some tasty waves, a cool buzz, and I'm fine, dude."

Rik shook his head. "Nope. Not happening. I'd rather get caught."

"By the way, where's your disguise?" Rik asked.

Billy grinned and pulled out a yellow CAT Tractor hat and promptly rolled up his mane and pulled it tightly onto his oversized head. The transformation was instant—he went from crazy, wild Native American to redneck truck driver in two seconds flat.

Rik sighed. "Do you have another one of those?"

Billy tossed him a spare, and Rik put it on. With that, the two good ol' boys fired up the big rig and rolled on down the road. Coincidentally, "East Bound and Down" crackled out their ancient AM/FM radio.

As they made their way south and west toward Key West, they passed familiar landmarks: Indian Key to their left, Robby's to the right, and tiki bars on both sides. Before they knew it, they were approaching the Seven Mile Bridge. The span could occasionally be deadly because of drunk drivers and the narrow proximity of cars, but Rik and Billy felt comfortable in their massive rolling cement-and-gold machine.

Their calmness ended abruptly when Billy muttered, "Uh-oh… we've got company."

Rik looked in the super-sized side mirror and saw them also—two black Suburbans approaching fast, full of nefarious-looking characters.

Traffic was light in the early morning, and the first SUV tried to pass them, its occupants brandishing guns and waving furiously. Billy veered left, blocking them. They quickly got the idea they couldn't bully the rolling mix master.

The Suburban passed them and then tried to slow down in front of the big truck. Billy responded by giving them a few "love taps" from the fifteen-ton vehicle. The goon's car spun out, slammed into the left guardrail, and came to a smoking stop.

Rik muttered under his breath, wishing he had one of his Coast Guard weapons, but that wasn't an option.

The second SUV sped past them and used a new strategy. Two men stuck their heads out of the rear windows and began shooting at the mixer's radiator and tires.

Rik was used to gunfire, but Billy clearly wasn't. Billy shouted, "What do I do?"

"Knock them into next week!" Rik yelled.

Billy accelerated, and when thirty thousand pounds meets eight thousand pounds, physics decides the outcome. The smaller vehicle crashed through the railing to the right, flew through the air, and coincidentally soared past Fred the Tree before landing in the water below. One could almost hear the goons yelling "What the hell is a tree doing here?" before their car hit the water and began to sink.

The four men emerged, more or less unscathed, and swam to safety—until they saw a floating log. Only it wasn't a log. The reptilian log saw their shiny belt buckles and accelerated. That's right—it was Jolene, the cocaine-loving croc. Moments later, she made quick work of the four. She then retreated to a desolate portion of No Name Key and lounged on the beach, enjoying her full belly and euphoric high. If she had a toothpick, it would have been put to good use.

Back on the bridge, Rik and Billy assessed the damage. The cement mixer was hissing. White steam poured from the engine, and one of the tires was completely shot. They jumped back in the cab, limped into Big Pine Key, and stashed the broken rig behind a mecca for RVs. Hopefully, they could shield the mixer temporarily from Carmen and her people.

"So now what?" Rik asked.

It was noon, and the two, tired and battered, walked along A1A, trying to find a place to regroup and come up with a new plan. Then the lights went out.

THIRTY-THREE

When they came to, they were inside a van with rent-a-thugs. One of the goons said, "Carmen wants to talk to you." Rik would have laughed, but the machine pistol pointed at his gut told him not to. The goons covered their heads with obligatory black canvas hoods, and Rik thought, *Not again…at least these bags don't smell like a donkey's ass. Not good, but not ass.*

They were driven to Marathon Airport, a small airfield that was dead at this hour. The van passed old beat-up Pipers and Cessnas and the occasional Gulfstream. They arrived at a hangar on the far side that housed a fifties-era DC-3 with only one wing and one motor. The goons forced the two up the boarding ladder, pushing them into the front two seats and tie-wrapped their hands behind them.

Billy turned to Rik and said, "Well, at least we're in first class." It was funny, but Rik didn't want to give him the satisfaction of laughing.

Soon, Carmen joined them.

"You guys are pissing me off!"

"How did you find us?"

"I ask the questions, but I'll indulge you. You two morons don't know much about concrete, do you?"

Billy and Rik looked at each other blankly. Admittedly, they didn't.

"Concrete must spin, or it will set. I have eyes everywhere. And concrete trucks coming from the mainland that aren't spinning are suspicious. Or hauling cargo I'm interested in. Well, you two jokers… we found you, and your cement truck full of gold. But guess what? It was fake."

"What?" Rik yelled.

Billy's voice echoed his. "What? That's impossible."

"Nope," she smirked. "You two idiots fought all this way for a bunch of fake gold. How can you be so stupid?"

"We were going to do something good with it!" Rik shouted, his frustration spilling out.

"Do something good with it?" Carmen laughed like a madwoman. "That gold was for me and my ventures. Now where's the real gold?"

"No idea, lady! But I know a place you can look."

She turned to one of her henchmen. "Bring El Ministro Loco here! When I get back I want answers!"

Billy and Rik exchanged confused glances, wondering who the hell she was talking about. They were left alone for a few minutes. Billy, ever the wisecracker, quipped, "These flight attendants suck. And don't get me started on the beverage service."

Rik jostled Billy and said, "Look, we have to get outta here, find the real gold and get it to an indigenous tribe called the Toucano."

"Whatever you say, Rik."

"The Toucano will lose their land and their way of life. They'll die if we don't help them!"

"At this point, Rik, you can give it to a bunch of gold-hungry dancing leprechauns. Let's just get the hell out of here!"

Before they could continue, they heard footsteps on the creaky aluminum boarding ladder. An elder, tall, thin man dressed in black, stepped in, greeting them with a chilling "Good evening, my children. It's time to find religion." It was Preacher Payne, from the traveling Church of Pain & Agony.

Rik was first. "Are you fucking kidding me? You work for her now? I made a large donation to your fucked-up church!"

"Ah, brother, so you did. But yours was not a donation from the heart. Carmen … she is a true believer, as evidenced by the generous size of her donation. It makes your minuscule tithe embarrassing, I must say. Remember, there is peace in pain. No pain, no gain. And tonight, we are going to make huge gains in his name. For ye are the children of the coming pain. You will be my apostles of agony, my precious monks of misery."

"Okay, we get it. We've been to this rodeo…remember, Pops? We can't tell you what we don't know."

"Oh, child…that is simply music to my unworthy ears. It means our worship service will go on till dawn. Nothing would please me more than to greet the birth of a new day with your hymnal cries ringing out in glory."

"Don't you think our yelling will bring the police? C'mon, this is a public airport."

"Exactly, my naive acolyte. So, when we fire up a radial engine or two, no one will hear you. Oh, the beauty of it all. I think I'll move my church here permanently."

"You've got a screw loose, you nutjob."

"Wait here, my new parishioners, I'll be right back." His cheery demeanor was a tad unsettling to our fettered duo.

The preacher disappeared for a few minutes, then returned with several boxes. One of them sloshed with water. He reached into the other one, marked "venomous," and approached Billy, holding snakes in each hand—rattlers in one, and writhing, nasty blackwater snakes in the other. Billy's eyes darted back and forth, landing on the blackwater snakes.

"Ah, I see," said the preacher. "You're familiar with the rattlers, but these blackwater snakes… they hold a special place for you, don't they, Billy?"

Billy's voice cracked. "No, not the blackwater snakes. Please, not the blackwater snakes."

What no one knew was that when Billy was a boy, he'd caught blackwater snakes for Dr. Hass at the Miami Serpentarium. The doctor had paid five bucks a snake. And like Dr. Hass himself, little Billy had been bitten so many times he'd developed a partial immunity.

The preacher put the rattlers back in their box and brought the blackwater snakes closer, letting them bite Billy several times. Billy moaned and yelled in agony. Rik felt terrible—this was definitely not going the way he wanted it to. Eventually, Billy feigned passing out, trying to formulate a plan while the preacher turned his attention to Rik.

For Rik, the preacher went to the water-filled boxes, donned thick rubber gloves, and pulled out a lionfish. Rik knew exactly how painful their venom was. With a cruel grin, the preacher pressed its quills into Rik's skin. The hot, searing pain was intense, but Rik had been down this road before. He could handle it.

The preacher yelled, "Where's the gold? Where's the gold?!"

"I don't know! Caesar fooled us!" Rik shouted back.

"Your friend has passed out. A few more bites,

and he'll die. If I were you, I'd confess here, at the altar of the Church of Agony, and tell me where the gold is."

Suddenly there was a disturbance outside with a lot of yelling. Rik was thinking the cavalry was coming, but the cavalry didn't know they were there. No one did.

Except that somehow, Barefoot Joe and Jimmy Legs did. Both arrived on the scene tumbling down the ancient bird's aisle, with more thugs behind them, armed to the teeth.

Rik was too stunned to say anything, and Joe muttered, "Leave the dog out of it. He had nothing to do with the rescue attempt. It was all my doing. Let him go." He was interrupted by the preacher's loud clapping.

"Glory. Glory Hallelujah! Hallelujah! More followers! And a dog. I can't believe it. My joy is boundless. My cup runneth over with pain and suffering. I've always wanted a dog to join my flock."

Rik shouted, "You're a sick fuck. Leave the dog out of it. Let him go."

"I won't harm the dog. I'm not a psychopath, ya know. Jeesh," the preacher muttered under his breath.

Barefoot Joe was soon tie-wrapped to a seat back in coach and Jimmy Legs was kicked to the back of the plane, where he stayed, whimpering. And listening.

The preacher resumed his whack-a-doodle

religious service.

Before he could start, Billy stirred, groaning. "Preacher! I have seen the light," he bellowed, wide-eyed. "Yes, I have seen the beautiful light!"

The preacher looked at him in amazement. "Hallelujah, brother! Hallelujah! This truly is a miracle. Tell me, what did you see?"

"Come closer, Preacher, and I'll tell you," Billy beckoned.

"What, my son?"

"I'll tell you everything. I'll tell you where the real gold is. But I'm parched, so parched. I just need a little piece of fruit. Please?"

"Fruit? What kind of fruit?"

Billy whispered in a raspy voice, "Ya know…it's orangey-yellow and tastes sweet."

"A peach?"

"No."

"Papaya?"

"No," he said weakly. "Its skin is greenish purplish."

"A mango?"

Jimmy Legs ears perked up and he sprinted to the preacher like the dinner bell had rung. With a ferocious vise-grip bite, he neutered Payne like a feral hog. The preacher screamed and whirled dervishly. Billy, adrenalized from the venom, snapped the ties, grabbed the two guards, who were in shock from seeing the worst bris ever, and banged their heads like cymbals at a Boston Pops Fourth of July.

Jimmy Legs retreated to a corner snacking on the preacher's peaches. To stop Pastor Payne's whimpering Billy shoved an oily rag in his mouth and hissed, "Shut up, you pyscho bastard."

The preacher had a bizarre expression on his face. Somewhere between abject rapture and immeasurable pain. As they moved to leave, Billy paused. "Wait, I've got something special in mind for the preacher."

"Billy, we have to go!" Rik urged him.

"This will just take a minute." Billy rummaged through the preacher's white van and emerged with Julieta, his prized anaconda. Staggering under her weight, he headed back up the steps, disappearing for a moment before stumbling back down.

"What did you do?" Rik asked.

"Let's just say Julieta is going to dine on 'Payne alla Castrati' tonight."

As the beat-up crew and a smirking Jimmy Legs snuck away, Billy asked how Rik was doing. Frankly, Rik's legs and arms were on fire from the lionfish toxins. He told Billy so and added, "You've got to pee on me. That's the only cure."

Billy looked at him and deadpanned, "You're going to die. Now, where is the real gold?"

"I have no fucking idea!"

THIRTY-FOUR

Turns out Barefoot Joe was working late on the Beaver when he noticed lights on in the usually quiet hangar. His rescue mission was unorthodox but thank goodness for Rik and Billy he acted. Barefoot Joe and the ever-grinning Jimmy Legs were able to catch a ride north on the back of a trap hauler, waving like they'd just closed a deal with Neptune.

Rik and Billy, however, needed to debrief—and preferably with alcohol and a minimal chance of surveillance—so they made for the Bottom Lime, a lurid, little lime-green bunker tucked behind a marine supply shop. It looked like it had survived both a hurricane and a tax investigation, and in truth, it had.

The place was owned by two ex-accountants who got sideways with the IRS and then had a full-on Shawshank Redemption moment. When they crawled out of the mess, they had a suitcase filled with enough embezzled cash to buy five years of silence. They poured their sins into the Bottom Lime, now famous from Key Largo to Marathon for its "Balance Sheet

Nights of Madness," where mild-mannered CPAs from across the Keys turned into limbo champions and where ladies in glasses reportedly did things that couldn't be itemized.

But tonight, there were no spreadsheets on fire. No tax-themed limbo. Just Rik and Billy in a back booth, soaking in the hum of an ancient ceiling fan and the smooth croon of Captain Sam Crutchfield on the jukebox.

Their waitress, Nettie Profitt, sidled up in heels that didn't belong on that floor and a sundress that might've once been a curtain. She had a pad in one hand, a notary stamp in the other.

"You boys look like you need a drink... or a forged receipt," she said.

Billy grinned. "What's the house special?"

She didn't blink. "Double Entry Martini. One sip, and you forget what you owe and who you owe it to."

Rik raised a brow. "What's in it?"

Nettie leaned in. "Gin, regret, and plausible deniability."

They ordered doubles.

"Well, now what are we going to do?"

"I don't know," said Billy. "How could we be so dumb? Man, I thought that gold was light. I just thought that all that weightlifting I do was doing was really paying off."

"Hey, quick fact...Arnold Shots-of-Jaeger; you

drink… you don't lift weights."

"I could!"

"Let's get back to basics. Where are we with this whole treasure quest thing?"

"Well, we have the Kahatee."

"Right. We unlocked its secrets. It led us to the tablet, which led to the treasure. Except the treasure was stolen and replaced. Why replace it?"

"Clearly someone got there before we did. But who?"

"Maybe we should give up. Carmen's not gonna bother with you now. You're useless to her. Go chase Lieutenant Wright. She's kinda hot in a military way. I've always liked women with formal handgun training."

"No, you like women of questionable morals and a proclivity for drinking too much. But what you say makes sense. But I know the treasure is out there. I can feel it. And we have to get it to the Toucano. It's the right thing to do. I can feel it in my bones. Ever since I touched the Kahatee, I've known things. Sensed things. It's hard to explain. It's like I have one foot in the past and the other in the future. The story doesn't end here."

"Well, Sheerluck Holmes, I think you've been working too hard. Let's make our way back to Rum Key and start over."

The two went back to their routines. Billy debauched his way through questionable company and late nights. Rik went fishing and spent time with Lieutenant Wright, discussing new assignments and logistics. Yet Rik couldn't shake the feeling—an obligation, a task he had to complete. Something that transcended time. It had been established long ago and had a timetable, a ticking clock. He could hear the clocks from the Pink Floyd song. They were all ticking, and he had to stop them. And Carmen.

After several days of welcomed normalcy, Rik woke up, went through his coffee ritual then then stepped outside to clean up what the seagulls left him overnight. And there, on the fighting chair, was a small wooden box.

It was orange-ish in hue and very well made. Unknown to Rik it was made of Brazil wood. Very rare and the name sake of its country of origin.

Rik looked all around, like an owl on the hunt, but there was no evidence of who delivered the box. His first inclination was to call the bomb squad but his curiosity got the better of him. He opened it slowly, carefully. Inside there were two objects. A note and an ancient key.

The note had seen better days. The paper was folded in half, the paper crinkled, sweat stained and the ink faded and smudged. Whoever wrote it was in a hurry and in rough surroundings. Rik unfolded it and read:

I'm with the Toucano. We are being hunted by the Tabasco cartel. The Toucano fight bravely but we are no match for mercenaries with machine guns and heat seeking drones. We can last another week, two at the most.

Bring the key to the man at number ten Tortuga Marina. You will know what to do.

There's a reason I raised you like I did. Why I taught you to fight, to listen, to stand between harm and the helpless. You're a Guardian now. Not because I said so. Because you always were.

I'm proud of you and I love you like a son.

Uncle Jax

The note shook him to his core. Uncle Jax was seeking redemption in the jungles of Brazil. Helping a stone age people battle extinction. Fighting a one sided battle. Blow guns versus machine guns. s. Rik knew his uncle wouldn't abandon these people. Not this time. He would die first.

He needed time to process the note. Especially the part where Uncle Jax said he loved him. He never uttered those words in person. Rik loved him too but for now, there was no time for emotion. Rik had a job to do.

He looked at the key. In contrast to the crude note it was a well-crafted brass key to a lock. An old lock too as the style resembled nothing in the modern world. The head of the key was cast as a beautiful turtle. With a blue head. Gemini had mentioned something about blue turtles and their connection to Caesar's treasure. *Could this be for real?* He went back inside to the galley. This situation required more caffeine.

After a few cups of Blue Mountain's finest, he called Billy.

"Where are you?"

"Um…I'm a little tied up at the moment."

"Put her on."

A sultry voice came over the line. "This is Mistress Dee Toxin. How can I hurt you?"

"Cut my friend loose. We're on a mission."

"You're a real buzz kill, Rik Duval," she replied as a whip cracked in the background. The call ended.

Billy showed up not long after, looking a little sheepish.

"Anything you want to tell me? Anything I should know? I knew you were a freak, but Jesus, Billy. Dee Toxin. Really? Does she have a friend? Maybe we can do a picnic or double date sometime?"

"Drop it. You get your kicks, I get mine."

Rik told Billy about the note and showed him the old blue turtle key.

"Damn. We need to help Uncle Jax. He's in serious trouble. Didn't Gemini mention a blue turtle? Who the hell put it there?"

"Don't know. Don't care. But I know the Tortuga Marina. It's in Key West and we're headed there at first light."

The next morning, on the way to the parking lot, they stopped by the dockmaster's office. The office was an ode to bad taxidermy. On the walls were every fish that could be found in the Keys. But just a little off. Some with mismatched eyes. Yellowtails weren't yellow and black grouper weren't black. Word was the original developer of the marina was a city boy. And a real cheapskate.

"Hey, Larry," Rik said, "There was someone on my boat last night. Do your cameras work?"

"No shit? Sure, we have ten cameras. One should have an image."

Larry accessed the feeds but didn't see anything. "Ya know, Rik, if there was somebody on the Bum Runner, they sure knew how to avoid the cameras."

As they started to leave, Larry whistled and said, "Wait. We have a still shot. Holy cow. You don't see that every day."

Rik and Billy did an about-face and leaned over Larry's shoulder to see what had made him whistle.

There on the screen, on Rik's dock, was a small, wiry man. Now the Keys are home to a wide variety of, shall we say, "special" people. But this guy was clearly out of his element.

He was small but looked strong. Thick jet-black hair, cut in a bowl shape, topped by a small headdress in the shape of a crown. It was made of colorful bird feathers. His forehead and eyes were covered in bright orange face paint. His attire consisted of a loincloth. Now if this had been Saturday night in Key West, you'd hardly turn your head. But here on Rum Key he would have been right at home in a National Geographic special on the People of the Amazon.

Larry asked, "Do you want me to call Deputy O'Malley? This guy can't be that hard to find."

Rik replied, "He knew where the cameras were. He wanted us to see him. But we'll never see him again," and abruptly left the office.

They jumped in Roxanne and headed west to the Tortuga Marina in Key West. The trip was uneventful, and Billy was surprisingly quiet. Until they hit a bump in the road. Then he would moan like a baby and Rik would smile. After a while Rik began searching for bumps to punish Billy. As if he hadn't been punished enough. Ha.

They passed Fred the Tree and noticed the large gap in the railing caused by their last misadventure. The traffic slowed to one lane as there was a significant construction crew working on the repair. Unseen to them, Jolene the crocodile, was resting under the bridge, still digesting her latest meal. With a minor craving for some croc dust if you know what I mean.

They reached the old Tortuga Marina, and while Rik strolled down the dock, Billy did a two-step bunny hop kind of a thing. Bizarre but effective.

They reached slip number ten. It was vacant. All that was there was a nice hole in the water with some seaweed and ancient gray dock lines hanging from the pilings.

Rik saw there was a guy working on his boat in the adjacent slip. "Hey," he said. "Is there a boat docked in this slip?"

"Nope. I've been here two years and it's never been rented. Hey, can I interest you in a charter? The fish are running. I won't even charge you for your Sasquatch friend."

With that, Billy glared at the antagonist. He considered drowning him, but his body wasn't quite up to the task.

The two dejectedly headed to Captain Tony's, one of their watering holes when in Key West. They desperately wanted to get drunk but stayed sober and mature for a moment.

Hanging out with Carmen had increased Rik's Spanish acumen, and he started saying Tortuga Marina in a Spanish accent.

After a moment he said, "Hey, Billy, grab your phone. See if there's any restaurants or bars called the

Loggerhead."

"Yep, on Stock Island. The Loggerhead Bar. How'd you know that?"

"It dawned on me that Tortuga Marina could also mean Sea Turtle in Spanish. We were being directed to a bar, not a marina. Let's roll!"

Rik and Billy prided themselves on knowing most of the bars in the Keys. The owners too. And many occupants. But they'd never heard of this one. It appeared to be a good blue-collar bar. Frequented by shrimpers. It certainly smelled that way.

They walked in and the joint was dark as a sin with obligatory sad country music on. There was a beat-up bar, an equally beat up bartender and some booths. Rik asked the bartender, "Which is booth ten?"

The barkeep pointed and replied, "Over there, but it's occupado if you know what I mean."

They walked over. It was inhabited by a skinny man dressed in faded priestly clothes with the Roman collar slightly askew. The occupant was drunk and looked like he had a long-term lease.

Rik was tired of beating around the bush, so he placed the blue turtle key in front of the priest and said, "Hey, Padre, does this mean anything to you?"

Without looking up, the haggard man said, "Go away," in a slurred but academic voice.

Rik and Billy slid into the other side of the booth—well, *Rik* slid. Billy did more of a grunt-loaded table push-up, wedging himself like he was trying on his high school jeans.

"Look at me!" Rik demanded. "I've been chased, shot at, and tortured, and you are going to look at this turtle headed key!"

"I said go away!" Huh? What turtle? Did you say turtle?" The man slowly looked up, and his eyes lit up at the sight of the blue turtle key. "Where did you get this?" he asserted, no longer slurring.

There was no way Rik would reveal the details behind finding the key so he simply said, "I found it on my boat yesterday in Rum Key."

"This is sig … very signif … We need to talk."

"Señor Gigante," the now sobering priest said, looking at Billy, "would you mind asking the bartender for some coffee? I need to study the key, and coffee would certainly help."

Billy got up with a grunt and came back with some surly coffee in a cup that had seen things.

The man finally said, "This is *muy importante*, my friends. I have a long story for you if you have the time?"

"We do," Rik said impatiently. "Go on."

"Well, my name is Emanuel Fernando Garcia de la Marcos. But my friends call me Manny. I am the Monsignor of our Lady of Lourdes Basilica by the Sea, here in Key West. And have been for twenty years.

"This blue-headed turtle key is a link to a mystery

that began several hundred years ago. So, again, if you gentlemen have time, I will regale with an improbable tale over several cups of awful coffee.

"It all starts with Black Caesar, the pirate, and the Tequesta Indians. Black Caesar plundered the waters off South Florida in the early 1700s and lived with the Tequesta, who were here for thousands of years before that. But like most Indigenous people, they were killed and pushed off their ancestral lands in the name of progress and pure greed. By the late 1700s, there were only sixty surviving Tequesta. They ended up in Key West and would have slowly died, but my predecessors, Jesuit priests from Havana, offered them sanctuary in exchange for their conversion to Catholicism.

"One night in Key West, a ship named the *Exquisita*—"

Rik interrupted, "The what?"

"The *Exquisita*. It was chartered by the Jesuits to bring the remaining band of Tequesta to Havana."

Rik's mind was racing at the coincidence but decided now was not the time for sharing. It was a time for listening.

"Please continue."

"The Tequestas made it to Havana. They were a peaceful people and the Jesuits in charge of their care and education were respectful of them and their plight. Their world was turned upside down. They had never seen buildings, cathedrals, or indoor plumbing. Can you imagine the shock?"

Billy and Rik nodded.

"There was a calm interlude for some time. The Tequesta assimilated. They learned Spanish, became educated, and began to wear Western-style clothing. But this period came to a halt when a priest was transferred from Mexico to help with the Tequesta's 'education.' His name was Father Toreador.

"He was not a nice man. It was rumored he eradicated thousands of Mayans and other indigenous peoples in Central America in an effort to "enlighten" them.

"At this time, two theologies began to emerge within the Cuban Catholic church. The first were of the Jesuit mindset, which focused on education and missionary work. It was this sect that rescued the Tequesta and acted with good intentions.

"The second sect were called the Maliviri. The literal translation in Latin was Bad Men. They were…how would you say? Sick fucks? Yes, they were sick fucks. They used beating, torture, and starvation to force religion onto indigenous people. Their focus was on Central Americans, such as the Mayan, Miskito, and Chorotega peoples. Father Toreador was a leader within this sect."

Billy said, "My roots are with people like that. I've never heard of the Mosquito or Chora somethings."

"Well, you can blame the Maliviri for this. Their mission was to eliminate the traditions, languages, and spiritual beliefs of those people and replace them with their own warped form of Christianity. "Father Toreador became aware of a rumor that the Tequesta had knowledge of a cache of gold that remained in the Florida Keys. It was cleverly hidden and only a special person would understand the clues to its location.

"Once they became aware of the gold, the Maliviri became obsessed with obtaining it for the greater glory of God. They believed the more gold they possessed; the more God loved them. And they would do anything to get it. As I said, they were sick MF'ers. Excuse my French.

"So, Father Toreador embarked on a plan of torture and starvation to discover the Tequesta's treasure. He tortured man, woman, and child until they revealed its location in the Upper Keys."

Rik and Billy tried to remain stone-faced, but after decades of listening to confessions and reading people's faces, the priest believed they knew more than they were telling. There was a lull while everyone in the booth considered their current position.

Rik eventually said, "Please continue, Father."

"The Maliviri knew where the gold was—but they lacked the means to retrieve it. So they waited. Patiently. Silently. For decades, they guarded the secret. Then, in 1898, they finally made their move."

"During that period there was civil unrest in Cuba, and they used this turmoil to cover an expedition to Shell Key, where they found the gold. They moved it to Cayo Hueso, I mean Key West, for transport back to Havana and the Church. They also left behind a hoard of fake gold to throw others off the scent."

Rik and Billy were now beside themselves. Billy hurriedly said, "So what happened to the real gold?"

"That's the mystery. They were arranging clandestine transportation for the gold when the USS *Maine* was blown up in Havana Harbor. There was so much chaos and scrutiny of vessels, it's believed they left the treasure behind in Key West. And gentleman I believe it resides here to this day. One would assume though, that it's cleverly concealed somewhere on the island.

"So, what now?"

"The wicked faction was eventually overthrown, but they purportedly left behind a scroll, hidden within church walls. This scroll that may hold the key to the treasure's location.

"How so?"

"The Tequesta revealed that Black Caesar was the source of the treasure. He split his bounty between two separate locations. The clues to his first treasure hoard were hidden inside a limestone turtle with a blue head. The blue head reflected Caesar's African Tuareg heritage. They were known as the blue people as their scarves used indigo dye, which stained their faces and heads. That treasure was found several years ago with the clues provided by the blue-headed turtle in the Miami Historical Museum.

"I'm at a crossroads in my service to the Almighty. I'm wracked with guilt. I don't sleep. I drink. I ponder the evils we committed in his Name. Past and present. I sit here most days and drown myself in bourbon. Not even the good stuff. I want to make the wrongs of my predecessors right.

"And now you, my friends, appear with an old key. A key with a blue headed turtle at the top. Clearly someone or something is pushing you towards a destiny. If you're willing, I want to help you find the gold. And get it to those it was intended for. Perhaps then my burden will be released."

So that evening, over a pot of bitter, angry coffee, a new chapter in Rik's bizarre life began.

THIRTY-FIVE

That night, after Father Manny's church fell silent, they all gathered in the sacristy. He led them to them a little used hallway where there was a metal plate mounted directly in the wall. It had a small hole at the bottom that didn't necessarily look like a key hole.

Billy looked at Rik as if to say, 'We've come all this way to look at an old metal plate on an old church wall?'

Father Manny, sensing their lack of enthusiasm pulled a small light from his pocket. "We use this to cull counterfeit bills from our weekly collection." They thought he also muttered the words 'those godless heathens'.

"Several years ago, I walked this hallway absent mindedly with the UV light on and noticed an image on the metal plate. I was in a hurry and didn't think much of it at the time. But now … watch!"

Father Manny held the UV light up to the plate. A fluorescent image slowly appeared. It was a turtle. He held the key up next. They were a match. This was a safe and Rik and Billy had the key.

Father Manny inserted the key and after some jiggling the metal face plate creaked open. He reached inside and brought out a small old box with a faded drawing on its lid. Sure enough, the drawing on the box and the turtle were an exact match. Whatever was in that box was connected to Black Caesar, the Tequestas, and possibly a hidden treasure.

Father Manny opened the box and produced a scroll. The parchment was faded, crinkled, and hard to decipher, but it read:

> *To whom possesses this scroll: The treasure belongs to the Church. The Maliviri are watching!*
> Your quest begins with the *Orb d'Lunacie,*
> When all can see it, in its entirety.
> For you to succeed and then to reave,
> The search must occur in the month of All Hallows' Eve.
> Collect the silver arrows on the *House of Agnus Dei,*
> Through the angel's lantern, shaped by Lepaute.
> The light of the stars will dance over streets, alleys, or even a knoll,
> But only you can unshroud the treasured soul.

The three of them were stunned. It was clear they were onto something, but the clues needed to be deciphered one by one.

Rik started: "The Orb D'lunacie. That has to be

the moon. Back in the day, people thought it caused craziness—that's where the term 'lunatic' came from."

Billy chimed in, quoting one of his favorite movies: "Check out the big brain on Brad!"

Rik rolled his eyes. "Come on, Billy, be serious."

"It says 'in its entirety,' so it must mean the full moon," Billy added. "But what does 'reave' mean?"

"It's old-fashioned," Father Manny said. "It means 'to reap'—to take the treasure."

"Okay," Rik said, "so we all agree our search must happen during the full moon in October."

"Shoot," Billy muttered, "Fantasy Fest is in two weeks. Somebody check the weather or the calendar for the full moon."

Rik pulled out his phone. "It's next week. Holy cow, that's exactly when Fantasy Fest is. You can't make this stuff up."

"Let's keep going." Manny ran a hand through his hair. "Collect the silver arrows on the House of Agnus Dei'?

Agnus Dei is Latin for 'Lamb of God," Father Manny said. "It could be referring to a church—maybe even this church."

"Collect silver arrows … angel's lantern…? Let's put that aside for a moment," Rik said. "Then there's 'the light of the stars will dance over the streets, alleys, or even a knoll, but only you can unshroud the treasured soul.' I'm stumped."

"Me too," Billy admitted.

Father Manny sighed. "Let's take a break. I make a mean Cuban coffee. Anyone want some?"

"I'll take two," Rik replied.

"Three," Billy said.

When Manny returned with the sweet little coffees, they continued.

"What the heck is an 'angel's lantern,' and who is 'Lepaute'?" Billy asked.

Rik again reached for his phone. "Let me Google 'Lepaute.'"

A moment later, he said, "Looks like it's a reference to André Lepaute, a master builder of lighthouse lenses. Many Florida lighthouses used Lepaute lenses."

So, the angel's lantern was a lighthouse lens. They all sipped their coffee in silence for a moment, letting the new discovery sink in.

Then Father Manny proclaimed, "I've got it! When I first arrived here the roof was being replaced. There was a bracket on top of the bell tower that no one could explain. The roofers wanted to remove it, but I insisted they leave it alone. I had a feeling at the time that it was important. Collect the silver arrows on the House of Agnes Dei. Don't you see?"

But Rik and Billy didn't see.

Manny continued, "A lens should be mounted on the church. On top of the bell tower. It all makes sense now."

Billy spoke first. "Where the hell are we gonna get a lighthouse lens?"

Before he could finish, Rik said calmly, "My great-great-uncle George Meade was the engineer for the Key West lighthouse. His last project is now a museum ten blocks away. That's where the angel's lantern is."

––––––––––––

Rik's mind was racing and he needed some time to think, so he left the group with a curt nod and headed down to the Chart Room at the Pier House. This tucked-away bar was rumored to be the first place Jimmy Buffett tested his brand of Gulf and Western songs on the Key West crowd.

The evening breeze off the Gulf clung to Rik's clothes as he stepped inside, his mind a carousel of questions. He took a seat at the far end of the bar, half-shielded by an old wooden column, and ordered a Cuba Libre. He yearned for a Coastie, but the Ball and Chain bar and that life were a distant memory.

It was quiet enough that the bartender's polite small talk faded into the background. Rik swirled his drink, letting the hum of overhead fans and the faint tinkling of ice in his glass fill the silence. His thoughts drifted back to the treasure, Carmen, the cartel, and the dangerous tightrope he'd been walking for weeks.

He barely registered the heavy footsteps behind him until a large iron grip clamped onto his shoulder.

"Hey, Rik. Rik Meade. How ya doin,' man? It's me—Reaper."

The voice was low, authoritative. Rik blinked himself back to reality and turned. A tall, broad-shouldered man with a square jaw and an air of military discipline stood there, grinning like he'd just found a long-lost friend.

Rik's instincts flared. He exhaled slowly and shook his head. "Sorry, pal. You're mistaken. I don't know you."

That line stopped Reaper short. His face twitched, halfway between annoyance and disbelief. "Fuck you, Coastie. Or should I say Puddle Pirate? I kicked your ass at Fort Benning three years ago."

Rik threw a quick glance around the bar, hoping to avoid a scene. "Look, buddy, I'm busy. Please just leave me alone."

But Reaper wasn't having it. In one swift motion, he jerked Rik up from the barstool and spun him around. The bartender froze midsentence, and a few patrons looked over with alarm. Reaper grabbed Rik's right hand and twisted it upward, exposing two surgery scars.

"Yeah, buddy," Reaper growled, "how'd I know you had these?"

Rik's gut tightened. He could sense the tension from three other figures at a nearby table—Reaper's SEAL buddies, clearly. All of them very dangerous and ready to back their friend in an instant.

"Alright," Rik muttered. "I give. Let's talk. But now it's not Rik Meade. I go by Rik Duval now."

"Really? Like the street? Man, you really need an operator name."

Reaper led the way to a small corner near the back of the room, out of immediate earshot. The three men at the table stood up casually.

"Rik, meet War Child, Thunder, and Tigger."

Rik nodded at each. Operator names were standard practice for SEALs or ex-special operators. Handles that kept their real identities hidden. He couldn't help noticing that Tigger, ironically nicknamed, was the scariest looking of the bunch.

War Child gave Rik a once-over, a ghost of a smile tugging at his lips. Thunder merely grunted a greeting. Tigger's expression remained unreadable; eyes dark with the kind of intensity that suggested trouble if you crossed him.

Trying to make a little conversation, Rik asked War Child how he'd gotten his operator name. Since Rik had some credibility with Reaper, he decided to answer.

"My therapists all say I'm only happy in a war zone. It brings out my childlike innocence. It involves

Jung's theory of the 'divine child.'" All Rik could think of was that *therapists* was plural.

Without waiting for the obligatory question, Thunder said, "Me? My name comes from the sound a neck makes when it snaps. I wanted Snap Crackle Pop, but a guy on another team had it. He's a little wacky if you ask me."

Tigger went next. "I like kitty cats," was all he said.

Rik inquired, "So you like A. A. Milne and his stories?"

"Never heard of him."

Reaper interrupted, "Okay, ladies. *The View* is over. What's going on, Rik?"

Rik rubbed his wrist, trying to slow his racing pulse. "Reaper… look, I didn't want to blow your cover, or mine. But I've got a situation on my hands."

"Situation?" Reaper echoed, crossing his sinewed arms. "Big enough that you won't even acknowledge an old friend? Tell me what's going on. You can speak in front of my team. Uncle Sam trusts with way more than he should." With that statement, his guys chuckled, and Rik could only imagine the wild stuff they'd seen.

Rik looked around, making sure nobody else was listening. Quietly, he explained his travails over the past several months: Carmen, the cartel, his new identity.

"Shit, man, we heard rumors in the community about a Coastie who shot some narco's head off. From a helo. That was you?"

"Yep."

Reaper let out a low whistle. "So, what the hell you are doin' here looking like you heard from a divorce lawyer?"

Rik then went on to tell them the rest of the story, just like an old-time Paul Harvey radio show.

"Damn, son, that's quite a tale. Pirates, Native Americans, treasure. Ya know we've moved billions through the Sandbox. Africa, South America—you name a shithole, we've been there. Bullion is our specialty."

"Really?"

"You have no idea," and with that his guys again chuckled.

Reaper clapped Rik on the shoulder, friendlier this time. "I owe this guy," he said to his team. "Best damn shooter I ever saw. And I mean, ever. He woulda beat me at Fort Benning. But for busting his hand."

"How can we help? Frankly, we're pretty bored taking our rebreather certification at the SFUWO up on Fleming Key."

"SFUWO?"

"Yeah, that's the Special Forces Underwater Operations center. Nice pool. Tough instructors."

Reaper continued, "Now we can't jump in guns

blazing, but we can sure help you plan. Hell, we could draw up a strategy tight enough to keep Carmen or the cartel at arm's length."

War Child nodded. "We've done riskier ops for less cause."

Thunder added, "Logistics, timing, infiltration—we can walk you through it all. But you'll be going in with just your guys."

Tigger finally spoke, voice a low growl. "If this cartel's half as connected as you say, you'll need every angle covered. We can at least make sure you won't walk in blind."

Rik exhaled, feeling like a weight had been lifted. He ran a hand through his hair, deciding whether it was worth dragging them deeper into his mess. But, seeing their readiness, he nodded.

"Alright," he said. "I'd appreciate any planning help you guys can give."

Reaper grinned. "That's what I like to hear, brother. Buy us a round, and we'll hash out the op."

Rik glanced back at his abandoned rum and Coke still on the bar. It felt surreal—coming in here to clear his head, only to bump into a ghost from his past. A ghost who was willing to help him find the treasure, but he couldn't deny the relief settling in his chest.

"Deal," he replied. "Let's get to it."

They all moved to a quiet table in the corner, conspiratorial looks on their faces. Rik and the SEALs hatched a plan that was so improbable that it just might work. But it all had to happen on the night of the full moon. Thankfully, that week was the peak of Fantasy Fest, the largest, craziest distraction he could imagine.

Outside, the neon lights of Key West blinked in the humid night, oblivious to the crazy and dangerous plot taking shape in the back of the Chart Room. The bartender was making margaritas, and you could … *smell those shrimp, they're beginnin' to boil.*

THIRTY-SIX

As dusk settled over Key West, the island transformed into a kaleidoscope of color and chaos. It was time for Fantasy Fest, the annual ten-day carnival that turned quaint streets into a sprawling playground of debauchery and imagination. The air buzzed with excitement, the scent of salty sea air, sizzling street food, and the sweet undertones of tropical flowers.

Crowds of revelers, clad in everything from glittering mermaid tails and flamboyant feathered boas to intricate superhero costumes and avant-garde masks, streamed through Duval Street. Music spilled from every corner—reggae beats, pulsating electronic rhythms, and live bands creating a symphony of sounds that kept feet moving and spirits high. Street performers captivated onlookers with fire-breathing acts, acrobatic displays, and mesmerizing dancers whose movements defied gravity.

Parades wound their way through the heart of the festivities; each float more extravagant than the last. One featured a fantastical underwater kingdom with shimmering scales and cascading fins, while another showcased a steampunk-inspired metropolis with gears turning and steam rising.

Vendors lined the sidewalks, offering an array of handmade crafts, elaborate masks, and "unique" accessories that glittered under the festival lights. The laughter of friends mingled with the cheers of impromptu dance-offs and the clinking of glasses from celebratory toasts. Everywhere, there was a sense of freedom and creativity, a temporary escape from the ordinary into a world where imagination reigned supreme.

At midnight, the energy would reach a fever pitch. Fireworks exploding overhead in bursts of color, illuminating the night sky and reflecting in the jubilant eyes of the crowd. For those few exhilarating days, Fantasy Fest was a time when the island itself came alive, embodying the spirit of unrestrained festivity that made Key West legendary.

In the middle of this hedonistic party, a piratical crew was planning a treasure raid. The plan would be conducted in three phases: 1) Remove the lens from the Lighthouse Museum, 2) Install the lens on the church roof and, hopefully, 3) Locate and remove the treasure.

The plan made perfect sense sitting in a bar with the most confident and able guys on the planet. But now with the phantasms of Key West floating and Rik's A team consisting of Billy and Father Manny, his confidence was waning.

The process started at noon on Halloween. Billy and Rik pulled up to the Lighthouse Museum in a boom crane truck from the Treasure Roofing Company, whose motto was ironically "Your Roof Is Our Treasure." With a pirate's gleam in his eye, Billy began positioning the crane.

As he was maneuvering the crane, Rik asked, "You sure he won't be a problem? And no violence?"

He was referring to the plan to distract Gus, the day overseer of the museum. The museum would be empty that day and Billy was in charge of luring Gus off the property. Billy replied, "Trust me, I got this."

"Of course, you always know a guy!"

"Nope. I know a girl."

"Huh?"

And with that, a dominating vision came strutting down the sidewalk. It was none other than Dee Toxin. The click-clack of her stiletto-heeled knee-high boots preceded her like a sultry Latin rhythm. As she passed by Rik and Billy, she turned her head and sternly said, "Stop drooling and close your jaws, my pets. You're embarrassing yourselves."

To which they immediately replied, "Yes, ma'am."

Dee Toxin was a beauty. That's not true. Margot Robbie is a beauty. The words to describe Dee haven't been invented.

In a prior life, Ms. Toxin was a Dolphins cheerleader who'd left the team's employment with a cool five-million-dollar payday. No, it wasn't the result of a sexual harassment lawsuit. It was a reverse settlement.

You see, she was hurting too many players during nightly "UTA's." or Unofficial Team Activities. So, the wives and ownership got together and offered her a healthy buyout. One she simply couldn't refuse. Then she set up shop on Rum Key and the rest was history.

For this assignment, Dee knew how to dress for success. As mentioned before, she wore black leather knee-high boots with stiletto heels designed to leave a "lasting" impression; if you know what I mean. Her fishnet stockings creeped from under the boots and up past her short black leather skirt. Elbow-length gloves, riding crop and a choker with delicate, petite spikes. Smoky eyes, black lipstick, and her raven hair pulled into a very tight, high ponytail. The ponytail was gathered tightly at the crown of her head, ensuring that every inch of her face remained sharply defined, emphasizing her commanding presence.

Her looks demanded attention, especially since she wasn't wearing a top but just accentuating body paint. After all, this was Fantasy Fest and women of all shapes and sizes wore just body paint. Some definitely should not. Dee should. It was easy to see through the paint that her breasts were exquisite. Elegantly shaped, contributing to her imposing yet captivating silhouette. Fantastic and natural.

She liked Billy and his 'attitude' and was therefore willing to help the cause. She would extract her payment soon.

She sashayed into the museum and was met immediately by Gus, who almost had a heart attack. "Sir," she implored, "I am a damsel in distress. I need your help."

Gus managed to stutter, "S-s-sure, what do you need, miss?"

"Well, me and the girls are having a contest around the corner and our judge backed out at the last minute. We need a man with good vision and soft hands urgently. Can you help us?"

"What do I have to judge?"

"Breasts, good sir. Nice young perfect breasts. The Fifth Annual Perfect Breast contest is about to start. Do you think you could do that for me?" With that, Dee leaned forward and grabbed Gus by the ears. "For example, if you had to judge mine, how would you rate them in terms of size and firmness?"

Shaking, he said, "Uh … er … uh … Perfect I guess?"

"Good answer. So, you're *up* for the task?"

"Yes ma'am!"

"Well, I like your go-get-'em attitude, sailor!" With that, Dee grabbed Gus's anxious hand and walked him around the corner where he would be occupied for a tit… I mean, bit.

With Gus gone, Rik ran to the top of the lighthouse tower and began disconnecting the brass clamps holding the overhead cupola onto the glass walls of the lightroom. Billy—who had watched a total of three YouTube videos and was convinced he was an expert crane operator—began swinging the crane boom around. In his confident mind, it was like pulling the lid off the top of a can of Pringles.

This process went surprisingly well. Off came the cupola and then the lens was lifted carefully up and out. As it was moving slowly skyward, Rik took the opportunity to glance under the large crystal array. Yep, there it was. The engraved signature of *Mssr. Henri Lepaute*. Seeing his signature sent a shiver through his spine. But it was way too early to celebrate.

Rik did have the courtesy to leave a note for the museum staff telling them where they could find their lens the next day. And a set of keys to the crane.

THIRTY-SEVEN

Phase one was complete. The truck-mounted crane crawled through the drunk and depraved crowds of Fantasy Fest, which, unlike the truck, were shifting into overdrive. Lusty pirates, sultry wenches, angels, devils, even satyrs and unicorns filled the streets. Don't even ask about the horn on the unicorn costumes.

Rik and Billy had one goal: set the lens in place by dusk. They didn't want to miss a minute of moonlight. Fighting their way slowly through the revelers and impromptu parades, they finally reached the church.

Billy maneuvered the massive Fresnel lens into position with surprising skill and set it deftly atop the church's bell tower.

The trio, climbed up to the top of the bell tower, taking up positions with a perfect line of sight to watch the anticipated beam. Now, all they had to do was wait. They chatted nervously for a bit and then Father Manny became clearly agitated.

The view from the church tower gave them a clear view of the Fantasy Fest activities on Duval Street.

"Pagans!" Father Manny suddenly exclaimed. "Hedonists! Heretics all! One day you sinners will feel God's wrath!" Rik and Billy were somewhat stunned by his outburst.

Billy said, "Relax, Padre, or else you'll be talking in tongues soon. Those are good people just blowing off steam."

"Of course, you're right, Billy. I just wish they'd stop by the church after their bout with immorality."

They all looked up, just then, to see the sun dip down in the west and the moon begin to rise in the east.

As nightfall approached, the lens came to life. At first, shards of moonlight scattered in every direction. Hour after hour, the beam intensified, sharpening as it moved across central Key West. Just like the poem said, *it danced across streets and alleys.*

Then, around midnight, it locked onto a single spot. The Key West Cemetery. Through his binoculars, Father Manny muttered, "It's lingering on the USS *Maine* Memorial."

Rik and Billy exchanged looks. They didn't hesitate. Three blocks. That's all that separated them from the cemetery. They ran, carrying shovels, crowbars, and whatever other tools they thought might help.

Father Manny, huffing, puffing, and tripping over his cassock, tried to give them a history lesson between gasps for breath. "This makes sense," he wheezed.

"The USS *Maine* exploded in Havana harbor in 1898. Hundreds died; God rest their souls. The injured were brought here to Key West. Those that didn't make it … were buried here. And this memorial was built for them."

Then he added, almost to himself, "I should've thought of this before. My predecessors were brilliant."

They reached the cemetery, and Rik immediately noticed a typical Key West tombstone. It said, "I Told You I Was Sick." He chuckled inwardly but didn't have time to share.

They proceeded to the center of the cemetery, where the moonbeam still bathed the USS *Maine* Memorial in ethereal light. The scene was almost beautiful. And eerie. Billy squinted. "Now what?"

Rik thought fast. "Check the names. Read them out loud." They all started searching.

Smith. Hawkins. Roberts. Forrester. Nothing.

Harkins. Robinson. Larimore. Schwartz. Still nothing.

Until…

Billy said. "Wait. Here's one. Kind of unusual."

Espectro Orquidea

Warrant Officer

Born: August 5, 1873

Died: February 15, 1898

Father Manny read it twice. "What an odd name.

'Espector.' Sounds like 'Spector'—that's Spanish for ghost. And 'Orquidea' means orchid. His name literally means ghost orchid."

Billy and Rik froze.

Father Manny sensed something. "What? What is it?"

Rik swallowed hard. "Father Manny… do you know what a ghost orchid is?"

The priest shrugged. "Never been much into plants. Just tending to my own garden of godless heathens and altar vultures tests my eternal soul."

Billy and Rik were again surprised by the venom in his voice, but Rik continued, "It's a rare, mysterious flower. Grows deep in the Everglades. Kind of looks like a ghost." Rik's voice dropped. "And it was the imprint on all of Caesar's gold. His maker's mark."

Feeling the discovery, all three of them whispered in unison, "Holy shit."

Father Manny quickly crossed himself. Rik and Billy—despite having zero religious affiliations—did the same.

Billy moved first. He jammed a crowbar under the warrant officer's sarcophagus lid. Like many waterborne cemeteries, Key West's dead were often buried above ground in stone crypts. But this was different. Using a flashlight, they could see a deep shaft descending underground.

Then—movement!

A slithering, shifting wave of multicolored snakes poured out. Dozens. Their skin covered in bright red, yellow, and black bands. Billy and Rik didn't panic, though. They'd spent too much time in the Everglades. But their brains raced. These could be harmless. Or highly venomous.

They both said out loud, "Red touches yellow, kill a fellow. Red touches black, friend of Jack." Their eyes locked onto the pattern. *Kill a fellow*. Shit. Coral snakes. The *deadly* kind.

"Father Manny, step back," Billy warned. "Those are coral snakes."

But Manny wasn't listening.

Instead, he was shaking and looked like he'd seen the devil. He reached down and grabbed two handfuls of snakes, held them high over his head, and shouted at the moon high overhead.

"Shala-randa kosi-lamah. Torrebah sanda-liah koreshita manah solekiah! Sharakai no'thoma! Sola'kesh!"

His voice rose and fell, as if channeling something ancient. And pretty damn scary!

Billy and Rik stared, horrified. Each thinking the moon really can make a man crazy.

Billy blinked. "What the fuck?"

Rik's jaw tightened and said, "Whiskey tango foxtrot."

Father Manny dropped the snakes and turned to

them. His face had changed. "Thank you, my heathen friends." His voice was different now—calm, measured, fanatical.

"Thanks to you, I can continue the good work of Father Toreador and the Maliviri. We have waited over a hundred years for this treasure. A treasure that will bring glory to God… and eliminate the remaining pagans who defile this earth."

Billy took a slow step back. "Eliminate?"

Father Manny smiled. "Yes. Like those filthy Indians in the Amazon. But it takes money to eradicate—I mean, *educate* them."

Father Manny pulled a revolver from his cassock. Rik recognized it as an old Astra model used in the Spanish Civil War. But it would blast a hole just like a new gun. "And now, my friends, you will complete the final part of the plan." He leveled the gun at their chests. "Your journey ends here."

Billy closed his eyes, said quietly to Rik, "It's been an honor, my friend," and prepared himself for the impact of a bullet.

"Drop your weapon, you psychopath!" This command came from out of the shadows.

Father Manny whirled around and aimed his pistol toward the voice. The last thing he saw was four green laser beams. Two on his heart. Two on his head.

Pfft-pfft-pfft-pfft.

The suppressed shots hit center mass, followed by

four wet cracks as Father Manny's skull received the rest of a double-tapped sacrament.

The priest plunged headfirst, or what was left of it, down into the crypt. A quick but fitting funeral.

Four men emerged from under a nearby oak tree. Walking confidently. They had the air of those who erase evil…like me and you tying our shoelaces. They were a special breed. Born and bred to be sheep herders who watch over their flock. Willing to die for the overall good.

Like the infamous spirit Charon, they escorted people across the river Styx into the underworld. Into Hades. Into hell. Where evil belongs. There would be no coin in Father Manny's mouth. He was destined to hell for an eternity.

If anyone saw this play out, they would wonder if this was a reenactment, with Fantasy Fest revelers dressed as Navy SEALs. But no. It was War Child, Thunder, Tigger, and the aptly named Reaper.

Reaper spoke first. "Man, what an asshole."

Billy blinked. "Who the hell are you guys?"

Rik quickly said, "These are the *guys* I told you about, Billy," adding sarcastically, "You know, the ones *who couldn't participate.*"

"We're here in a strictly observatory capacity. Now let's see what's in that hole and get it the hell out of here."

War Child fixed a rope and rappelled down into

the crypt. His boots hit the bottom with a dull thud, flashlight cutting through the darkness. He took no notice of the priest or his pooling blood. This wasn't the first body he'd stepped over.

"What's down there?" Rik yelled excitedly.

"Nothing," was the depressing reply.

The men up top slumped.

"Nothing but several hundred small casks filled with gold. Little ingots with a funny flower stamped on them."

Billy let out a low whistle. "Well, let's get this shit out of here."

For the next two hours, they worked in controlled chaos. The SEALs operated with military efficiency, hoisting box after box of solid gold up from the pit and loading it into a deuce-and-a-half truck they "appropriated" earlier.

As they worked, the chatter turned to war stories. "This reminds me when we hauled Saddam's bullion through Fallujah." Thunder grinned, securing another cask. "That was easy."

"What about humping Assad's secret stash out of Syria?" Tigger muttered, sweat dripping off his brow.

Then Reaper spoke up. "Nah, my favorite was taking all of El Cojón's gold. I'll bet that one-balled prick was hopping mad when he found out it was missing."

Rik froze mid-lift. "Say what?"

Reaper shrugged. "Yeah, sometimes we're more like bank robbers and armored car couriers than warriors."

Rik's brain went into overdrive. "No, no, no—back up. What did you say about El Cojón?"

Reaper gave him a curious look. "Yep, we stole his 401(k). We took all his damn gold. It was stashed in an abandoned mine in the Sierra Madre del Sur. We went in one night with three stealth Blackhawks and a Chinook and left two hours later with four hundred million dollars in gold bullion. I heard through the grapevine that Uncle Sam split the haul fifty-fifty with Tío Sam."

Rik's stomach twisted. *Holy shit.* He had assumed, back in the bar, that Reaper knew he'd killed the Painter. El Cojón's only son. And also Carmen's husband.

"Reaper," he said. "The guy I shot was El Cojón's son."

"No shit? I assumed you took out a Sinaloa. Or Michoacán. Not a Tabasco cartel dude."

Reaper and his guys had unknowingly thrown gasoline on his personal firestorm. No wonder he needed gold.

After that bit of crazy news, the entire group worked in silence. Soon the last cask came out, the sarcophagus lid was slid back in place, and they disappeared into the Halloween night… like the ghosts they were.

———————

Rik and Billy were in the front of the truck, driving, while their heavily armed SEAL friends were literally sitting on a pile of gold. The poor truck's suspension groaned like a couch potato on gym day, but they'd make it.

"So, now what's the plan?" Billy asked Rik, who was driving.

"I'm gonna take South Roosevelt by the airport. That'll avoid a lot of traffic."

"And then?"

"Head over to Stock Island."

Rik and Billy had kept different parts of the plan secret for operational security. But now, Billy couldn't stand not knowing.

"Rik," he said, exasperated by the late hour, possible dehydration, and because he'd just witnessed a man in a cassock turn into pink Swiss cheese, "How the hell are we getting the gold to Fort Jefferson?"

"Relax, *I know a guy.*"

"Get outta here. You don't know anybody. Wait, you know Lieutenant Wright. Is your girlfriend or her boss, that Dumbledore guy, gonna swoop in with the Coast Guard and save the day?"

Rik replied indignantly, "First off, Billy, she's not

my girlfriend, and her commanding officer is Captain Eisendorf, not Dumbledore. And don't knock the Coasties. They could save the day."

He continued, "When are you and Miss Toxin getting married? I'm sure the tribe will love her. I can't wait to see the dress. Honeymoon at a good S&M club?"

"Leave Dee out of this. We have a special relationship!"

"No… the Clintons have a *special* relationship. I don't know what you have. But I bet you have a special relationship with the urgent care on Rum Key. Met your deductible yet?"

"Enough! What's the plan?"

"We're almost there."

The deuce-and-a-half bumped along the dirt washboard road into Stock Island. Rik could only imagine the swearing going on in the back.

Stock Island, unlike its drunken neighbor to the west, was more businesslike in a Keys kind of way. It was home to many commercial fishing ventures and all manner of nonrecreational boats. At this time of night—or morning, as it turned out—it was also less subject to curious eyes.

Rik pulled over near a large banyan tree, and a fellow came over to the truck. The stranger said, "You made it. Your tires look like they're gonna pop, but you really made it."

"Hey, Dale, glad you made it too. Yep, piece of cake. Where is she?"

"Just past that coastal freighter over there."

Rik kept the heavily laden truck in first gear while they rumbled up to … none other than the *Lil' Annie*—the beat-up nondescript USCG buoy tender that was going to get the gold to Fort Jefferson and the Phat Man.

Billy exclaimed, "Shit, you really do know someone!"

Rik jumped out and said, "Hey, Dale, how's the baby? How's Brenda?"

"All good, thanks."

Quick introductions were made, and Dale couldn't help but notice the blood on Billy and Rik's clothing. "Relax, we just ran into a vampire on Duval Street. It's fake blood."

"Uh-huh, sure, right?"

"Hey, let's get a move on, okay? Some characters are sniffing around."

Dawn was starting to break, and they busted their asses to load up the *Lil' Annie*. With the gold loaded, it was time for quick goodbyes.

Still sweating, Reaper approached Rik and said, "Hey, man. I'm not good at apologizing. I know I was a major dick at Fort Benning. That dude was gonna clock me from behind and you saved me from a major concussion. So, this is my apology. You're a good dude and a hell of a shot. The SEALs could use you." Reaper extended his hand. Rik paused before he shook it. Not because he doubted the sincerity. He was truly taken aback by the gesture. They shook, and in an instant, an old wound healed, then disappeared.

Reaper continued, "So, we're square?"

"We're square. Very square."

Reaper continued, "Hey, me and the team held a meeting in the back of the deuce-and-a-half while you were trying to break our kidneys. You've been through a lot and you're clearly doing the right thing."

"And?"

"We picked your *operator* name."

"I can't wait."

"You're Guardian now."

Rik thought it over. Operator names aren't given out lightly. Especially by a team like Reaper's. From early childhood through joining the Coast Guard he knew being a guardian was his calling. Just like first time he'd met Lieutenant Wright he thought, *that'll work.*

"Thanks man. I won't take it lightly. I'm glad to have it."

Billy muttered under his breath, just like a kid seeing his best friend get a new bike, "I want a *cool* name."

Rik next said, "You guys need a lift?"

"Nah, thought we'd relax a little and swim home.

Gonna take Cow Key Channel to our post on Fleming Key."

Rik was startled. He knew these guys were tough, but that was crazy. "That's a five-mile swim from here!"

"Damn, you're right. Too short. We'll take the long way."

With that, Reaper and his team said, "*Vaya con Dios*," slid silently into the dark water like the seabound ghosts that they were and headed to their next adventure.

"*Go with God*," Rik said to himself.

Then Billy said, "Man, those guys are the real deal. Glad they're on our side."

It would take Dale and the *Lil' Annie* some time to make the trip to Fort Jefferson, so Rik and Billy needed to rest up and then arrange transportation. It was time to bring in their personal pirate air force. Barefoot Joe and Betty the Beaver.

THIRTY-EIGHT

Rik and Billy climbed into Joe's Beaver at Key West International Airport and noticed two pilots in the cockpit. The first was Barefoot Joe, as expected. The second was his new copilot, Jimmy Legs. They hoped to see their four-legged buddy, but looking like this was a complete surprise.

He stood proudly on the right seat, wearing an old-time leather flying helmet. It was fur-lined and had built-in goggles. In addition, he had a custom-made headset for noise protection and so he could hear the air traffic control chatter. He was turning into quite the aviation buff. To top off the ensemble, Jimmy Legs had a white silk scarf wrapped around his neck, Baron von Richthofen style.

Seeing his old friends in the back, Jimmy Legs seemed to signal to Joe, "Our VIP passengers are buckled up. Let's get this bird in the air!"

Barefoot Joe landed Betty downwind from Fort Jefferson, hoping to minimize the noise of landing. Rik and Billy waded, then walked a half mile before arriving at the entrance to the fort. Rik's wet shoes reminded him of the wet foot–dry foot policy the Coast Guard was previously in charge of enforcing.

The moon was still bright and created eerie shadows around the foreboding brick monolith. This was not an ideal condition for stealth, but they had no choice. This was the only chance they had left to save the Toucano's and their land.

To get to this point had not been easy, to say the least. Their quixotic quest was nearing the finish line, and the Brazilian land sale was just two days away. In order for the Toucano's to maintain their way of life, nothing could go wrong now.

The only sounds they heard were the ocean waves and the wind rustling the few trees on this barren island. The fort itself was silent, like an abandoned abbey, silhouetted against the night sky.

Fort Jefferson was an unusual place for their rendezvous, yet perfect. Built in the 1800s, it had tremendous naval military significance back then. Now, sitting on top of the remote Dry Tortugas, seventy-five miles west of Key West; its remoteness made it the ideal spot to transfer the gold to the Phat Man's shrimp boat. The fort's deep-water harbor had been one of the reasons for its construction, and now that it was closed for repairs, it made an ideal, out-of-the-way meeting point.

They crossed the small footbridge over the

saltwater moat and were now inside the fort. The Phat Man could be anywhere, and Rik and Billy found themselves navigating this desolate, haunted place, their nerves fraying with every step.

But something was off. Very off. Rik had been trying to reach the Phat Man on his satellite phone for hours, but there had been no answer. Worse, there was no sign of him, his crew, or his shrimp boat. Rik and Billy exchanged glances, both shrugging, unsure of what to do next.

They searched the barracks, the galley, even the dungeon…nothing. Just as they were going to give up, a familiar, sinister voice came out of the darkness.

"*Hola, mi amor.*" It was Carmen, emerging from the shadows, carrying, with some difficulty, what appeared to be one of those black hooded bags Rik never wanted to see again.

By now, Rik should have been ready for anything, but her sudden appearance caught him off guard. He said, "How did you know we were here? How did you get here?"

"That's a lot of questions, big boy, for someone who has five machine guns pointed at him." At this point, her goons appeared from the shadows carrying Heckler & Koch submachine guns, a particularly vicious assault weapon that could turn Rik and Billy into mist with the pull of a trigger.

"But I'll humor you," she said. "I took back *La*

Exquisita. You named her *Bum Runner*? Really? So crass, my dear. We've been behind the lighthouse on Loggerhead Key, waiting for you and your Shrek-sized friend to arrive."

Rik clenched his jaw as Carmen continued. "How did I know you'd be here? The Phat Man was very talkative. Oh, by the way, he won't be meeting you tonight. Or any night, for that matter."

With that, she grunted, undid the black hooded bag, and with a menacing grin reversed it, letting the Phat Man's severed head roll out and hit the dirt with a nauseating thud. His lifeless eyes were still open, frozen in eternal confusion.

Rik felt something snap inside him. Too many people had suffered—now more blood spilled for the damned gold. He exploded, "You didn't have to do that! You're insane!"

Carmen just smirked. "Oh, but I did. He was going to steal the gold, my naive darling. Someone has to protect you from people like him... and me. Now tell me…where is the gold, *chéri*?" she asked sweetly with an undercurrent of venom.

Rik said nothing and Billy clenched his jaw. Both were furious and sick and tired of this woman. They both imagined a horrible demise for her but snapped back to reality.

Carmen knew that these two would not talk readily, so she told one of her goons to throw them in

Dr. Mudd's cell so she could prepare for their interrogation. Did I forget to mention that Fort Jefferson was home to the infamous Dr. Mudd—the man who assisted John Wilkes Booth after he assassinated President Lincoln? As I told you, this fort had a long, storied past and many park rangers believe the ghosts of deceased soldiers and prisoners haunted the passageways and bulwarks at night.

They hit the far side of the damp cell hard. It was now two in the morning and both were incredibly tired, hungry, and thirsty. They also knew that their next meeting was going to be very unpleasant, adding more stress to an already traumatic situation.

Billy said, "Man, I'm hungry. I could eat the ass end of a rhino. You know what I could go for?"

Rik, ever stoic, ignored his friend.

Billy continued, "A big steaming dish of creamed possum with sweet potatoes garnished with hot coon-fat gravy. My old man used to make that for Sunday dinner. Man, that's livin'! I'd kill for some right now."

"Are you fucking kidding me? That sounds disgusting. We're about to die and you're thinking about food that sounds like roadkill?"

"Ooh, and some fried possum on the half shell!"

"What the hell is that?"

"Armadillo, baby. The *other* gray meat."

Billy, ever the entertainer, was good at gauging a room. And this room needed a mood change, so he asked, "Are you ready for a good ghost story, Rik?"

Rik was in no mood and was trying to think through their options, which appeared bleak. Billy pressed on, saying a good ghost story would be a real stress reliever and fun.

"Okay, fine, tell me your silly story."

Billy began, "They called him the Tapping Doc, a prisoner here at Fort Jefferson, but no one knew his real name. Legend has it that he'd been a surgeon with the Union Army, accused of sabotage after a series of medical supplies went missing. He'd been thrown into one of the fort's darkest cells, stripped of his dignity, and left with nothing but chains and damp stone walls. Some say he was innocent, that he'd simply been a scapegoat for someone else's theft—but the men who guarded him didn't care. To them, he was just a traitor.

"Days turned to weeks, and in the relentless heat, he grew feverish. With no doctor willing to treat him, his condition worsened, and his fever rose to dangerous levels. He began to hallucinate, murmuring about surgical instruments, phantom patients, and field hospitals. And then, one night, the tapping began.

"It started as a faint sound, barely noticeable over the rustling palms and distant waves, but as his fever climbed, the tapping grew louder. Guards on night duty reported that the tapping followed a specific rhythm, as if he were mimicking the slow, fading heartbeat of a patient on the operating table.

"One night, when his fever peaked, the tapping suddenly stopped. When the guards opened the door to his cell the next morning, he was gone. His fever-burned body had vanished, leaving only a set of iron shackles, rusted and still, lying on the floor.

"To this day, visitors hear a strange, rhythmic tapping from within the abandoned cell. Some say it's a warning to those who neglect the sick; others believe it's the surgeon's desperate attempt to call for help from another dimension, tapping out a ghostly heartbeat that no one can answer.

"And if you ever find yourself alone in that cell, pay close attention. You might hear the slow, relentless tap-tap-tap, like a surgeon checking for a pulse on a fading patient. But by then, it's too late—the fever has taken hold, and you're just another ghostly echo in the haunted halls of Fort Jefferson."

Billy let the last sentence hang in the air.

Then they heard tapping. Tap. Tap. Tap. Tap. Like a heartbeat.

Rik scowled at Billy and said, "Very funny, Billy. We're both going to be tortured and killed soon and you're playing silly games. Quit tapping, will you?"

Billy turned to Rik's shadowed face and slowly said, "That wasn't me, Rik. I swear. Look, my hands are in the air."

Tap. Tap. There it was again. Their gaze turned to the wall from which the sound was emanating.

On the far wall, one of the bricks slowly began to move. Rik practically jumped into Billy's arms and Billy fell backwards.

THIRTY-NINE

The brick moved a bit more, then fell onto the floor, sending a small plume of dust into the stagnant air. Two beady eyes peered eerily out of the opening. There was a moment of silence before they heard a scratchy voice say, "You boys need some help?"

Rik answered first, "Who the hell are you? And yes!"

With that, a small doorway creaked open, revealing a haggard and ancient man and a narrow secret chamber behind him. With a vise-grip handshake that belied his age, he introduced himself. "I'm Silas P. Fletcher, Senior Ranger Emeritus of the National Park Service. But everyone calls me Whiskers." His long scraggly beard resembled Spanish moss hanging from an old oak tree. The ranger looked like he was from another century and would have fit in well with the prior occupants of Fort Jefferson.

Whiskers was tall and lanky and wore a threadbare ranger uniform. His pants were held up by an old leather belt that seemed to wrap around him twice before being buckled. Rik got the feeling his superiors didn't visit the fort much. He was right. Fort Jefferson was Whiskers' home. Billy and Rik were now his guests, and Carmen and her narco thugs were intruders. These invaders didn't know that Florida was a stand-your-ground state and deadly force was on the legal menu.

Rik said with some urgency, "Whiskers, I don't have a lot of time to explain, but these people are going to steal a shit ton of gold from its rightful owners way down south. As in South America. I thought I saw a radio tower when we came ashore. Can we get a message out?"

"Yes, but it's guarded by one of those Spanish fellers with a machine gun."

"Don't worry, I'll take care of him."

"Then follow me. These passages were created to move gunpowder safely throughout the fort, but I'm the only one who knows about 'em. Well, me and Ol' Sam."

Rik quickly followed Whiskers and then Billy, who tried to squeeze through the small doorway. But Billy announced, "Houston, we have a problem." His frame and girth would not fit through the opening. He backed out and continued his discussion from the cell.

"You guys are gonna have to go on without me. There's no way I can get my big ass through that tiny porthole!"

"Come on, Billy. One more time. Stick your hands out and we'll pull you through!"

"No way, man. I've been to this movie before. I like my arms and ribs just where they are. Seriously, get a move on. Get the cavalry. I'll hold them off as long as I can." Both Whiskers and Rik knew he was right. They said their farewells and pushed the mysterious door back in place as well as replacing the spyhole brick.

Whiskers and Rik crawled their way through a maze of ancient, tiny passages. While doing so, Rik asked, "Whiskers, what the hell are you doing here?"

Whiskers replied, "Well, the big brass were planning a big renovation project for some time. But I knew something wasn't right. There were some characters posing as construction guys. Alarm bells went off in this ol' brain of mine. With the timing of the repairs and the shutting down of my old fort, my bones told me something wasn't right.

"The on-site staff were told to take one of the boats to Key West for temporary reassignment. But I could never leave this place. This place is my home. I'll be buried here. I even have a nice place picked out next to Ol' Sam Smith under the big buttonwood tree."

This was the second time he'd mentioned Ol' Sam. But the ever-curious Rik had no time now to follow up.

Whiskers continued, "So, I stayed behind when

the last boat left to see what all the shenanigans were about. I watched that mean Spanish lady yell at you and I figured you fellas could use some help. Man, she's a scary bee-atch! Did you see that feller's head roll around on the ground?"

Rik grinned inward. Whiskers' take was right on.

Whiskers vectored them around the fort so that he arrived silently on one side of the radio room guard and Rik was situated around the corner, armed with the only weapon he could find—a rusty old shovel. It would do the trick.

At the appropriate time, Whiskers popped up by the guard and said, "Hey, sailor, got a light?"

Rik wanted to laugh out loud but instead whacked the distracted guard over the head and sent him into La-La Land. Rik wondered if he had killed him, but at this point, he could care less.

They entered the radio room and Rik found the VHF. He turned it on, dialed in channel 16 and immediately said, "Mayday. Mayday. Mayday. We have an emergency at Fort Jefferson. Bogeys on site. Repeat, bogeys on site. We need a QRF ASAP. Repeat. Need QRF at Fort Jefferson." Just then they heard footsteps coming and they couldn't stick around. Key West was seventy-five miles away and he hoped someone heard him.

Rik and Whiskers resumed crawling through the secret passageways and Whiskers asked, "What the hell is a QRF, son?"

Rik replied, "QRF stands for Quick Reaction Force. It's a unit designed to respond rapidly to emergency situations. If there was a military branch out there listening, they would know we would need help immediately. Mobile help. Heavily armed help." He continued, "Key West is the home of the Army Special Forces Swim training school. There could be a Delta team in the area. There's also a Coast Guard base in Key West and I'm sure there's always some special ops guys hanging around Naval Air Station Key West on Boca Chica. I just hope somebody heard our message. And the cavalry comes. Whiskers, I have another idea. Can you take me unseen to the flagpole on the west parapet?"

"Is a frog's butt watertight? Hell yeah, I'll get ya there."

Again, they wound their way through the passages to the top of the fort. As they were crawling, Rik thought he could make out the letters of a tattoo on Whiskers' arm. It was dark, but Rik's marksman eyes missed little. It looked like the word *rat*.

"Hey, Whiskers, I'm not judging, but why do you have the word *rat* tattooed on your arm?"

"Ya noticed, did ya? Well, it wasn't the highest-quality job. All I had was ten bucks on Duval Street in the sixties, and I was full of piss and vinegar. I just joined the Coast Gua—"

"What! You're a Coastie?"

"Damn straight. Four years on the cutter *Androscoggin*. Based in Key West."

"But *rat*?"

"It faded over the years, but I got *Semper* on my right arm and *Paratus* on my right. It wasn't always rat. Ha ha ha."

Rik knew he could trust Whiskers. "I'm a Coastie too. Retired. I used to be on the aviation side of things."

"Well, I'll be a whale's toenail. Two Coasties crawling through this ol' fort."

"Why did you leave? You already had the tattoo!"

"Well, the *Androscoggin* would stop here regularly. We'd stretch our legs, and I fell in love with the place. After my four years, I showed up, asked for a job, and never left. This is my home. They'll have to take me outta here in a box. Even then I'd rather be buried here."

"Well, I'll be damned. Once a Coastie, always a Coastie. Let's get rid of these hostiles so none of us have to worry about a box."

"Copy that, Sonny!"

They soon stepped out near the flagpole. Rik, stiff from too much crouching and creeping, straightened his back and moved to the halyard. He unfastened the American flag, lowered it carefully, then turned it upside down and sent it back up the pole—the universal distress signal.

As the flag rose against the sky, a line from the

Coast Guard's official song echoed in his head:

The flag is carried by our ships,
In times of war and peace.
And never have we struck it yet...

The Coast Guard had never surrendered—not once. Not in war, not in peace. Not on any sea.

In his mind, he heard the words as clear as a gunshot: *We hoist them higher... and fire back harder!* He looked up at the inverted flag snapping in the breeze. Anyone who saw it would know—there was danger at the fort. Real danger. And they needed help. Now.

He prayed that was the case and even thought he heard a small plane to the north. But that was probably his ears playing games with his tired brain.

Unknown to Rik, Billy had been dragged roughly from his cell and was now standing stiffly in the middle of the parade grounds...with a pistol to his head.

Carmen had a megaphone and said, "Rik, come on down, We see your little flag trick. Come down here or Yeti Billy gets a bullet in that Cro-Magnon skull of his." With that she fired a bullet in the air for emphasis.

Billy yelled out, "Get the cavalry, I'm—"

Before he could finish, a thug delivered a blow to his solar plexus that would have downed a normal-sized man.

Rik couldn't take a chance with Billy's life. Carmen had turned full-blown psychopath. He had to keep stalling and hope someone heard his call.

While he was thinking, Whiskers said, "You go there and save your extremely large friend. I've got an idea that will stall them for a bit."

When he arrived, arms up, Carmen yelled, "Where's the gold! Playtime is over. Tell me or the Hulk here is going to bleed out before your eyes." With that she pulled out a fillet knife and pressed it against Billy's jugular vein.

While Carmen was threatening Billy, ol' Whiskers was discreetly wheeling an ancient swivel gun around. It was used on Fourth of July for ceremonial purposes and not considered a weapon. But Whiskers … well, he was pissed and had other ideas.

He pushed the small cannon into position and filled it with gunpowder, then all the egg rock he could find, and finally a wad of old rags. Now this doesn't sound so deadly, but not many people could survive being hit by rocks flying at them at one thousand feet per second. Whiskers was counting on this.

He only had enough gunpowder for one shot, so he was hoping to take out Carmen and a few goons all at once. But she stayed within arm's reach of his new friends. Then he saw his chance. Three guys wandered in his direction, so he carefully aimed the small cannon.

Right before Whiskers pulled the lanyard, he stood up and yelled, "Get the hell outta my house, you bastards!"

The three were startled to see the scarecrow-thin figure yelling at them but had no other subsequent thoughts. The cannon exploded and the rocks tore them to bits. They resembled the ragged sails of a ghost ship. But much bloodier.

Their remains slumped to the ground while Whiskers jumped up and down and yelped, "Take that, you sumbitches," then disappeared into one of his secret passages.

Rik stayed silent, and so did Billy, but Carmen was quick. She yelled, "Find that geezer and throw him off the top of the fort!" She was oddly silent for a few seconds. Rik could see the gears turning in her mind as she pieced it all together. "The gold's not here at the fort, is it?" she muttered. "You didn't have time to move it. Where the hell is it? Where's the gold?"

Then, suddenly, she understood. "It's on that beat-up construction boat by the old coal dock, isn't it? Chico! Rodrigo! Go check it out! *Vámanos!*"

Rik's heart raced. Her men would be back any minute with the news that the gold was on board the *Lil' Annie*. Once they knew, Billy and he would be useless to her.

Sure enough, her men returned, confirming the gold was on board. They also carried a beat-up canvas banner that had hidden the USCG emblem. Rik must have looked confused because Carmen gave him a wicked smile.

"Wondering how we're getting the gold off the island?" she sneered. Inwardly, he was. *God, I hate that woman.* She picked up a radio and said, "Hey, Babycakes. We have the gold. Come on in."

Who the hell is she talking to? Rik wondered. Then he heard the sound of an approaching helicopter. But this was no ordinary sound. Or helicopter.

Its arrival was preceded by the "wop-wop" unique to the Chinook. The sound was intensified as it echoed off the old brick walls. These birds are known for their incredible lifting capacity; twenty thousand pounds to be exact.

Now, they all could see it—a helicopter with not one but two rotors, coming in from the southeast. It was huge, the kind that could easily lift an elephant. Or a cache of gold. His mind raced. *Who the hell is piloting this bird?*

The large helicopter landed on the north side of the old parade ground in a cloud of dust. As the rotors wound down, the rear ramp descended slowly. Three figures emerged through the haze. Rik immediately recognized the gait of the first one, and his heart sank. It couldn't be him—a man he trusted with his life.

FORTY

It was…Tony. Tony was the mole!

Things began to fall into place for Rik. It all made sense now. Tony must have arranged the encounter with Carmen at the Ball and Chain. Tony had observed them from the helo when Billy and Rik had traveled to Porgy Key to talk to Gemini. Was he really on a nearby mission to the Featherbeds? He was in debt up to his eyeballs. He knew everything about their missions and operations. And Carmen had gotten to him. *I've been such a fool.* He loved Tony like a brother, but he wasn't going to get away with this.

Two other figures emerged from the din—a man and a girl. It was Erica, Tony's daughter! *What the hell is she doing here?* Rik asked himself, squinting to make out the man shoving her. Did he know him? *What is happening?*

Commander Eisendorf! Holy shit. The man who'd orchestrated everything regarding Rik's new "life." *Was he the scumbag behind everything? And Tony was in the wrong place at the wrong time?*

As the trio walked away from the helicopter, Rik struggled to wrap his head around it all. He had been so wrong about Eisendorf. The commander had a pistol in one hand and was gripping Erica by the neck with the other, holding her hostage.

Like a giddy schoolgirl, Carmen ran over to Eisendorf and greeted him with a sickening, tongue-twirling heavy kiss. Even her goons looked away in disapproval. Just how depraved was this woman?

Rik's mind was still racing. Eisendorf needed Tony to fly the gold away for him. And Carmen. This was why he'd arranged Tony's sudden training for tandem rotor helos.

Carmen turned to her men and barked, "Move the gold to the helicopter. Kill them," pointing at Rik and Billy.

Billy puffed in size and said to Rik, "It's been an honor, my friend."

Rik seethed in a low whisper, "This isn't over, Billy. Not by a long shot."

Eisendorf sauntered over to Rik. "Hiya, Chief Meade—I mean, Duval. Bet you didn't see that coming, huh? That Carmen! Man, she is one special lady. A real wildcat in bed, too. I can see how you could fall head over heels for a woman like that. I know I did—I was just several years ahead of you."

"You're a son of a bitch, Eisendorf. You're going to rot in hell, and I'm gonna put you there!"

"Riky, Riky. Relax, will ya? You got to know when to throw in the towel. Just like you let a little cold stop you at the sniper competition. Winners push through adversity. Like me and my hot tamale Carmen. While you're becoming fish food, I'll be sipping margaritas in my hacienda with my Carmencita. Yep, all is right with the world."

Rik wasn't done yet. He wasn't going to let this prick fluster him. He had to stall for time. "Carmen, there's a squadron of Coast Guard gunships on their way from Key West," he bluffed, his voice steady. "A lot of angry Coasties with .50-caliber machine guns. If you survive that hail of lead, honey, you're gonna look great in prison orange. It's the new fall color, ya know."

At the mention of helicopters from Key West, everyone turned to the east. Rik was just as stunned as anyone. Sure enough, there were airborne navigation lights headed their way. Rik didn't know what or who it was, but he prayed they were the cavalry.

It was a plane, not a helo. As it approached, Carmen's six lookouts on the upper level raised their guns but didn't fire. It was simply too strange a sight. Definitely not military, so they relaxed a bit. Rik knew this wasn't the cavalry. *Maybe Billy was right...it's been an honor, my friend.*

The large amphibious aircraft had enormous radial engines mounted on top of its wings. Rik had seen photos of these beasts from out west in California and Arizona. They were called Super Scoopers and fought forest fires. But it would be no help today.

As he was still gathering his last thoughts, the aircraft was directly over them—fifty feet off the deck. The plane's release doors opened and out plunged two thousand gallons of seawater. Nine tons of water moving at one hundred twenty miles per hour, stunned and knocked everyone to the ground.

They had been hit by a saltwater stun grenade, like the kind that SWAT teams throw into a room to incapacitate everybody. The effect was the same.

If that crazy pilot wanted to knock everyone senseless, it worked. Good guys and bad guys alike were dazed and sputtering, some retching saltwater and holding their ribs. Even Billy looked like he had been hit by an NFL linebacker.

All that remained standing were the six sentries, stationed on the upper level. They immediately fired on the departing Super Scooper, which took evasive maneuvers. Rik was in a daze, but he thought the mystery plane looked like a wobbly albatross as it evaded the gunfire.

Rik recovered quicker than most and grabbed Erica from Eisendorf. Billy stood up, dripping like Niagara waterfalls, and Rik handed Erica off to him. He knew Billy would protect her with his last breath.

A drenched Carmen looked at Eisendorf for

direction. As with most bullies, Eisendorf only felt confident and in control when he held the upper hand. And now the tide was turning. He ignored her glare and was thinking through an escape plan just in case.

The fort was eerily silent, and Rik's senses were on edge, listening for something he hoped to hear. A distant rifle shot. Then, *thump!* A dead sentry landed next to him. With a very large hole in his torso.

Another rifle shot. *Thump!* A second sentry landed, again with a similar hole.

Within seconds, all six sentries thumped and lay dead around the perimeter of the courtyard.

Rik, having just been stunned by a wall of water, was now equally stunned by this event. *Huh? How can that be?* Rik's well-tuned ear and shooter instincts knew the shots came from at least half a mile away. *Holy shit, HITRON is here. There are airborne snipers out there. But that's impossible. I don't hear any helos...*

His mind raced as six dark gray, almost invisible helos emerged over the fort's walls. They came from all points of the compass. Silent. One for each side of the fort. One per sentry.

They were the Coast Guard's new stealth models. The kind that Rik and Tony had tested in Andros. The kind that had taken out Bin Laden.

Thick ropes were dropped, and men began fast-roping down to the fort. Twenty-four heavily armed operators quickly converged onto the scene.

Two different teams, twelve each, encircled the parade grounds. One from the east. One from the west. They had the air of operators—guys you wanted on your side when you were outnumbered and your back was against the wall.

He could now tell the west group was a USCG Maritime Security Response Team. They were identified by their dark navy tactical uniforms and weapon of choice, the short-barreled Mk 18. They might rankle at the comparison, but they were often referred to as a nautical SWAT team. He didn't know anyone on this team but knew their reputation and trusted their abilities.

From the second team came a recognizable voice with a tinge of the islands in it. "Need a hand, mon?" It was Pinder and his Commando Squadron team, all carrying their unmistakable Uzis. Pinder extended his hand and then withdrew it. It was a bloody mess from fast roping. Rik started to say something, but Pinder grinned and said, "Sorry, no time for gloves, brother."

"You have no idea how glad we are to see you. I guess our training in Andros paid off. How the hell did you find out about us?"

Pinder pointed to a figure running towards them.

The runner's gait was more lithe and sinewy than the operators'. *Is that a woman?* Damn, it was Lieutenant Wright.

She ran right up to Rik and put a big fat kiss on him. And it was returned in kind. So much so that Billy started coughing. Loudly.

The two separated reluctantly and Rik finally said, "How the hell did you find us?"

"Thank your buddy Barefoot Joe. After dropping you off, he saw a boat behind Loggerhead Key and got suspicious. So, he circled the fort from a distance and saw the upside-down flag. He called me from the air. I swear I heard a dog barking like crazy. Anyhow, I called the cavalry. Lucky they were training in the Marquesas Keys. And you've been acting a little strange lately. I knew you were up to something."

Both special ops teams were expert operators and quickly disarmed Carmen's goons. Rik was starting to catch his breath and thought they were almost out of the woods.

Eisendorf approached Rik under guard. He implored Rik, "You win. You got us. But I can't live the rest of my life in a box. Do you know what they do to officers at Leavenworth? It's going to be a living hell. Please, Rik, let me take the Chinook. It's on fumes. Let me die with dignity. I'm begging."

Rik looked briefly at Tony, who offered, "It's true. We came in on fumes. He and his Queen of Cocaine intended on refueling here before heading to Mexico. That bird couldn't fly another couple of miles."

"Let me die a hero. I'll run out of fuel and crash

into the ocean. My family doesn't need to know about this. Carmen tricked me. Having an unlimited supply of Florida nose candy didn't help either. I made some bad decisions, I know. I'm begging. Please?"

Hearing his painful entreaty, Carmen spat on the ground and hissed, "Fucking gringo. You were lousy in bed, too."

Eisendorf looked deep in Rik's eyes and implored him silently.

"Ya know what? Eisendorf, you deserve to rot in a box."

"Well, I tried the easy way."

He whipped out a belt buckle knife, grabbed Tony, and put the blade to his neck. "I'm leaving in the Chinook and he's my pilot. *Comprende?*"

They entered the Chinook's rear cargo ramp, which had been lowered to receive the gold treasure. Now it was entered by a disgraced officer and Tony, who had made mistakes but didn't need to end up with this prick.

Tony did as he was told, and the helo took off. Once clear of the fort walls, the big helo turned south.

Multiple radios squawked. It was Eisendorf. "See ya, suckers. They love me in Havana. Oh, I had a few auxiliary fuel tanks installed. *Semper Paratus,* right?"

Rik grabbed a radio and said, "How dare you speak those words! I'm going to send you to hell." Without waiting for a reply, he turned to Pinder and they both sprinted to the south Bastion Tower. They flew up the ancient stairs two at a time. At the top, Pinder unslung his Remington 700 and handed it to Rik.

Pinder was very aware that Rik possessed world-class marksman skills, and they were much needed now! The Remington wasn't quite like Rik's Barrett, but it would have to do. Without a word, Pinder hunched over, indicating to use his shoulder as a stock to steady a shot. As Pinder put his fingers in his ears Rik went through his internal and external checklist. He quickly adjusted the scope for windage and elevation. Then he started to slow his breathing and heart rate.

But now he hesitated. He had doubts. His plan was to put a .300 Win Mag through one or both turbine engines, which would surely cause the big bird to crash. In a few more seconds, Eisenberg would be out of range. He couldn't let that SOB get away. He needed to rot in a box.

He made his decision and began to apply the required four pounds of pressure to the trigger, considerably less than his Barrett.

Before he finished pulling the trigger, the eggbeater turned to the left. Rik immediately knew what Tony was up to. He was exposing Eisendorf's head for a kill shot. Now there was a commotion in the copilot seat. Eisenberg also figured out was Tony was up to.

Rik's finger hovered over the trigger. There was Eisendorf's exposed head—he could take him out in a second. Many thoughts raced through his mind. He was a criminal responsible for the deaths of people. He needed to die, and Rik was in a perfect position to do it.

Slow is smooth. Smooth is fast Slowly, Rik squeezed the trigger…the port engine exploded. Rik was no murderer. A military tribunal judge and jury would put Eisendorf in his place. Not Rik.

Coast Guard personnel were trained to survive helicopter crashes, and they had some of the world's finest rescue teams just half a mile away. This was Rik's quick rationalization for his decision. The helicopter fell from the sky and slammed into the water. For a brief moment, the twin rotors churned the ocean into sea foam, then silence descended under the moonlight.

Without waiting for orders, one of the stealth helicopters, with a full crew, launched to rescue Tony and Eisenberg. Multiple radios then crackled to life, and Tony's voice came through, "Rik, pick up."

Rik hesitated; he wasn't sure he wanted to hear what Tony had to say. It was too soon.

"Rik, pick up," Tony urged, his voice tense. "I don't have much time."

Pinder handed Rik his MBITR radio. "Go ahead,

Tony, I'm here."

"Rik, this is for your ears only. Get everyone off the command net."

Rik gave the cutthroat motion, and the multitude of radios went dead.

"Okay, Tony, it's just you and me now."

"I can't believe you shot me out of the sky! I set you up for a perfect head shot on Eisendorf."

"I know," Rik replied, his voice heavy with guilt, "but I couldn't pull the trigger. I'm not a murderer. I already have one kill I've got to live with. I didn't want another. What's happening? Are you okay?"

"I'm unbuckled, maybe a broken arm."

"And Eisendorf?"

"He's alive... but not for long."

Rik could hear muffled noises in the background. "Why?" he implored. "Get out now. The rescue helo will be there in two minutes."

"He doesn't have two minutes," Tony said gravely. "Listen, Rik, I messed up. Eisendorf blackmailed me, knew about my debts, and the cartel cleared them. Then he threatened to ruin me and harm Erica. He said he'd sell her into slavery and the sex trade. He's a demented POS."

He continued, "I didn't know anyone would get hurt. They kept me in the dark. And all the while you were helping me and Erica with fishing trips and raising money with her mango stand. I feel like the biggest dirt bag on the planet. But I'm going to fix it. Now!"

"Don't do anything stupid. Think of Erica!"

Inside the Chinook, Tony turned to Eisendorf. "Damn you, you bastard, you're going to hell."

"Tony," Rik pleaded, "He'll get what he deserves. Now get out of there!"

"You're right, Rik. He'll get what he deserves. And he for damn sure will never utter the Coast Guard motto again. In this life or the next!"

Then the radio went dead.

Almost instantly, orange smoke began billowing from the cockpit, forming an eerie moonlit cloud over the water.

Down below in the parade ground, someone yelled, "We got a squirter!" Carmen was running towards the gate and moat, hoping to swim away. Lieutenant Wright was hot on her heels. She raced after her, dove through the air and tackled Carmen like a linebacker on Sunday. They rolled and tumbled and stood up to face each other. Rik, looking down from the parapet wall, was afraid for the lieutenant— Carmen would be a vicious opponent and a dirty fighter.

Carmen, sharpened hairpin in hand, launched a right thrust at the lieutenant, but Wright fended it off. The lieutenant, quick on her feet, delivered a swift left-right combo to Carmen's face, knocking her out cold.

Guess she had been paying attention to Billy's boxing lessons.

Lieutenant Wright was quickly on top of Carmen and slapped her into consciousness. Then she slid Billy's brass knuckles off her hand and seethed in her face, "Semper Paratus…bitch."

Carmen was now shrieking, but her missing teeth gave her a speech impediment. All those within earshot thought she sounded like a Latin Elmira Fudd. Carmen sat up and shrieked, "You foolth! Thupid gringoth with your thupid idealth. Wiff the Phat Man gone; you'll never make the Brathilian auction. Governor Imperiotha will thell the Toucano'th land and they'll be gone for evuh. They don't thtand a chanth. Poor pitiful naketh children, thick and thtarving…all becauth of you!"

Rik ran down the stairs to the south end of the parade ground. He wanted to engage in Carmen's rant but thought better of it. The entire chaotic scene was beginning to evolve into some semblance of order. Pinder and his men had corralled her miscreants. Rik, Billy, Erica holding Billy's hand tightly, and Lieutenant Wright huddled up.

"So, now what are we gonna do?" Rik said aloud, "We have a fortune in gold here but no way to transport it. She's right. We'll miss the deadline for the auction. My uncle and the Toucano are fighting for their lives and I'm letting them down."

FORTY-ONE

Dawn was approaching the island citadel, and the sun was gingerly sending out scout rays in advance of her arrival to see if it was safe to make an appearance. Who could blame her? It had been a hell of a night. The fort was now quiet, and the adrenaline level was starting to lower. The air was a mix of salt air and three-hundred-year-old brick.

Billy looked knowingly at Rik and said, "There is a way. We know a guy."

"You mean *you* know a guy?"

"Nope, we both know a guy," Billy replied. "Lieutenant Wright, hand me your sat phone."

Billy hit a few buttons and then said in his best air traffic control voice, "Bull Gator to War Eagle. Bull Gator to War Eagle. Come in."

Rik thought, *Well, I guess Billy has an operator name now.*

The sat phone crackled back with an annoyed, elderly voice. "Hold your horses, Andre the Giant. War Eagle here."

"Bring the Big Bird in," was all Billy said.

With those instructions, the Super Scooper that had been circling the fort banked to the west, landed in the south channel, and pushed itself onto Seaplane Beach. Two long-haired pilots emerged, wearing colorful patchwork flight suits in the Pahokee style. One old. One young. The elder was Toby Cypress, the Pahokee chief who had given Rik the Kahatee at the beginning of this tale.

The younger was Kenny Tiger. Recovered from the airboat accident but still with a pronounced limp.

Rik was dumbfounded as the Pahokee elder approached, smiled, and said, "Sorry about the saltwater bath. I'll bet it was refreshing, though."

"Good to see you, Chief Cypress, …you saved our lives."

"I'm proud of you, Chief Rik Duval. You have done the right thing. You listened to your heart and helped a people who can't fight the modern world. Now, please let the Pahokee Nation lend a hand."

"Huh? What are you talking about?" Rik stammered.

"We've been aware of the Toucano's troubles for years and now it's our turn to help. The Pahokee tribe has been honor-bound by an obligation created hundreds of years ago by a revered member of our tribe. His name was Chitto, and we've been encumbered by his words for too long. Now, we can make things right. We couldn't help the Tequesta three centuries ago, but we can atone for that now and aid another ancient people. The Toucano."

Pointing to the Super Scooper, he continued, "That baby carries one thousand five hundred gallons of water, which weighs ten thousand pounds. So, we can carry all the gold to Brazil. We'll refuel in Yucatan and, God willing, get to the auction site in time. We will transfer the gold to the Toucano people and advance funds on their behalf if needed."

"We also know about Uncle Jax and his demons. He is alive. There will be enough resources to help him and his brothers ensure the safety of the Toucano from the outside world."

Rik looked at the old chief with admiration. He had so many questions but at the moment was too tired to talk.

"There's no time to waste," Toby Cypress announced, and so everyone on the desolate island helped move the gold. Some under gunpoint, including Carmen, who was actually crying at this point— whether from the physical exertion, her missing teeth, the thought of the lost gold or the fact that she really did look terrible in orange.

When the last ounce was placed on board the Super Scooper, the chief said his goodbyes and yelled to Kenny, "Grandson—let's kick the tires and light the fires! Let's get this bird in the air!"

As the chief was about to climb the boarding ladder, Rik quickly approached him and asked, "I need to know something, Chief Cypress. How did you know we were here? That we needed help?"

"Guardian. Are you asking a pure-blood Pahokee whose people have been here for a millennium? A people who speak to the wind and the stars. A people who own lots of casinos. You're asking me how I know things? Like your operator name?"

"Yes, Chief."

"Nah. You'll figure it out one day. Oh, and next time you visit our casino, put a hundred bucks on red."

And with that, Chief Cypress and Kenny were airborne for Brazil. To save a people. And Uncle Jax.

Their rapid departure was offset by the arrival of the stealth helo from its rescue mission. After the pilots and crew, only Tony emerged, holding his arm in a makeshift sling. He walked stiffly over to Rik.

"Where's Eisenberg?" Rik demanded. "The crash didn't look too bad."

In a distant voice, Tony replied, "He didn't make it."

"What do you mean? He needs to rot in hell."

"He will. He'll slowly rot away at the bottom of the ocean."

Rik looked into Tony's eyes. These were not the eyes of his friend. The friend that he shared beers with and floated all night with, in the Gulf Stream. The eyes that guided Rik safely over the ocean on risky narco interdiction missions. His eyes were different now. Darker. Hollow. These were the eyes of a killer. Eisendorf never had a chance to leave the Chinook. Tony had jammed his safety harness, put a flare gun in his mouth, and pulled the trigger.

Rik thought, *If you threatened my blood, I'd do the same. Without remorse.*

All this was unspoken, but Rik thought, *He'll never be the same, but maybe Dr. Krak could help.*

It took some doing, but the bad guys were finally bound, some gagged, and ready for transport to—if luck would have it—a dark, distant black site where no one would bother to remember their names. Carmen yelled like a wildcat with a prominent lisp when she was covered in her own personal foul-smelling hood.

Dawn broke, a soft glow cresting over the edge of the horizon, casting a pale light over the fort's rugged walls and quiet, weed-covered parade ground. Rik had one last task.

With every muscle crying for rest, he hauled himself up the spiral staircase back to the parapet where the flagpole stood. The old iron steps creaked under his weight, groaning in a ghostly echo. As he reached the top, those on the ground below stopped and looked up, sensing something significant was happening.

Whiskers, his tired frame leaning on Billy, asked,

"Billy, what's going on?"

Billy, eyes wide with understanding, replied softly, "Rik's lowering the distress signal. The upside-down flag."

Rik's hands shook as he gripped the halyard. He undid the clips, each snap feeling like a somber heartbeat, and held the flag in his hands, feeling the coarse fabric and weight of the years embedded in every stitch.

Memories crashed over him—a flood of ceremonies, parades, solemn salutes, and caskets draped in these colors. He had seen Old Glory fly proudly and folded in sorrow, but he had never held the Stars and Stripes with his own hands before.

As he stood there, cradling the flag like a sacred relic, a wave of gratitude and grief washed over him. He felt for all those who had fought, bled, and fallen to preserve the ideals it stood for. A tear slipped down his cheek. With a deep breath, he reversed the flag, then, with deliberate care, raised it high once more.

As he pulled the flag upward, the first light of dawn broke over the parapet walls, bathing Old Glory in a golden glow. A gentle breeze picked up, catching the fabric just as it reached its peak, causing it to stretch outward and wave. A proud reminder of resilience, just like its ancestor had flown over another fort, Fort McHenry, two hundred years ago.

Below, all those on the parade grounds stood at

attention, hands snapping to salute. Even Whiskers, with Billy's support steadying him, managed a salute, his frail frame quivering with effort and pride.

As the impromptu ceremony ended, the various units began to disperse and Whiskers looked up at Billy, his eyes distant and reflective. "Would you lean me up against Sam Smith's gravestone over there?" he asked, nodding toward the old buttonwood tree shading the resting place of his closest friend.

"Are you alright, Whiskers?" Billy asked, worry evident in his voice.

"I'll be fine," Whiskers replied, his voice softer now. "All this excitement just got to me. Just fetch me a little water, would you? I think I'll have myself a quiet chat with Sam."

Billy left, casting a concerned look over his shoulder, but Whiskers was already lost in his own world.

His hand rested on the cool stone, a wry smile crossing his face. "Well, Sam," he muttered, "we kicked their asses, didn't we? Wickedness came to our beloved fort, but we stood our ground. Some new friends, me, you, and this old fort. We beat 'em, Sam. We beat 'em good."

Whiskers let out a soft, shaky breath, eyes slipping shut as he sank against the gravestone. "I'll be seeing you soon, old friend." With that final whisper, his heart gave a gentle flutter, and he passed on.

Moments later, Billy came rushing back with a flask of water, his footsteps slowing as he approached. He found Rik on his way back and they shared a look of dawning sadness. Together, they hurried to Whiskers' side, but it was already clear. The old ranger and former Coastie's weary heart had stopped, but the peaceful smile on his face told them all they needed to know. He had passed away happy and content, in the place he loved.

FORTY-TWO

Rik knew, it was once again, time to get the hell out of Dodge. Especially given his task to "stay under the radar" while in the Keys. But that order had been given by a guy who was in an aluminum coffin at the bottom of the ocean, so he was more than a little confused about his current station in life.

He stepped onto the bridge of the reclaimed *Bum Runner* and began preparing her for the two-hour run to Key West. He was waiting on his crew to say their goodbyes, both official and unofficial. Rik was more of an Irish goodbye kinda guy.

He noticed a crumpled envelope wedged into the steering wheel. He opened it carefully. Very carefully. After that night, he was not in a real trusting mood.

The note read, *Chief Rik, Look under the console. Signed, Toby Cypress.*

Rik slid the small door open. *I'll be damned!* he thought. There was a beautiful pair of python boots, and a belt made out of alligator skin. *How the hell did Chief Cypress know?* Rik had only uttered his desire for the boots inwardly when he'd begun the python hunt with Kenny Tiger.

Lieutenant Wright was the first to arrive onboard. She hugged Rik for a long time, and he knew their relationship changed that night. Without Jill and her quick thinking, he and Billy would be dead and the Toucano people, too.

Jill's sat phone beeped loudly and they ended their embrace reluctantly. Jill answered, then, stone-faced, handed the phone to Rik. "It's for you."

"Hello?"

"Master Chief, this is Robert Cutter, vice commandant of the United States Coast Guard. Bravo Zulu, Chief! Bravo Zulu. We suspected Eisendorf was a bad apple and you and your team rid us of a nightmare. I like your resourcefulness. You took the bull by the horns and ripped its goddamn head off. Take a few days off, son. Rest up. The Coast Guard is going to need you again, though. Are you up for it?

"Yes. Yes, sir…I am, sir."

"Good. Good. Lieutenant Wright will continue to be your liaison. So long, Chief. I mean, Guardian. Out!"

The phone went dead. *Holy shit. That was the number two guy in the Coast Guard. And I'm in his contacts.* Rik had spent most of his Coast Guard career trying to stay off the brass's radar, and now he was front and center.

He handed the phone back to Jill, who went down below to prepare some snacks for the ride home. Everyone would be starving. This left Rik alone with his thoughts.

It was quiet on the bridge. Fort Jefferson in the distance seemed so isolated, almost lonely. Sitting on a tiny limestone bed in the middle of the ocean. An old sentry still guarding America from bad guys. This beautiful setting gave him time to reflect on the past few months.

He thought about the phrase truth is stranger than fiction. Maybe I should write a book. Nah. The Coast Guard would probably frown on that crazy idea.

His thoughts turned to family. *Uncle Jax was his last remaining relative. Would he see him again? He didn't always understand his lessons but they were starting to become clear.*

And the USCG was like a family. But more like a fraternity. Brothers and sisters you could count on. But when holidays rolled around, they weren't true family.

Now his life was upside down. Or was it? Maybe he was supposed to be here. He was a card-carrying adrenaline junkie and these past months certainly had been exciting. And his crew of mavericks. Well, who could explain them? Other than they would do anything for each other.

His crew was now joining him on board. Billy was carrying a sleeping Erica. Pinder and Tony brought up the rear. They all gravitated toward the bridge.

As Rik motored out of the channel, he glanced around the bridge and counted his blessings. To his left, Pinder, his hands bandaged, was stretched out, resting. Billy was deep in conversation with Tony, who had his arm in a sling. Erica was sound asleep on the port lounge and hopefully recovered emotionally from tonight. And beside him, Lieutenant Wright—I mean, Jill—sat quietly holding his arm. In that moment, everything felt right. He couldn't believe his luck. This was only the beginning, he hoped. A future full of new adventures with his new family.

He was about to push the throttles down and bring the Bum Runner up on plane when he saw a flare go up near Loggerhead Key. He reached for his bino's and saw a man waving from the pontoon of a seaplane. It was Barefoot Joe. And Jimmy Legs.

He motored over and Barefoot Joe hopped on board with Jimmy Legs, who looked a little sheepish.

Rik yelled down, "What the hell happened to you?"

"You know my good luck charm, Layla?"

"Yeah."

"Well, we hit a little turbulence, and she started shaking and Jimmy Legs got all excited and ate her. That's when my luck ended. The engine quit and we emergency landed here. Can you give us a lift to Key West?"

"Sure. Come on up."

As Barefoot Joe reached the bridge, he looked around and said, "Did I miss anything?"

This brought out a round of laughter, which was interrupted when Billy jumped up and announced loudly, "Man, I'm gonna hit Key West like my parachute failed! I know a bartender who makes the best Bloody Mary's on the planet. Two of those and you'll end up shooting craps with chickens on Duval Street. They open at 7:00. First round's on me."

Typical Billy—and the group all nodded their approval.

As they sped eastward, Rik spotted an osprey circling overhead, screeching loudly. *Odd*, he thought, *they usually stay closer to land.* Still, the sea was calm, the engines settled into a slow, deliberate rhythm a mechanical heartbeat that echoed through the hull. All felt right in the world.

The bow rose and fell with the gentle swells, and Rik tilted his face to the sky and muttered, *Why me? Am I part of something bigger*?

He didn't know for sure. But in his gut—in the marrow of his bones—he knew the answer.

Yeah. I am.

EPILOGUE

Hell's Bay, Everglades
1783

Tulec slumped weakly against an old cypress tree covered in Spanish moss. His breath was ragged and shallow. His skin was turning clammy and the young warrior's heart raced frantically, trying to outrun the inevitable.

For the past week, Tulec had survived only on coontie root paste, his body growing weaker, hungrier with each passing day. He was desperate to fulfill his father's wishes, but he needed more sustenance, more strength to continue. When he'd spotted the deer and silently tracked it through the hammock, his hope had been rekindled—until he stepped on the old rattler.

With reflexes honed by a lifetime in the Everglades, Tulec grabbed the snake and severed its head with one swift motion. The body writhed and coiled in his grip, but the damage was done.

In his left hand, he clutched the scrimshaw rod his father had entrusted to him seven days earlier. In his right hand lay the limp, headless body of a six-foot rattlesnake, its tail still rattling like a shaman's last incantation.

He looked down at his calf. Two large, venom-filled holes marred the skin, their edges angry and inflamed. A rush of remorse surged through his mind. *How could I have been so reckless?* he thought, a pang of despair settling in his chest. *I'll pay for this mistake with my life. And worse, I will break my promise to Father. To my people.*

His vision blurred, the world around him dissolved into vague, wavering shapes, but his ears remained sharp. He heard the soft crunch of footsteps, and he turned with great effort, his body trembling. Out of the Everglades haze stepped a tall, dark man, moving softly, as if he were part of the forest itself. The stranger took in the scene with a quick, knowing eye.

Tulec instinctively reached for his yari, the oversized bow the Tequesta favored, but the man spoke calmly, his voice like the whisper of the wind through the trees. "There is no need, my brother. I will not harm you. Here, have some water." He produced a small leather bag, lifting it gently to Tulec's cracked, dry lips. The cool liquid poured into his mouth, easing his parched throat, and Tulec drank gratefully. The stranger took the serpent from Tulec's hand and flung it into the brush.

"My name is Chitto. I am a Pahokee of the Panther

clan. How can I help you, my young brother?" he asked, his voice filled with a sincerity which caught Tulec off guard.

Tulec's mind swam with confusion. The Pahokee and Tequesta were not allies. The Pahokee were newcomers to this land—hunters, fishermen—encroaching on the territory the Tequesta had called home for thousands of years. They were part of the reason his people had been forced to migrate south, into the Keys.

"Why would you help me?" Tulec asked weakly, suspicion and disbelief mingling in his fading voice. "Why should I trust you?"

Chitto knelt beside Tulec, his eyes steady and warm. "It's obvious—the Creator chose us to meet. We walk the same path, my brother. You have nothing to fear. What is that strange stick you are holding?"

Tulec's strength was almost gone, but he knew this man was his only hope. He lifted the scrimshaw rod, his voice strained. "It's called the Kahatee." He began to speak, revealing his people's plight—the hope they placed in this mission. He spoke of his father's dreams, the vision that had guided him to this task, and how he had entrusted Tulec to see it through.

As Tulec spoke, Chitto lit a small fire, and they sat in silence, the flames casting flickering shadows across their faces. Tulec's thoughts drifted back to a week ago when he and his father had had their last conversation, their faces lit by the glow of another fire.

Suddenly, Tulec's eyes opened wide, a surge of determination pushing through the fog. "I need to stand! Please help me." Chitto moved quickly, lifting Tulec to his feet. Tulec grimaced in pain, his face contorted with the effort, and tears sprang to Chitto's eyes at the sight. With the scrimshaw rod acting as a staff, Tulec drew himself up, shaky but resolute.

He declared to the heavens, his voice ragged but forceful, "I am Tulec of the Tequesta tribe ... my soul will not rest until my father's wish is fulfilled." His words rang out, echoing into the stillness of the clearing like a pebble dropped into a universal pond, rippling outward beyond their world.

Chitto watched Tulec's face intently. Abruptly, Tulec's eyes grew wider, his expression one of astonishing wonder, as if a vision had gripped his soul. "I see it. I see the path!" he exclaimed.

"What is it, Tulec?" Chitto said, his voice urgent. "What did you see, my brother?"

Tulec tried to speak, his lips moving, but his voice failed him. He managed only a raspy whisper, the words barely audible. Chitto knelt beside him, placing his ear close to Tulec's mouth, listening intently as the dying Tequesta struggled to speak. When Tulec had finished, Chitto nodded solemnly.

"I understand, my brother," he whispered. "You have my word. And the word of the Pahokee people."

Hearing this, Tulec smiled, then loosened his grip on the scrimshaw rod. It fell softly to the ground. The venom in his blood claimed him and now his soul was wandering free.

Chitto knew what he had to do. He rose slowly, standing straight and tall above the body of his Native brother. He took a deep breath, the duty of the eternal vow settling within his soul. Tears welled in his eyes, and he let them fall, to honor the young warrior lying next to him.

As an osprey screeched overhead, Chitto proclaimed, "Tulec, you have my eternal vow that my people will, one day, bestow the Kahatee to a great Chief and Guardian.

"To the one called Riqdou-Vahl … so others may live."

The End… or is it?

I hope you enjoyed reading <u>So Others May Live</u>. It was my honor to write it for you!

Want to know what happened to the characters?

Visit <u>bwilliamhoolihan.com</u> for that information and interesting tidbits about the people and places mentioned in the book. Use the secret code USCG to gain entrance.

If you enjoyed "So Others May Live" and want to read more, please e-mail me at <u>bwh@bwilliamhoolihan.com</u> and let me know your thoughts.

Oh, and Rik and Billy would appreciate it, if you give <u>So Others May Live</u> a five-star review!!

B. William Hoolihan

ABOUT THE AUTHOR

B. William Hoolihan was born into a world steeped in storytelling. His grandfather, a masterful teller of tales, grew up in rural Kentucky in the early 1900s. Letters describing his childhood adventures on Uncle George's farm first ignited a passion for storytelling in young Bill.

During Bill's formative years, his mother—a single parent and schoolteacher—surrounded him with a vibrant tapestry of adventurous and colorful characters who further inspired him. She nurtured his thirst for adventure by taking him on a journey to the Middle East. Together, they explored the Valley of the Kings, swam in the Dead Sea, and roamed the ancient ruins of the Parthenon. His quest for adventure deepened as he absorbed tales of distant lands and seas, particularly the Caribbean, told by a family friend.

These days, Bill can be found cycling through the back roads of Florida, contemplating new stories and adventures to chronicle. If you see him, feel free to say hello, but tread carefully—you might just become a character in his next tale!